Jassy Mackenzie wa̲ and moved to South Africa when she was eight years old. She lives with her partner Dion, and two horses and two cats. She enjoys traveling, cooking, cycling, and competes in dressage on her thoroughbred.

She also loves the energy, danger and excitement of Johannesburg, believing there is no better place for a thriller writer to be, and wishes to share its 'terrifying, exhilarating, essence with readers across the world'.

From a book-loving family where TV was banned from the house, she is the second youngest of five daughters. Her mother Ann Mackenzie was a well-known short story writer, and Jassy's sister, Vicky Jones, now living in New Zealand, is a prize-winning author of children's books.

As a youngster, Jassy seemingly had an uncanny knack of choosing unsavoury boyfriends who were involved in everything from cocaine dealing to smuggling. Then, she was hijacked at gunpoint outside her home, and had her car taken from her by force. This experience led to her first novel: 'Random Violence'. She has since written several more thrillers, a 'Jade De Jong' detective series, and erotic romances.

Combining her writing career with editing a 'Hair and Beauty' trade magazine, Jassy has also had numerous non-fiction articles on a wide variety of subjects published locally, and internationally, over the years.

Soaring

Jassy Mackenzie

Soaring

Copyright © 2016 Jassy Mackenzie
Typography © Astor + Blue Editions

The right of Jassy Mackenzie to be identified as the author of this work has been asserted.

This Edition Published by:
Astor + Blue Editions LLC, 1330 Avenue of the Americas, Suite 23A, New York, NY 10019, U.S.A.
www.houseofstratus.com

ISBN: 978-1-941286-95-X (Paperback)
ISBN: 978-1-941286-97-5 (ePdf)
ISBN: 978-1-941286-96-8 (ePub)
ISBN: 978-1-681200-08-8 (Mobi)

A catalogue record for this book is available from the Library of Congress and the British Library.

Cover Design: Kate Murphy

All rights reserved. No part of this publication may be reproduced, stored in a retrieval system, or transmitted, in any form, or by any means (electronic, mechanical, photocopying, recording, or otherwise), without the prior permission of the publisher. Any person who does any unauthorised act in relation to this publication may be liable to criminal prosecution and civil claims for damages.

This is a fictional work and all characters are drawn from the author's imagination. Any resemblance or similarities to persons either living or dead are entirely coincidental.

DEDICATION

To Dion, with all my love.

ACKNOWLEDGEMENTS

With thanks to my incredible agent, Stephany Evans of FinePrint Literary Management, and to Jillian Ports and the wonderful team at Astor + Blue Editions.

A special thank-you to Natalia Tyshler, of Tyshler School of Fencing in Johannesburg, for her enthusiastic assistance in educating me on the competitive sport of fencing.

CHAPTER 1

Occasionally I can glimpse what's going to happen in the future. It's a strange ability. It happens randomly, but it's never been wrong. It comes in pictures and it feels as if a new memory has unfolded in my mind…except it's a memory of something that hasn't happened yet. It made me dizzy the first few times, but I became used to it after a while.

The first time it happened when I was eight years old. I saw our family's first rescue cat, a long-haired gray and white Norwegian Forest cross, before we'd met her at the shelter. I thought I was getting carsick on the drive to find an adopted pet, but then the giddiness passed, and there she was, bright and vivid in my mind, all the way down to the last whisker. I couldn't believe she was so beautiful, and when we reached the shelter, I ran inside, turned left, and went straight to her cage. "This is our new cat," I told my parents proudly. "Her name is Shadow." I think Shadow had seen a picture of me, too, because she was standing at the cage door, waiting for me like she'd known all her life I was coming.

I was in seventh grade when my friends and I went sledding on trash bags down the hill at the back of Heidi Baker's house. Before it was Heidi's turn, I had to sit down in the snow for a while because my head was spinning, and when I stood up again, I saw she was going to end up in the holly bush near the bottom of the slope. I told her so, but she didn't listen. Off she went and sure enough, she headed straight for the holly, getting wedged into its branches with her backside sticking out into the snow and her scarf tangled up. It was a very funny picture; just as funny as the one I'd seen in my mind, and everyone was too busy laughing to help pull her out of the bush.

And who did Heidi blame for that incident? Herself? Nope.

JASSIE MACKENZIE

The holly bush? Also nope. Me? You got it. I don't think she spoke to me again till senior high. It would have been more helpful if I could have seen a picture of my mother having the fall that paralyzed her from the neck down when she went rock climbing on her fiftieth birthday. I remember the shock of the news vividly, and how my father and I stared anxiously at each other over her bed in the ICU as we waited to hear firstly if she was going to live, and secondly if she would ever regain the use of her arms or legs.

She'd lived, but was forever without feeling or movement in her limbs. It was a tragedy for a lively, athletic woman like her, and the repercussions had a huge impact on our future. I hated myself for having not been able to predict her fall, and wished I could have seen a picture in time to warn her. But as I said, it's an occasional ability, and it happens when it wants to, not when I need it.

Anyway, I'm skipping ahead in my story, because my mother's accident was in my future the day I boarded the business class flight from JFK to London. I was eighteen-years-old at the time, and I'd been invited to an awards ceremony in London hosted by a sports gear supplier. I was sitting up front for the journey. There were a small group of us going over from the U.S., but I was flying separately from the others, on a British Airways flight, due to scheduling issues.

The sports gear supplier was one of the major outlets for all sorts of equipment, including everything needed for my sport, which was fencing. I'd started it a few years ago and had quickly discovered that I was very good at it. My footwork was fast, I was well coordinated, but more than that, all my coaches expressed puzzled admiration for the fact that I sometimes seemed to know in advance exactly what my opponents were going to do. My strange ability at work again? Perhaps. All I knew was that when I was in the zone, feeling one with my blade, it was as if I could foresee what the next few moments would bring. And in fencing, that gave me enough time to score points. I'd captained my college team, and I'd gone on to win junior gold in saber in the North American Cup. And now, here

SOARING

I was, heading overseas for the first time in my life.

I felt somewhat overawed as I followed the flight attendant into the hushed, spacious realm of business class, wheeling my carry-on past these huge cubicles, more like hotel rooms than seats. I couldn't help glancing into them to see who was sitting there. Who was lucky enough to fly like this all the time? Seeing as I was going to be here probably once in my life, I was curious.

A gray-haired Indian man was in the first row, frowning down at his laptop as I passed him by, a pale drink in a crystal glass ignored on the table next to him. The next row was empty. Then I saw a woman with the glossiest, most immaculate mahogany hair—the perfect complement to her gleaming deep-red nails. She was slim and beautifully dressed, and every stitch of her clothing looked designer. I saw her watching me as I passed and I wondered if she was assessing me the same way I was her, looking at the denim skirt I'd purchased a while back from the outlet store, my long sleeved top, which was a flattering turquoise in color but a no-name brand, and my nails, short and unpolished, because practicing with a saber six hours a day is not conducive to having a glamorous manicure.

"This is your seat, ma'am. Shall I stow your bag for you?" the attendant asked.

There was just one other person in my row, sitting across the aisle from me, and he looked up just as I glanced at him.

I wasn't anticipating what happened next. The shock hit me with all the force of a runaway eighteen-wheeler.

This man was a few years older than me—in his mid-twenties, I guessed. He was extremely good looking in a powerful, yet charming way. His lean face had the most classic bone structure—defined cheekbones above a strong jaw, a sensuous mouth, a perfect nose, and eyes that seemed to light up as I looked into them. In contrast to the steely perfection of his face, his dark brown hair had wayward, tousled bangs flopping over his forehead in a way that only added to his masculine appeal.

Gorgeous as he was, it wasn't the sight of him which had forced the breath right out of my body.

It was the picture which appeared, briefly, but vividly and

clearly in my mind. I saw the two of us together, arms entwined, bodies pressed close. I could see the ripped, muscular definition in his left arm, wrapped around my back. We were sprawled, half-sitting and half-lying, in semi-darkness on one of these wide airplane seats, made up into a bed with white sheeting. Our lips were touching—no, not just that. They were mashing together as we kissed passionately, unstoppably. And his right hand…his hand was roaming…

The image sent a bolt of heat right through me and I felt so dizzy, I grabbed onto the seat for support. It was shocking; so unexpected, so hopelessly erotic. I'd never, ever visualized anything like this happening before. How could it be possible? With a stranger? On a first-class flight?

I sat down fast, scooting into the plush, private cubicle that was my seat. I was relieved that the high sides of the seat were shielding me from his gaze, because my face felt as if it was burning.

The flight attendant offered an aperitif and I said yes to champagne without really thinking about what I was doing. While she brought it, I opened my purse and took out my compact mirror.

My pink scarf had unwound itself from my neck and slipped down over one shoulder, dragging the neckline of my top with it, of course, so my white bra strap was peeking out. Above this disarray, I saw my startled blue eyes, my chestnut hair pulled back in a ponytail with wisps curling out from either side. My full mouth was still half open from shock and my cheeks—I knew it—already crimson.

I took off the scarf, rearranged my clothing, undid my messy ponytail and ran my fingers through my hair. I checked the mirror again, barely noticing myself, seeing only the way my fingers had been smoothing over his broad, strong shoulders.

The champagne was sparkling on the side table where the attendant had placed it. Suddenly, I needed a big gulp of it. Of course, to reach the glass, I'd have to lean forward again, which would bring me into my handsome neighbor's view.

Worth the risk, I decided. I grasped the glass and, as if I

couldn't help it, my head turned to the right and I saw he was looking at me.

His gaze felt like hot water cascading down my spine, suffusing my body with warmth. His mouth curved into a smile and I found myself smiling back, seeing his own expression warming further in response.

I noticed the color of his eyes for the first time—a bright hazel-green with flecks of gold. Really, he was model-gorgeous, but I sensed a hardness to him, a streetwise edge that convinced me he hadn't made his money shimmying down catwalks. And a model would probably be wearing something smarter than that well cut, but equally well worn, gray sweatshirt, with the sleeves pushed back to reveal the whipcord muscles of his forearms…

I felt suddenly self-conscious as I realized he was staring at me with the same intensity as I'd just been devouring him with. Where was the flight attendant, to turn the plane's AC up a notch?

He raised his glass to me and I lifted mine in response, sipping the icy bubbles. A few seconds later, we were leaning across the aisle, speaking to each other. He introduced himself as Patrick, and I told him my name was Claire. After take-off, he came to sit with me in my cubicle, on the padded footrest opposite my chair. Our knees brushed and my heart went into overdrive.

What did we say? I wish I could remember more clearly. Parts of our conversation are etched into my memory, but a lot of it was lost because of the tumult in my mind. I was intensely, viscerally attracted to him in a way that was making me feel nervous and excited and short of breath. When I looked at his mouth, I wanted to lean forward and kiss it, and I actually had to physically hold myself back by wrapping my fingers around my armrest.

His voice was deep, and when he spoke to me, it felt like a caress. I couldn't place his accent, but understood why when he told me he had been born in Ireland before moving to the U.S. when he was twelve, and that he'd lived in London for a year now, after starting up a company there.

When he asked, I told him I was a student and a fencer, going to London to attend a sports awards ceremony. He told me that running and cycling were his passions when time allowed, which wasn't often enough, but that he'd completed the Lake Placid Ironman last week and had stayed in New York to do some business.

He asked me what I was studying and where I lived, and I found out about the town in southwestern Ireland where he'd grown up. It was Castle Hill, near Kenmare, a place which he said was one of the most beautiful in the world.

"If you get the chance to go there, take it. Stay at the Park Hotel. It's rather rundown, but its location is incredible. Right in the center of town, and the rooms on the upper floors have the most amazing view over the bay."

It wasn't all about what we said, though. It was the energy that seemed to spark between us, making me realize that while my airplane neighbor was good looking, interesting and charming to a fault, our communication went beyond that. After we'd talked a while, our legs remained touching, his knee warm against my inner thigh, pressing harder as he or I leaned forward. Once or twice, our fingers brushed, and when I laughed at one of his jokes, I put my hand on his arm, my fingers briefly clasping his tanned skin and taut muscles.

Although his eyes were mostly focused on mine, from time to time I noticed how his gaze roamed over my body, lingering on the curve of my breasts, moving down to my legs. It made me feel excited that he might be thinking of me in that way—in a sexual way, because I was beginning to realize that under that urbane veneer, Patrick was an intensely sexual being.

I found it impossible not to take in his own body in quick, stolen glances...the breadth of his shoulders, the way his leanly defined muscles gave shape to the soft fabric of his sweatshirt, the length of his legs. And once or twice, my eyes couldn't help straying to the crotch of his jeans, the bulk of his manhood faintly visible under the faded denim.

When the beds were made up and the lights dimmed, our conversation tailed off into a short and slightly uneasy silence. I didn't want him to go, but it was quiet now, people were sleeping. Even in this spacious cabin, our voices would carry and might cause disturbance.

"Well, I'd better let you get some rest," he said in a low tone. "It's been great meeting you, Claire."

"Same here," I said, not quite sure if my response made any sense. I couldn't think sensibly. Every fiber of my body was screaming for him to stay, and even after saying those words, he didn't get up to go.

A strange thought suddenly occurred to me: what if he felt the same way as me? Could it be possible that I wasn't the only one who had just fallen hopelessly in lust?

"Good night," he whispered, a shadow of a smile illuminating his face as he leaned toward me. My heart started hammering violently as I realized he was going to kiss me before leaving. A quick brush of the mouth; surely that was all it would be, and during that fleeting contact I could not dare to show my longing for him.

His left arm slid around my waist, pulling me close as his right hand stroked my face, gently pushing aside a stray lock of hair. I found myself touching his leg, my fingers hungrily exploring the toned steel of his thigh. As his lips met mine, the image I'd had earlier came back to me in raw, explicit detail, and I knew that there was no way this kiss was going to be brief or superficial…that the spark between us had ignited into a flame, which would sear its memory into my life forever.

CHAPTER 2

Ten years later, and as my Aer Lingus flight from JFK to Dublin began its descent, I found myself thinking obsessively of that night, that handsome stranger, who'd come into my life so briefly and then was gone again. It was strange how such a chance encounter could have left such vivid memories.

And it had been all too brief. Early the next morning, as we'd prepared to disembark, Patrick had asked, almost shyly, if I would like to stay in touch. And I'd made a decision that I had never stopped kicking my eighteen-year-old self for. I'd said no.

Who knew what my deranged reasoning had been? I couldn't remember. Perhaps I'd been embarrassed or ashamed, thinking of the raw sexuality he'd briefly unleashed, a side of myself I had barely explored until then. Or maybe I'd thought staying in contact with a man who lived in London would only lead to an inevitable fizzling out—a series of increasingly terminal goodbyes.

I could never fly without thinking of Patrick, wondering what he was doing, and where he was now. His memory would stray into my mind at unexpected moments—sometimes when I was happy, occasionally when I was sad. And I wondered if he ever thought of me, or if he might have seen me on television or read about me in the newspapers.

I thought of him when I'd traveled to the London Olympics a few years ago to represent my country. I was the reserve for the saber team, who had excelled at the Olympics by winning their first-ever team medal: bronze. As reserve, I was the only one of the four of us not to set foot on the piste. I felt like a fraud during the medal ceremony. There's almost what you could call a tradition of minor "injuries" occurring in Olympic team fencing—twisted ankles, and the like. Everyone wants a medal but everyone's terrified by the pressure, so most reserves get to compete. But my teammates didn't suffer a twinge.

My life took an unexpected turn after a talent scout saw me standing on that podium, and a few days later I received my first modeling contract. For the next year, I juggled my modeling and my fencing career, and ended up presenting the first two seasons of the "Games of Skill" program, which aired nationwide on Fox Sports. It didn't pay very well, but suddenly everyone knew who I was, and as a result I received a few more modeling contracts, as well as the lucrative College Sports sponsorship. Modeling and presenting sports had propelled me into the public eye far more than fencing could ever have done, but if I hadn't won that medal I might never have been noticed.

I thought of Patrick whenever I was posing for the camera, looking into the dazzling lights with the photographer behind the glare encouraging me for "more personality please, darling, we need you to smolder…oh, yes, that's the look! That's it. Great, darling, just great."

I'd thought of Patrick the very first time I'd smiled nervously at the television cameras when I was on air. I wondered if he'd been watching. I'd even thought of him, guiltily, when my manager Dave, who had become my boyfriend soon after I'd met him, proposed marriage. I'd been so happy then, believing that a golden future lay ahead of us, that Dave and I would build a wonderful life together. Of course, it hadn't worked out that way.

In the last few weeks, scandal and injury had derailed my career. My sponsors were threatening legal action, my marriage was on the rocks, and Dave had told me he was going ahead with the divorce.

Now I sat alone, watching out of the window as the plane cut through a blanket of cloud to reveal the landscape beneath—a patchwork of green fields, their colors subdued on this drizzly morning. Dublin was gray and gloomy, the perfect match for my mood. No bright emerald vista to welcome me, no storybook landscape as promised by the tourist brochures. The countryside gave way to the city, and that too was dull, grim-looking, its charm hidden away.

"Thank you, have a nice day, Ms. Harvey," the flight attendant called as I disembarked.

"Thanks," I muttered. I couldn't meet her eyes. Did she know who I was? Had she read the headlines? Was she going to gossip about the woman on the flight? "Was that Claire Harvey? You know, the fencer who used to be on TV, who's just been in all the tabloids?"

I hadn't checked in any bags. My trip had been a sudden, spur-of-the-moment decision. Desperate to flee the country, I'd used my accumulated voyager miles to pay for the flight. I wasn't even booked into a hotel. I was used to having my life organized, regimented. Not to mention traveling with truckloads of luggage. Now, holding the handle of my compact carry-on awkwardly in my right hand, I walked through the airport and then paused, deciding.

Cab or rental car? How far did I want to go?

"Claire!" A man's voice cried behind me and I flinched, my left hand flung protectively in front of my face as I turned, expecting to see the sight I'd dreaded: somebody with their camera or iPhone, gleefully brandishing it to capture me in their lens.

But the speaker, a middle-aged businessman, was calling out to somebody else, another Claire, who was browsing a newsstand a few yards away. The short, dark-haired woman turned, recognition in her eyes, a smile lighting up her broad face.

"And there you are, Gerald Kilblane, late as usual."

"I'd be late for my own funeral," he admitted, striding over to give her a hug.

I let out a deep breath, and looked away from their happy embrace, lowering my arm. My wrist throbbed from making the sudden movement; eight weeks was long enough to heal a bone, but the muscles were still weak and the arm, painful if I twisted it in a certain way.

I walked over to the newsstand that the other Claire had just left and glanced at the headlines.

SOARING

A gale had capsized a sailboat off the northeastern coast. The economy was still struggling, but exports of potatoes were on the rise. The tabloids were full of excitement about the Duchess of Cambridge, who was arriving for a royal tour.

I was relieved to see that the news was all so unfamiliar, so normal-sounding, and that none of the recent hysteria had followed me across the Atlantic.

It was a storm in a teacup, I told myself. It would blow over quickly.

Talking of storms, though, it did look as if the southwest of the country was having the better weather.

I decided to go there.

"Castle Hill, near Kenmare. It's the most beautiful town in Ireland, Claire. If you have the chance to travel there, you should take it."

Words of advice from the stranger I'd never forget. Whose lips had closed over mine in what I still, somehow, thought of as my first real kiss. That moment had sent my hormones raging, making me feel wild and reckless, because ending up in an intimate embrace with a stranger on an airplane was not what good girls do. The caress of his lips had been soft at first, but the strength I'd sensed in his lean, strong body and the carnal intent blazing in his green-gold eyes…well, that had been so powerful it had blown my mind.

I remembered the advice he'd given me; the words he'd spoken about that beautiful town. If I was going to hide out, why not choose the prettiest place in Ireland? Perhaps I could even stay in that rundown hotel he'd talked about, centrally located, with a stunning view over the bay. What had he said its name was? The Park. I decided to find out if it was still in business.

I walked briskly out of the airport, headed for the car rental, and ten minutes later, I had the keys to a VW Polo Classic, and my GPS programmed to guide me to Castle Hill.

"Take the Ring of Kerry route," the woman at the counter advised. "It's a beautiful drive."

"Left side of the road, right side of the car," I reminded myself as I popped the trunk and stowed my bag.

This freedom felt scary and wonderful all at the same time. Nobody back home knew where I was. Not Dave, not anybody. They couldn't get in touch with me. Nobody could arrive on my doorstep begging for an interview, or call me up asking how it felt to be a whore.

That had been the last anonymous call I'd received yesterday.

It was straight after that I'd decided to leave the country for a while.

"How does it feel to be a whore?" the woman had shouted down the phone at me. I'd been paralyzed by shock, unable to press the disconnect button in time to cut off the rest of her diatribe.

"You cheated on your husband. God will judge you for that, and he will make sure you get what you deserve! I saw you on Fox Sport. I heard you speaking about how your husband's management helped you succeed. You're nothing without him. He's going to divorce you, and your life is going to be destroyed. And you deserve it, the Bible says so, you immoral, whorish…"

I'd finally managed to guide my trembling hand to the disconnect button.

I still had not turned my phone back on.

Now, driving out of the airport, I switched it on with trepidation. I felt cold inside. What if the abusive woman had called back?

I had ten messages. None, thank God, were from her. Five were from journalists wanting my comment on my current situation. Four were from friends, including my best friend, Monika, checking whether I was okay.

And the most recent one was from my estranged husband, Dave.

"Claire, where the hell have you gone? The shit's hit the fan on this side, big-time. Please call me as soon as you get this. I'll be available on my cell, or at my lawyer's."

"The shit's hit the fan?" I repeated aloud, my voice high. I thought it had done that before I left. Distracted from my driving, I almost swerved into the wrong lane. The warning flash of lights from an oncoming vehicle corrected me just in time.

I didn't know, couldn't dare to think, what else might have gone wrong.

Reflexively, I dialed his number. He picked up within two rings.

"Claire. Where are you?"

I hesitated before replying, "Out of town."

I didn't want to tell him I'd fled the country. It was none of his business now that we were separated.

"You've lost the Tempest sponsorship," he told me, his voice grim. My heart sank.

Tempest rental cars, with whom I'd had a small reciprocal sponsorship agreement, was the second of my sponsors to pull out, after College Sport. At least they weren't threatening legal action and demanding their money back, like College Sport was doing.

"I'm sorry," I said.

Nobody wanted to be associated with a tainted heroine. My career cut short through injury, and now my reputation indelibly smeared.

Dave sighed heavily. "I'm doing what I can. But we don't have legal grounds to fight this."

"Don't fight it then." My voice sounded small and trembly. "Just let them go."

"We have to fight it, Claire. There's a lot of money at stake."

I couldn't argue with that. Money was something we both needed—Dave because he had expensive tastes and a love of fast cars, and me because I was desperately trying to help my parents, who had recently gotten into a tough financial predicament after my father lost his job. It was only after I had started trying to help my parents out that I'd realized how Dave's lifestyle was causing us to hemorrhage all the money we made. I'd felt a sense of panic as I looked through the account statements. The mortgage on the house was costing a huge chunk every month, and had it really been necessary for Dave to buy a brand new luxury car? I frowned down at the numerous cash withdrawals. What on earth were they all for? Was Dave remembering to keep the slips for tax purposes? Somehow, I doubted it. I had to scrape together enough to pay for my parents' rented house, and cover my mother's enormous medical expenses. Perhaps I could dip into our savings account…but another bombshell had been waiting when I opened those statements.

It had seemed bad enough at the time, when I'd assumed there would be more money coming in. Now, with my sponsors canceling and demanding payback, our situation was an unmitigated disaster.

"Let me know what I can do to help," I said to Dave.

"I would have hoped you'd be thinking what you could do. Not waiting for me to tell you."

"I'm sorry," I repeated.

There was a pause. Then he let out another breath. "Whatever, Claire."

"I'll speak to you later," I told him. "I'm losing signal."

"Okay, then," he said and disconnected.

I put my phone back into my purse. It rang again almost immediately, but it was an unfamiliar number, so I ignored it. Rain spattered the windscreen. Above me, clouds were gathering, but ahead, to the southwest, the sky was clear.

I was going to get to Castle Hill as soon as I could; try to outrun the storm which was pursuing me literally and figuratively.

I turned on the radio, cranked the sound up high, and headed for the Ring of Kerry highway.

The drive to Castle Hill took place in increasingly glorious weather. By the time I reached my destination, soon after lunch, the sun shone brilliantly from a sky flecked with clouds, casting a magical green brightness over the trees and hedges that lined the road.

The Ring of Kerry proved to be as magnificent as the rental car attendant had promised. The highway curved through idyllic farmland, passing quaint farmhouses set among patchworks of fields, and hugged the coast, where the cliffs dropped dramatically away toward the sea below.

SOARING

I pulled into a service station for fuel when I was just a half-hour away from my destination. I was glad to get out of the car. My muscles felt stiff and sore from their cramped position, and my left wrist was aching from grasping the wheel. I was surprised by how tired I felt. I told myself that it was no surprise, given the stress I'd been through. But the truth was that my body was leaden with an exhaustion which felt like it had been accumulating for years.

How long since I'd properly rested, since I'd gone more than a few days without the endless regimen of gym, training, training, gym? How many years since I'd eaten anything other than the strict diet which Dave had prescribed, after consultation with experts?

I remembered the conversation we'd had, a few years ago now, when he'd called me to tell me the good news.

"Claire, you're not gonna believe this! We've gotten you a really great sponsorship here. With College Sport. My brother Daniel's just been made a partner in the business and he's organized it all for you. They're expanding, going big, getting into all kinds of different gear—running, fencing, football—specializing in sales to schools and colleges. And they're looking for a frontline girl. I suggested you, and Daniel and the other partners agreed."

"Oh, Dave, that's amazing! How wonderful!"

"You're gonna fence professionally for them, but it's more than that. They really like your looks. Part of the deal is you become their face, appearing at events, doing PR, modeling for some of their new lines. It'll mean losing a few pounds – yeah, yeah, I know you're normal weight, and that's fine for fencing, but the camera fattens. And you need to be thin to look good in sports gear. So, you up for it? I got a diet sheet here for you already!"

Since then, I'd been hungry so often that it seemed like a constant in my life. If I wasn't getting fit for competition, I was gymming and dieting. Staying thin for the cameras. To please my sponsors.

The array of chocolates on the shelves inside the service station seemed to call to me, their colorful wrappers luring me in. Sugary bliss, no longer on the forbidden list.

I chose a bar of milk chocolate with caramel and hazelnuts,

and to drink, a strawberry shake. I stabbed the straw through the lid of the shake and the smell filled my nostrils, saliva flooding my mouth.

I sucked hungrily at the shake, savoring the cold, creamy, faux-strawberry taste. And then, my thirst quenched, I turned my attention to the chocolate. I peeled back the wrapper, breathing in its cocoa-rich fragrance, before sliding it between my lips and sinking my teeth into its delicious softness. Caramel stretched out in rich, syrupy strands; the crunch of the nuts added another dimension to the texture.

I wanted to laugh aloud from childish delight, but instead I found my eyes flooding with tears. I attacked the sweet, cramming it into my mouth, craving it all, suddenly starving. I closed my brimming eyes, wiped away the wetness on my cheeks as I chewed voraciously on the enormous mouthful of fattiness and sweetness and sin.

A half-hour later, I drove into the town of Castle Hill, feeling slightly sick from my bingeing, but awake and alert thanks to the sugary energy.

Where to stay?

The Park Hotel that Patrick had mentioned was still open. More than that, it seemed to have been recently refurbished. It didn't look rundown, the way he had described it. It looked shiny and up-market, a five-star establishment in a town center that was quaint and beautiful, but also looked to be busy and thriving; a mini-hub of commerce.

I was suddenly tempted to turn away from the town center and drive out into that glorious, green countryside. Find a cheap and friendly farmhouse or a B&B and hole up in quiet, rural tranquility.

I decided to allow myself a short stay in the hotel. My remaining voyager miles, which were about to expire, would cover two nights there. I might as well use them. After that, I'd find somewhere else to go.

But while I checked in, I started to feel I'd made a big mistake.

The young, dark-haired receptionist was polite and charming, but I couldn't help noticing that she raised her eyebrows when she looked at my passport, and I felt a knot of dread tightening. At a five-star hotel, with satellite television and guests from all over the world, the staff might be more up to date with international news. I didn't want to be recognized, but I feared that it was too late.

"There's your room key." She slid the card across the polished mahogany counter. "Breakfast is from seven to ten a.m., and I'm giving you the brochures for our two restaurants. Booking is advisable, especially for the Terrace. It can get very popular in the evenings, especially with our Associated Press conference on."

She smiled again, and I smiled back, my lips feeling tight.

The press? Just what I didn't need.

"How big is the conference?" I asked her.

"Oh, it's four hundred people. About two hundred are staying at the hotel—the ones from out of town and the international delegates. The others are coming in for the meetings. The conferencing area is very busy today, and the restaurants will be booked up later."

Four hundred journalists?

Suddenly this spacious hotel seemed very small. I glanced behind me and saw a young, slim man with a short, black beard. He was obviously waiting to be attended to. He had a camera bag slung over his shoulder and was wearing a Boston Red Sox T-shirt.

American journalists?

I knew I should have kept driving and looked for an old country house with milk churns outside the barn and an Accommodation Available sign at the gate. And now, here I was, sharing the hotel with four hundred journos who would sell their sister to get the scoop on my story.

"The conference finishes tomorrow," the receptionist told me. "So we'll be back to normal then."

That news made me feel better. All I had to do was lay low for the rest of the day. That would be possible, wouldn't it?

The porter wheeled my bag across the marble tiles and we

rode up to the fifth floor, where he showed me my room. It was lovely—spacious, airy, beautifully decorated, and the view was as glorious as Patrick had described, but I had the Associated Press on the brain, and to me, it felt claustrophobic. When the porter left, I opened the window, staring out over the bay while I breathed in the fresh sea air.

I glanced into the mirror, not liking that the woman staring back at me was all too recognizable. My broad shoulders, my too-lean body, my blue eyes, and my mane of hair which fell past my shoulders and which over the years had been artfully (and expensively) highlighted into tones that were more sand and honey than its natural caramel. I wished I'd brought a black wig with me, but all I had in the way of disguise were my Tom Ford sunglasses, which were courtesy of a small sponsorship last year, and my baseball cap.

Perhaps a walk on the beachfront would do me some good. The press would all be in their conference, and when that was done, they'd flock straight to the pubs and restaurants. I knew what journalists were like. They wouldn't go out for a walk, especially now, with the wind starting to freshen and light clouds obscuring the sun.

I changed into capris and a blue T-shirt, scraped my hair back into a ponytail, and put on the baseball cap, taking a light jersey from my bag before making sure my sunglasses were safely stowed in my purse.

As the elevator doors closed, I wondered whether it would be more sensible to walk or drive to the beach. Walking would be better exercise, but driving would mean I'd get there quicker. I was still undecided, but happily so, when the "Lobby" button lit up and the doors slid open again.

The man waiting in front of the doors was as impatient to get in as I was to get out. We almost collided before he stepped hurriedly back.

"So sorry," he said. He moved aside and, with a chivalrous sweep of his hand, invited me to walk out and past him. But I was rooted to the spot. I couldn't move. I could barely breathe. I'm sure I must have looked as if I'd seen a ghost…and not your everyday, common-or-garden specter, but something way more terrifying.

I recognized this man. Tall, broad-shouldered, his build as lean and rangy as I remembered it. His face…the rugged handsomeness of his bone structure more defined than it had been back then. His hair—slightly shorter, perfectly cut, although not so perfectly styled—those wayward locks still falling over his forehead. His gold-hazel eyes, that seemed to be lit from within by a flickering flame. He was arching his right eyebrow slightly, just the same way he'd done when I'd first seen him. I took in his chiseled mouth, which had kissed my own with such expert, melting tenderness…

Patrick was standing in front of me—the physical embodiment of all my thoughts and dreams.

I remembered exactly how it had felt when I'd slid my hands underneath his sweatshirt and let them roam over his body, touching his abs, moving round the leanness of his waist, to press into the thick muscles flanking his spine. Taut as his skin looked, it had been silken soft to the touch and surprisingly hot, as if the same fire that flickered in his eyes was also smoldering in his core.

Now, he wore dark pants and a perfectly cut black jacket. His white dress shirt was open at the collar, no tie. He looked like he'd just started undressing after a formal function, and for just a moment, it scared me to think how badly I wanted to tug that shirt out of his pants, to pull the buttons open so it hung loose, to slide my hands under it and touch him again.

I stared into his eyes and saw my own emotions reflected there. First confusion, then surprise, and finally I saw, dawning, the same incredulous realization that I felt.

This couldn't be! It was impossible. This was a man I'd met once, an encounter I'd fantasized about forever after…and now, here he was. Just inches away from me. In the same hotel, in the exact town where I had chosen to run.

Oh, God, my cover was so totally blown now. And in that instant of self-awareness, humiliation swept over me. Who had I been, when this handsome rogue had last seen me? An athlete on the brink of a promising career. A young woman with a bright future ahead of her. No scars on my body. No blemishes on my record.

Now, ten years later, I was a has-been, hated by the media, fleeing from scandal as sponsors severed their ties. I had broken everything that was precious to me. I was broken myself.

And that knowledge, finally, unfroze me.

He was already moving toward me again, starting to say something as I pushed past him, my hands cold and my heart hammering in my throat, and headed for the exit at a run.

I heard his voice calling behind me—deep, commanding. "Claire? Claire!"

This time, no doubt, the words were meant for me.

I did not stop, but sprinted out of the hotel, past the startled doorman, and out into the fresh, cloudy afternoon.

CHAPTER 3

Out in the streets, I just kept walking. No way was I turning back to the hotel now, not even to get my car. Wherever I was going, I wouldn't drive...on foot was safer.

Spying a gap in the light afternoon traffic, I jogged across the road and glanced behind me. The glass door of the hotel was closed. Nobody had followed me out. I prayed no one was watching.

Even so, I kept up my swift pace, with the wind tugging at my ponytail and the sights and smells of the town surrounding me. So different from the repetitive slog of a gym treadmill, where I'd put in most of my miles in recent years.

I headed inland, following the main road for about twenty minutes until I was out of town, before making a left turn onto a quieter road. It took me up a hill, over its crest, and half an hour later, I was walking through the farmland I'd seen from the plane. At times, my view was blocked by the overgrowth of trees and hedges that lined the road, but every so often a gap in the greenery allowed me to see wooden gates leading on to emerald fields where cows and horses grazed.

I turned again twice more, going deeper into the countryside and choosing narrower roads each time, including one that was little more than a tarred footpath and had grass growing down its middle. Hardly any cars passed me now; just the occasional farm vehicle or horse trailer. I was wished a good afternoon by a gray haired woman walking her two red setters, and a man riding a large chestnut horse tipped his hat in my direction as he trotted past.

I had no idea how I was going to find my way back. I had my purse and my phone with me...perhaps I'd call a cab. But the idea of heading back to that hotel terrified me. Should I find another place to stay? I knew I'd have to make a decision soon, because the shadows were starting to lengthen, the sun was hovering above the hills, and in another hour, it would be getting dark.

Now that I thought about it, I remembered there had been occasional signposts for B&Bs along my walk. I just couldn't recall how far back the most recent one had been. But it was worth a try.

I turned around and began the long walk back.

This crossroads…had I gone straight here, or turned? I gazed around me, mystified. Nothing looked familiar. Or, rather, the problem was that it all did. There were only so many bushy hedges, five-barred gates and Jersey herds you could pass before everything started looking the same. My sense of direction was unreliable even when there was a recognizable landmark within view—the Eiffel Tower, for instance. I'd gotten lost in Paris more times than I cared to remember. And now, for the first time, I was getting lost in County Kerry, Ireland.

I decided to go straight, knowing that it would probably be wrong, and then kept walking out of sheer stubbornness, as if by not giving up, I could make the right road come to me.

A half-hour and two more turns later, it was almost dark and I was ready to admit defeat. The only reason I was still going was in a vain quest to find the name of the lane I was on, so I could tell the cab driver where to come.

And then, I saw it: a hand-painted sign on a white board propped against the edge of a stone gatepost.

"Room Available. Enquire Within." It was followed by a phone number. The gate was open and, straining my eyes in the gloom, I saw that the winding driveway snaked its way between apple trees, up to a quaint farmhouse that looked to be built of the same stone.

I took a deep breath. Perhaps this sign was fortuitous—a signal from Fate. Or perhaps I was simply too tired to realize what a bad mistake I was about to make. Hoisting my ever-heavier purse onto my shoulder again, I trudged up the long gravel driveway.

CHAPTER 4

I was about fifty yards from the farmhouse door when a bloodcurdling yell stopped me in my tracks.

"Guinness!"

It was a woman's voice, furious, pitched midway between a roar and a scream. I could almost feel the sound waves battering me. I glanced back toward the gate, wondering whether I should make a hasty retreat.

"Guinness, come here!" I'd thought it impossible for her to shout louder, but this second wrathful cry made my ears ring.

Decision made, then. Clearly, a madwoman lived here.

I turned my back on the farmhouse and began hurrying to the gate, but a moment later, the scampering of paws on gravel made me spin round again. A large black and white dog—a collie, I realized—was heading my way at a run, letting out a volley of sharp barks.

"Um—good dog?" I tried, hopefully. "Shush, now!"

But the barking grew louder as the collie came closer.

"Guinness!"

Light streamed out as the farmhouse door was flung open, and a sturdily built woman marched outside.

"Come here! Now! Bad dog!"

Guinness's barks trailed off into a whine. He slowed to a walk and crept up to me, his ears laid apologetically against his head.

"Who's out there?" the woman called. "Can I help you?"

Guinness licked my hand, then wagged his tail.

"Come here, you thieving dog!"

Guinness left my side and scampered back to the farmhouse. The woman flicked a dishcloth at him as he trotted inside. "What is it with you and baked goods, Guinness?" she chastised him in a musical Irish accent. "I could leave a roast out, ready for the oven, and go into town and you wouldn't touch it. But put a cake on the cooling tray for five minutes..." She grimaced in annoyance before turning to me. "Sorry for the shouting. How can I help you?"

"Good evening." I made my way up to the door—a kitchen door, I now saw. The smell of baking biscuits wafted out to meet me.

Up close, the woman looked less scary than her voice had sounded. She was shorter than me and in her mid-forties, I guessed. Dark hair in an outgrown bob was held back from her face by a tortoiseshell clip, and her ample bosom strained against the confines of a blue apron.

"I'm Claire," I said. "I saw your sign at the gate."

"Noreen Neville." She nodded in response. "Which sign would that be? Free-range eggs? I meant to take it down until after the weekend."

"No, no. The one about the room for rent."

Noreen tilted her head sideways and regarded me shrewdly. "It's only a room," she said. "I don't think it's suitable accommodation for a tourist."

I nodded. "I wasn't looking for anything fancy."

"This is very basic," she explained further. "Just a small bedroom, with a bathroom down the passage. I normally rent to people who work around here. You know, riding the hunters, that sort of thing."

She must have seen the confusion in my eyes, because she added, "The horses. Riding the horses."

I felt my face grow hot. "I don't mind how basic the room is," I said. "I'd like to take it."

She regarded me for a moment longer, smoothing her fingers, which I noticed were floury, over her apron.

"Well, you'd better have a look at it then. Give me a minute while I wash my hands. Do you want to bring your car into the yard?"

"My car's—um—it's somewhere else. I walked here."

That comment earned me another narrow-eyed glance.

But Noreen said nothing more. She ushered me into the kitchen, which looked like the main living area of the house. It was spacious, with a polished wooden floor, white-painted cupboards and grey granite surfaces with a large table in the center. An empty cooling rack stood on the nearest surface, surrounded by the evidence of crumbs that had spilled onto the floor. From its perch on top of the refrigerator, a large, long-haired tabby cat regarded me inscrutably.

"The room belonged to my daughter, Marian," Noreen explained, leading the way down the passage. "She's gone to England, so I've been letting it out."

The floorboards squeaked under my feet. I followed Noreen up a flight of stairs. The house smelled good: the sweet, crispy aroma of cake, with a warm undertone of polish. And when she opened the door at the end of the corridor, the first scent I picked up was the fragrance of pot-pourri.

The room was tiny, barely big enough for the double bed, wooden wardrobe and small desk and chair it contained. It had a beige carpet and curtains that looked new. The duvet cover was patterned with roses.

"Basic, as I told you," Noreen repeated.

"It looks perfect," I reassured her.

I asked Noreen what the address was here, and she wrote it down for me.

"If you'd like some dinner, I've more than enough for two in the oven," she told me. "I can't offer you cake, though," she added, with a mock-frustrated sigh.

"Thank you," I said.

"We'll eat at seven."

She closed the door and I heard her footsteps going back down the passage, over those squeaky boards, and down the stairs.

I checked my phone.

There were a couple of missed calls and messages, none from anyone I knew. Ignoring them with an effort, I called the hotel instead.

"It's Claire Harvey here," I told the receptionist. "I was

checked into room number 507, but my plans have changed and I'm now staying at…" I consulted the piece of paper, "Mulligan Heights Farm, Shepherd's Lane, Drewes' Folly."

I waited while the receptionist took down the address.

"Could you possibly send my bag to me tomorrow morning?" I asked. "If you can't, then I'll come round for it, but if you could organize a courier, that would be wonderful."

I could do without the rental car for now. Maybe in a day or two, I'd summon up the courage to sneak into the hotel's parking and reclaim it. It was not urgent; my bag was. Apart from my toothbrush, toiletries and clothes, it also contained my cellphone charger—an essential, since my phone couldn't go twelve hours without needing to be charged.

"Of course we can do that, Ms. Harvey," the receptionist told me. "We'll send your bag with a courier."

I put down the phone with a sigh of relief.

I would not have to set foot in the Park Hotel again. I would not have to run the risk of being recognized by a curious journalist keen for a story. And I would not risk bumping into the man I'd spent far too much time thinking about over the past years.

That thought gave me an unexpected jolt of disappointment, but quickly, I suppressed it.

I walked down the passage a few yards to find, as advertised, a bathroom. A clean towel was hanging on the rail, and a bathmat was folded on the lid of the wicker laundry basket. There was a cake of soap in the shower and lavender bath gel on the shelf next to the claw-footed tub.

The tub looked too sumptuous to resist. I filled it halfway with steaming water, folded my clothes on the laundry basket, and climbed inside.

I lay down with a sigh, carefully positioning my left arm, fearing the usual stab of pain when I moved it, and was relieved to find that there was none. Only the usual residual muscle ache, but even the water was soothing that.

Looking at my body dispassionately, I could see it only as a tool—a tool that had been useful to me but which, ultimately,

SOARING

had failed me, or I had failed it. My legs, toned and sleek from hours of arduous gym sessions. My protruding hipbones and concave belly. The left arm, more firmly muscled than the right from the endless hours of thrusting and parrying with my blade. Even after the weeks of rest following the injury, you could still see the difference. It was one of the reasons I didn't like wearing sleeveless tops; I was embarrassed about the visible disparity in the size of my arm muscles.

I looked down at my breasts, which were firmly rounded, but otherwise average in every way. Perhaps I should have made more of the cleavage I had, flaunted it, worn lacy push-up bras and low-cut tops. But that would not have suited the image of the blonde, decent, all-American sports icon that College Sport wanted me to portray. It had been conservative necklines for me during my photo shoots. Even the gym tops hadn't been very revealing.

Now, my image was indelibly tarnished.

I soaped myself in the essence of lavender. Scooped hot water into my cupped hands and let it cascade over my breasts, and as I did so, I found my thoughts straying back to Patrick.

After so many years of existing only in my memory, I'd almost been able to believe he had never been real; that he'd been a figment of my dreams. And it was there that he reappeared, sometimes. I'd wake up alone in my hotel bedroom, or in my lonely bed at home on the many occasions when Dave was away. I'd be breathless and tingling with desire, still feeling the audacious brush of fingertips across my throbbing mound… only to realize with a stab of guilt that I'd just spent the night, figuratively, with another man.

The shrilling of my cellphone interrupted my reverie. I scrambled out of the bath with a curse, water streaming down me, grabbed my towel, and did a quick foot-drying dance on the bathmat before hurrying down the corridor to grab it just before it rang through to voicemail.

It was the hotel calling.

"Ms. Harvey, would it be convenient for us to deliver your bag later this evening?"

"That would be wonderful," I said, surprised. "Thank you."

I would be reunited with my toothbrush sooner than I'd hoped, and I'd be able to plug my pesky phone in before it died on me.

I put my capris and jersey back on, and went downstairs, where more delicious aromas were starting to fill the kitchen.

"You're not a vegetarian or anything, are you?" Noreen asked.

Even if I had been, the smell coming from that oven would have converted me.

"I do eat meat," I told her. Lean chicken or turkey, normally, in rationed portions doled out for me by Dave.

"Well, I've done a beef roast," she said. "It's been a cooking day, because I had to make something for the Castle Hill Women's Guild. They've got a home crafts shop in town. Proceeds go to charity, and we all take turns baking. I was going to do scones and cake. Turns out they'll just get scones."

She frowned in the direction of the dog basket near the door, and Guinness thumped his tail.

"That sounds like a lovely initiative," I said.

"Between you and me," Noreen explained, "it's a right pain in the backside, and the Women's Guild members here are a load of egotistical little interferers."

I wasn't sure how to respond to that. My gut instinct was to giggle, but I thought that might be unwise, so I pressed my lips together firmly.

"Do you want a beer?" Noreen asked. "Or elderberry wine?"

"I'd love whatever you're having," I said. Alcohol was forbidden to me for most of the year. I'd practically forgotten what it tasted like.

"Elderberry wine it is, then," Noreen said, handing me a glass of pale pink, fragrant liquid. "It's also from the Women's Guild shop. Mrs. Miller makes it. It's better than most of the other shite they sell there."

I almost snorted my first sip of wine out of my nose at that comment.

"It's very good," I said, when I'd gotten my laughter under

control. Sharp and tasty, I could almost feel it filtering into my bloodstream, making me lightheaded and amazingly relaxed.

"Can I help you with anything?" I asked. Noreen was dividing her attention between three different pots, including the sizzling pan of beef she'd just removed from the oven, the sight of which was making hunger claw at my belly.

"Yes," she said. "There's a colander in the cupboard on the left. No, not that one, the next. There you go. Could you be a dear and drain the peas?" She pointed to the smallest, steaming pot. "And there's mint growing in the flower bed outside. The one to the right of the door. If you wouldn't mind picking some, it'll go nicely with them."

Peas and mint. My culinary repertoire was not large, but I felt confident with managing that. I tipped the contents of the pot into the colander, and then, leaving it in the sink to drain, unlatched the door and stepped out.

It was fully dark now, and Noreen's farmhouse didn't have an outside light. Would I be able to identify mint by feel alone? My luck, I'd end up garnishing the peas with deadly nightshade by mistake.

I closed my eyes, hoping it would help them adapt to the darkness quicker. When I opened them, it was to see a pair of powerful headlights winding their way up the drive toward me.

A barking Guinness shot out of the house and past me, and Noreen appeared swiftly at the door, calling him back.

"Who's that?" she asked. "Somebody you know?"

"I think it's a courier, or a driver from the hotel where I was staying," I called back. "The Park. They said they'd deliver my bag tonight."

As the approaching vehicle curved round the final bend, the headlights shone onto the flower bed. Quickly, I stepped forward and broke off a sprig of mint from the leafy bush I saw there.

"Posh car for a hotel to use," Noreen offered doubtfully, before retreating inside.

I looked up again, to see the sleek, gleaming lines of a silver Mercedes SUV, and had time to think that Noreen was right; it was an extremely fancy car. The Mercedes stopped at the top of the drive, the lights cut, and I saw a gleam as the door swung open.

I peered into the gloom, seeing a tall man get out, hearing the scrunch of footsteps as the driver went round to the trunk. And then he walked toward me, and as he approached I felt my spine prickle…because he looked somehow familiar.

Then the light from the open door shone onto his face and confirmed my suspicions, causing me to let out a gasp.

It was Patrick. For the second time that day, we were standing just feet away from each other. His eyes were fixed on me; his mouth was quirked up at one corner. And he was holding my bag.

CHAPTER 5

The mint slipped from my fingers, which felt suddenly icy.

"Good evening, Claire," Patrick said softly.

"What—what are you doing here?" My voice sounded high and breathy. My heart was hammering. I couldn't believe this… it was surreal. How had he known where I was?

I was unable to look away. I watched the way his delicious mouth was curving up in that half-smile. The manner in which he was looking at me was just as intense…that green-gold gaze taking in the detail that my clingy jersey offered before fixing steadily on my own eyes.

"I've come to bring you your bag," he said. He stepped forward, coming closer to me, and at that point, the light from the open kitchen door was shadowed as Noreen appeared, once again, in its doorway.

"Excuse me, but who are you?" she demanded of Patrick, striding over to where we were standing. She was bristling with righteous anger, which made her seem taller than her five-foot-nothing. She stood next to me, her hands on her hips, her chin jutting. "Because this lady here is running scared, and she's obviously afraid of something. And if you're that something, I suggest you get the hell off this property right now, or I'm calling the police!"

Patrick's eyes widened at her words. Noreen's anger was an elemental force. Her irate expression barely softened as he turned the full force of his charm onto her.

"Good evening, ma'am," he said. "I hope I'm not the reason why Claire decided to leave the hotel. But I've brought her bag to her, and I wondered if I might have the chance to speak to her for a minute."

My body wanted that chance. My body was begging for the

opportunity to be alone again with him. My mind wasn't quite so sure.

"I don't understand why you're here," I said, faintly. "How did you know where I'd gone? Did—did someone at the hotel tell you?"

"Yes, how?" Noreen echoed fiercely.

Patrick blinked, looking briefly confused.

"Claire, I own the hotel," he said gently. "I was standing in reception when your call came through."

His words silenced me. Luckily, they did not have the same effect on my ally.

"You own the Park?" Noreen sounded incredulous.

"I do, yes." Patrick gave her a courteous nod.

"But it went bankrupt in January last year."

"That's when I bought it."

"So you're…"

They spoke the words at the same time, Patrick extending his hand to her.

"Patrick Maguire?"

"Patrick Maguire."

I hadn't known his last name till now; had not known who he was. Now I knew something about him…a fact that seemed to have mollified Noreen.

"So you took over the Park?" she said. "I haven't been there, but I heard it's very nice now. Refurbished, and all. It's brought a lot of business back to the town."

"My team's done a good job," Patrick nodded.

Noreen sighed. Then she turned to me.

"Do you want to speak to him?" she asked me.

"Yes," I said in a low voice. "Yes, I do."

"Five minutes," Noreen said, in a voice that brooked no argument. "Then dinner's ready."

She bent down and picked up the sprig of mint that had fallen onto the gravel. Then she took my carry-on from Patrick, refusing his offer to bring it inside. She hefted the bag in her right hand and marched back into the kitchen.

Patrick watched her go, and the corner of his mouth twitched upwards again.

Then he turned to me. He stepped closer.

He'd changed out of his smart clothes and was wearing jeans and a soft leather jacket. I could smell a hint of musky spice from the jacket; or maybe that was from his skin. I could feel my cheeks growing warm, my mouth parting slightly as I stared up at him; my body's responses betraying the flood of lust that was consuming me.

"Claire," he said again. "I can't believe you're here."

I nodded. "Likewise," I said. I didn't actually know what to say. I had the feeling nothing that came out of my mouth would make much sense. I wanted so badly to touch him, it was scary. I could feel the tension sizzling in the air, the electric thrill of attraction between us. It seemed safer to keep my hands behind my back.

I couldn't stop looking at him, though. My eyes wanted to make up for lost time. I couldn't get enough of staring at the perfect planes of his face. The sweep of his brows, his straight nose, firm jaw—all hard, angular, masculine, softened only by the warm sensuality of his mouth, and the golden fire in those unusual eyes.

"I'm sorry you left the hotel," he said. "I think I understand why."

He understood why? How much about me did he know?

"You don't need to say sorry for anything," I said. My mouth felt dry. The words came clumsily from my lips, as if they would rather not be speaking, but instead, kissing his own.

"Can I see you tomorrow?" he asked, and the question took me completely by surprise.

"T-tomorrow?" I stammered out.

"If you have time, I'd like to take you out. For lunch."

I couldn't believe what I was hearing. He was inviting me out? This was…well, it sounded to me as if I was being asked on a date.

There was a resounding silence as if the world around us was as stunned as I was by his question. Then sounds filtered back in. I could hear the faraway barking of a dog. A car purred slowly down the lane, its taillights glinting red as they retreated into the night.

"I do have time." I told him.

"Well, then," he said.

I suddenly picked up that he was feeling as awkward as I was; knocked way off-center by the rollercoaster of emotion we were riding.

"One o'clock?" he asked.

"That's good for me," I said, and saw his mouth soften in anticipation, or perhaps relief.

"I'll pick you up here, then."

I nodded. "That'll be fine. I—I look forward to it." This formality was killing me, but I didn't know what else to say, or how to say it. Perhaps it was killing him, too. I had no idea.

"Well, have a good evening." He turned and started back to the car.

He got only a few steps before he said, under his breath, "Oh, fuck it."

He turned and in three giant strides, he was back, and I could see the intent in his eyes, the abandonment of the control he'd been battling to maintain.

His arms crushed me close. He pulled me against him, groaning in pleasure as our mouths found each other once again. This was no Hollywood kiss. It was raw, rough, and desperate. We were insatiable. Our teeth knocked together as I parted my lips, wanting him, no, needing him to devour me. I felt the hot, urgent friction of his tongue on mine and let out an audible moan, sliding my own deep into his mouth. I locked my arms around him and dug my fingers into his back and closed my eyes as I kissed him back, as hard and hungrily as he was kissing me.

The spicy smell of his skin, the ravishment of his lips, the taste of him. I remembered how it had been, as clearly as if it had been imprinted on my senses. I was amazed to realize nothing had changed. Time had not lessened the astonishing, visceral attraction between us. Whatever chemistry had sparked our reckless behavior back then, ensconced in that luxury airline cabin, was still scorching every nerve ending in my body now.

Finally, we broke the kiss, still holding each other. He was breathing hard, and I supposed I was, too. I wanted nothing more than to mash my face into his own again, to bruise his lips with my own, to thrust my hips against the throbbing hardness of his groin.

Somehow, perhaps thanks to Noreen's dire warning about five minutes, which I did not doubt she would enforce, I found the strength to let go, to step back. I stared at Patrick, unable to believe what had just happened. His hair was tousled, his shirt was tugged sideways and pulled half out of his pants in a way that was begging me to finish the job.

"Tomorrow," I said. My knees were weak and my lips felt swollen. My face was tingling from the friction of his stubble.

He closed his eyes briefly, and gave a small shake of his head. "Claire," he said again, his voice husky. He spoke my name as if he was tasting it. "Claire."

His eyes met mine, pinning me in that golden gaze.

"Tomorrow," he promised, before turning and striding back to his car.

CHAPTER 6

I'd thought I wouldn't be able to sleep after the shock of seeing Patrick again, and the anticipation of our date—please, let it be a date—the next day. I'd thought I'd be too excited to eat, either, but I was wrong on both counts. I devoured the plate of tender beef and sweet vegetables, swimming in rich gravy, that Noreen served up. It was as if the taste of sensory delight I'd had with Patrick had whetted my appetite for other physical pleasures.

After another glass of the elderberry wine, I'd thanked Noreen for her hospitality, helped her tidy away and stack the dishes, and then stumbled upstairs where I'd fallen asleep as soon as my head had hit the pillow.

I slept for nearly eleven hours. That was unheard of for me. How exhausted had I been? I woke blinking in sunshine, checked the time on the travel clock on the bedside table, and was amazed to see it was quarter past eight in the morning.

A sensual memory flitted through my mind, but was gone before I could grasp it. The hunger that tugged deep inside me, and the tingling of my skin, told me that Patrick had spent the night with me again, captured in one of my dreams. I couldn't recall the details now. What a pity.

Tentatively, almost shyly, I slipped my right arm under the covers. I smoothed a hand over my thigh, parting the softness of my lips, and my eyes widened as I felt the slick wetness there.

"Your body's turning into a hormone factory," I scolded myself, even though this evidence of my own arousal made me smile; like springtime after a long winter. I'd have to use all my self-control when I met Patrick for lunch. Imagine if he knew how turned on I could get just from having him visit in my dreams?

SOARING

From the focused, hungry intent I'd seen in his eyes last night, I knew I wouldn't stand a chance, and at that thought, I let out a shuddery breath, and then stretched, languidly, enjoying the smooth caress of the cotton sheets on my skin.

It was time to get up. Perhaps there would be some chores to do, something I could help Noreen with to pass the time until one o'clock, when that silver Mercedes would scrunch its way up the gravel drive again.

I hoped we weren't going anywhere fashionable. I had packed no dressy clothes. I had yoga pants, a skirt, jeans, and one other pair of capris, together with a few casual tops and T-shirts. A pair of sandals and running shoes completed my wardrobe. For now, I pulled on a T-shirt and yoga pants, put on the running shoes, and made my way downstairs.

There was no sign of Noreen, and Guinness's basket was empty. The spot on top of the fridge was occupied by the magnificent long-coated tabby I'd seen last night. Standing on tiptoes, I scratched him behind his head and was rewarded with a thunderous purr.

"Noreen?" I called, but the house was silent.

A picture of a horse flickered into my mind—a tall gelding with a handsomely arched neck and a gray coat. His ears were pricked forward as he trotted through the short grass toward an outstretched halter. He was followed more reluctantly by a smaller, brown-coated horse that kept stopping to snatch at an occasional dandelion. The image solidified and became real, part of my memory. Animals often gave me clear pictures. I knew Noreen had gone out to fetch these horses. Perhaps she planned to ride them this morning.

I noticed a clean mug and spoon on the counter, near jars of instant coffee and sugar, and a china jug with a lid labeled, "Cream." Clearly, I was invited to fix myself some coffee. I put on the kettle, and while I waited for it to boil, I decided to explore the downstairs area of the house.

Opposite the kitchen, a glass-paneled double door led into a formal lounge. Here, two brown settees and two floral armchairs were placed around a wooden coffee table, on which were piled some hardcover books. One was a photographic collection of Irish scenery; another was a volume of art through the ages, another was a compilation of Charles Addams cartoons. The curtains were open, providing a view through the French doors of the colorful flowerbeds. Beyond that, a grassy field was dotted with trees.

The lounge led into a dining room with a table, six chairs, and a Welsh dresser, upon which was a collection of photographs and a number of trophies. Curious, I walked closer to look. Several were of the daughter Noreen had mentioned. She was blonder than her mother, smiling in every snapshot. In one, she was sitting on the grass with her arms around Guinness. In a few of the others, she was mounted on a tall gray horse that I recognized from my recent vision.

I saw several photos of Noreen with a sandy-haired, cheerful looking man. Her husband? I wondered where he was now. Divorced? I hoped not, from the happiness that was evident in the snapshots; Noreen's arms wrapped affectionately around him as he smiled down at her.

I was entranced by the framed artwork on the walls. Two large countryside scenes graced the lounge, while in the dining room, smaller still life portraits of fruit and flowers were displayed. They were skillfully done, with a captivating quality to their design that made me want to keep looking. Were they all painted by the same artist? The signature looked the same—the initials, "CN"—but I had no idea who he or she could be. I made a note to ask Noreen.

The whistle of the kettle sent me hurrying back to the kitchen. I spooned coffee into the mug, added a lump of sugar, and then opened the lid of the cream jug, which felt cold, as if it had recently come out of the fridge. To my delight, it was half full of real, thick, clotted cream. How sinfully divine. I spooned so much of it into the coffee that if Dave had seen, he'd have bawled me out and banished me to the gym.

I put the cream jug back into the fridge, and walked outside with my coffee, blinking in the brightness, taking in the vivid colors. The emerald fields, the azure sky dotted with small, fluffy clouds, the riot of hues in the flower beds. And the smells…I could smell the rich, earthy aroma of compost or manure, underscoring the clean scent of wet foliage. Breathing it in made me feel happy, as if I were renewing a connection with nature that I had lost, and missed, without even knowing it.

I'd almost finished my coffee when I saw Noreen approaching. She was leading the two horses along a pathway that curved down the hill. The majestic gray was accompanying her calmly. The smaller bay was dancing impatiently sideways, shaking its head and trying to pull the halter rope out of her hand. He was the dandelion snatcher; the naughty one.

From where I was standing, I could hear Noreen swearing.

Probably, she could use some help.

Quickly, I put my mug back in the kitchen, then jogged down the hill, slowing to a walk as I drew closer so as not to startle the misbehaving bay.

"You little varmint, if you try to pull my arm out of its socket once more, I swear to God I'm going to take you to the market! Stop trying to bloody well run off. We'll get there soon enough, dammit…oh, morning, Claire."

"Morning! Could you use a hand?"

"I could, thanks! Are you okay to lead this one?" She glanced at the well behaved gray.

"Yes, I've had experience with horses."

That had been fifteen years ago at summer camp…I'd loved caring for them, and had excelled at my riding back then. I hoped I hadn't forgotten what I'd learned.

Gratefully, Noreen passed me the gray's halter rope, and I held it as I remembered being taught, hoping it was correct. The large horse didn't challenge me or try to pull away. He simply turned his head in my direction, nostrils flickering, then continued walking steadily along the pathway.

With two hands to manage the smaller horse, Noreen had gotten him under control again, even though he was rolling his eyes, as if in disgust, and jogging sideways.

"I'm taking them to a fresh pasture," she explained. "They

always get excited on the way to a different field. Or rather, Murphy does. Titan's a real gentleman. Clever enough to know the grass isn't always greener."

"Are they hunters?" I asked.

"Yes," she said. "And you probably won't believe me when I tell you Murphy never puts a foot wrong on hunting day. As soon as he hears the sound of the horn, he's an angel. Titan also does dressage. My daughter used to compete with him, before she bought the horse she owns now."

That must have been the large bay I saw in the photos. "And where is that horse now?"

"She shipped him over to England." Noreen sounded sad. "She got it into her head she wants to try to get to the top in dressage. So she's boarding him at that Carl Hester's yard. Maybe you've heard of him? He's a famous dressage rider. He was on the British team, who won at the last Olympics."

I hadn't heard of him, but even so, I nodded knowledgeably. I wasn't going to tell Noreen that I'd stayed in that exact same Olympic village and I, too, had competed for my country at that event. I hadn't met any equestrian competitors while I was there. And, of course, with Dave managing me, I had not attended many of the parties.

Noreen sighed. "I'd rather she'd gone to university. But she has her heart set on trying to make it big in her sport. I think it was the wrong decision. But I'm only a parent…what do I know?"

"I guess you have to let her try," I ventured. "To follow her dreams, I mean."

What was I saying? It wasn't as if following mine had worked out so well for me long-term. Probably, I would have done better to give up on fencing and study economics or accounting. Why then was I leaping to the defense of a teenager who'd made the same stupid decision as me?

"Yes, I know," Noreen admitted reluctantly. "It's just that… life with horses is hard. Very hard. She hasn't chosen an easy road."

"It's the same with any sport at top level," I said carefully. I

SOARING

didn't want to give away too much to Noreen, but I knew how many arduous hours of practice, practice, and more practice was required. Long sessions of perfecting my lunges, parries, and footwork, with and without a partner. I'd repeated the moves until the muscles in my hand were too sore to continue holding the saber and my left arm was aching.

Most times, my best friend Monika had trained with me. We'd fenced together for years, and had competed in many national and international events together. Her encouragement, uttered in her husky, Eastern-European flavored accent, had always spurred me to push harder, parry faster, take myself to new limits. Monika was a great training partner, whether it was fencing practice or fitness. Slight, lithe and surprisingly long limbed, she was perfectly coordinated and had seemingly endless stamina. At the end of a hard training session, while I was trembling with tiredness, she'd be laughing at me over her Diet Coke and suggesting that we go out clubbing and dancing later.

Training with Monika made fencing fun, and I sometimes wondered how much our love of the sport hinged on the friendship and support we gave each other.

"Life is short! Live it once," Monika liked to say, usually just before opening a fizzy alcoholic drink. Perhaps the memory of her cheerful words prompted me to tell Noreen, "If dressage is your daughter's passion…she has to try and succeed in it."

Nonsensical as I believed my own advice to be, I was surprised that my words seemed to reassure Noreen.

"Well, it's good to hear your opinion," she said. "Makes me feel I wasn't completely crazy for allowing her to go."

She turned left, where a wooden gate leading into a large, grassy field stood open.

"Now, hang on to Titan's rope," she said. "Murphy's going to bolt."

She unfastened the halter, and as she slipped it off the bay's head, he tore away from her, kicked up his heels, and set off up the grassy slope at a full gallop.

Titan stood like a statue, watching his departure with pricked ears, obedient even though every muscle in his strong body and arched neck was tensed.

I slipped the halter off him carefully and he waited for a few moments more, until we were safely back at the gate, before squealing in joy, and launching himself away with a drumming of hooves to join his friend.

"You're welcome to ride while you're here, if you like," Noreen said. "Titan's very steady, and I haven't had time to start fitting him up for the hunt season."

"Thanks," I said. "I'd love to."

I wasn't sure if I meant it. Would my still-weak left arm hold up if I rode? And what would it be like doing a sport that was considered dangerous? I'd been banned from all of them for years, because of the risk of injury. Skiing was a no-no, and Dave had even balked at the idea of mountain biking. And then injury had happened anyway. A freak occurrence…there had been no avoiding the car accident that had resulted in a broken left wrist.

"How big is this farm?" I asked as we walked back up to the house alongside the undulating fence line.

Noreen made a face. "Too big. It's actually two separate farms. There's a large, fallow section of sixty acres to the south, which we bought years ago as an investment, and the smaller farm of twenty acres that we live on. Our plan was to sell off the bigger portion." She sighed. "But that hasn't worked out, with the economy the way it is—nobody wants to buy undeveloped land. So we've ended up stuck with it as an expense, which is why my husband, Connor, had to stop what he was doing, and go back to his old work."

"What does he do?" I asked, remembering the photograph of the smiling, dark-haired man.

"Connor recently started out as an artist. He's always loved to paint, and he's really good. He picked up a few commissions; he was making a name for himself."

"Did he do the paintings in your house? They're stunning. I was looking at them this morning."

"He did them all," Noreen told me proudly. "But the

economy really suffered here a few years ago, and we needed more money than his artwork and the farm produce could bring in. It wasn't the right time to launch a new career. He was in the police force before he married me, so he went back into that line of business. Security guarding. In Afghanistan." Her voice was tight and emotionless. "It's very risky, but the pay's good, and we need it. I just pray he gets back in one piece."

"I hope he does," I said, feeling worried on her behalf. I liked Noreen a lot. She seemed to be a forthright, fun person who was dealing with her challenges bravely. I'd only known her for a day, but I wanted her to be happy.

"Now, have you had breakfast?" Noreen asked as we walked back to the farmhouse, as if I hadn't eaten enough for three people last night before falling asleep like a lazy log.

"I had coffee," I told her. "I'll skip breakfast because I'm going out for lunch."

She raised an eyebrow at that, but she didn't ask where I was going. And, as I thought of seeing Patrick again and of the dizzying passion of our kiss, I was glad I didn't have to speak, because I felt suddenly breathless.

As we approached the stone farmhouse, I saw there was a battered green Land Rover parked outside. The driver climbed out when she saw us approach. She was a tall, imposing woman with short, curly hair that was such an impressively bright shade of red. I could only assume it was natural—who'd dye their hair to look like a ripe tomato?

"Noreen!" she called.

I thought that I heard Noreen say, very quietly, "Oh, God, not her," before replying, loudly and more enthusiastically, "Geraldine!"

"I'm on my way into town. I thought I'd come round and see if you're done with the baked goods. If you are, I'll take them through for you."

"Yes, they're ready."

Geraldine turned and regarded me, staring down her beak-like nose.

"This is Claire," Noreen hastened to introduce me. "Claire...

er…?"

"Harvey." Reluctantly, I supplied my surname.

"Claire Harvey," Noreen repeated. "And this is Geraldine Page, who lives across the valley and heads up the Castle Hill Women's Guild."

"Pleased to meet you," I stepped forward, and Geraldine crushed my hand briefly in a powerful handshake. I remembered that Noreen had said the Women's Institute ladies were egotistical interferers. I guessed she'd been partly referring to her red-headed neighbor.

"Claire Harvey? Now, why does that name sound familiar?" Geraldine asked, her words sending a chill of fear through me. "You're from America, by the sound of it?"

"Yes, from New York," I said. "I've never been to Ireland before. I'm here for a holiday. To see the countryside."

"I can't think where I've heard that name," Geraldine mused. "You're not a dressage rider, are you?"

"No," I said, smiling, even though I was cringing inwardly because guessing any competitive sport was too close for comfort, and I was worried her next question might be, "Did I see you at the Olympics?" in which case I'd have to tell a lie.

"Lovely meeting you," I said quickly. "Sorry to be rude, but I have to get ready to go out."

"Nice to meet you, Claire. I'm sure I'll figure out where I've seen you before. I'm very good with faces. Now, Noreen, where are the scones and cakes?"

"One of them's inside Guinness," I heard Noreen retort, and I had to suppress a smile at that answer.

Turning away from Geraldine's eagle-eyed stare, I hurried upstairs to check my phone. Dave had called me, and so had Monika. It was 7:00 a.m. in New York, and I knew Monika would just have finished her early training session. I called her first, smiling at the thought of speaking to her again.

"Well, look who it is!" she answered. "The prodigal. Where are you? I was trying to find you this morning, to see if you knew where my black scarf was. I think you might have taken it after our last training session. Accidentally, of course."

SOARING

"I left the country," I told her.

"Scarf theft is not such a serious crime!" Monika retorted, giggling, and I found myself smiling.

"That wasn't the only trouble I had to escape," I told her. "Dave's home, if you want him to look for your scarf."

"Thank you," Monika said. "But talking of trouble, the news is moving on to more important matters. Beyoncé has had plastic surgery, and Michelle Obama changed her hairstyle."

It was my turn to laugh. Monika had a way of putting things that made them seem less serious than they were. We were good at comforting each other. When I'd found her in tears one afternoon in the change room, devastated because she hadn't won an award she'd been nominated for, I'd been her shoulder to cry on. I had cheered her up afterwards by suggesting we bunk training for the day, and that I take her to the bar down the road for beer and fries. I never forgot what fun that illicit outing had been, and how happy Monika had seemed afterwards.

She'd been able to cheer me up, in turn, after my mother's accident. And more recently, she'd provided a listening ear when I'd discovered that Dave had taken a large chunk of our savings and spent it on playing the stock market…and losing.

"That was money my parents needed," I'd sobbed to Monika, who had done her best to soothe me.

"Dave's just an idiot man," she'd told me. "Wooden-headed moron! I don't know why you put up with his shit, seriously. If I were you, I would kick him out. He probably thought he was helping you by trying to invest it. But imagine if he'd doubled it! Then we'd all be laughing now."

It felt reassuring to be able to get her take on the dismalness of my current situation.

"I went to Ireland," I confessed. "But please, don't tell anybody, because I just want to be away from it all for awhile."

"I thought I would see you at training this morning. It's been more than eight weeks now. Has the doctor not cleared you for getting back to work?"

"Not yet. I don't know if I'm going to come back. It depends on what the sponsors decide." I sighed.

Monika was quiet for a few moments. Then she spoke in a softer voice than usual. "I never apologized to you."

"Apologized? For what?"

"It was my fault you ended up in…that situation. Because I introduced you to Hassan."

Hassan. The handsome Moroccan fencer whose name would now be linked with mine forever in a thousand gossip columns and web pages. I remembered the first time we'd met up at the opening of a local athletic stadium. I'd been intrigued at how somebody so physically imposing, tall and strong with bulky muscles that seemed hewn from mahogany, could be so shy and humble. But I'd liked Hassan from the start, and the relationship between us had quickly grown closer.

If I'd known back then how things would end, I would never even have greeted him that first time. But it was not Monika's fault.

"You couldn't know," I sighed.

"Now I have lost a friend," she complained. "Warming up is boring without you. Running is not as much fun without a partner. I never get to sneak off to bars when I am upset. And I have to wave a sword around on my own."

"I promise I'll come back soon and wave mine around with you," I told her, even though I didn't know whether I would be able to keep my word. What would I do, if I was forced to retire? Never mind how I'd be able to pay College Sport back if they carried out their threats of legal action.

I realized with a shock that I did not feel my usual passion when I thought about my sport. I needed to rekindle that love for competing. I had at least four more years at my peak and a chance at the next Olympics. Why was I suddenly finding it so difficult to want to make a comeback?

"You take care, then. Where are you staying?"

Telling Monika about the farmhouse seemed too complicated. "At the Park Hotel, in Castle Hill."

"My lips are sealed," she said, and we both laughed before saying goodbye.

My next call was to my soon-to-be ex-husband.

Dave answered sounding more cheerful than he had the last time we'd spoken.

"Hey there," he said. "Listen, I have some good news, I think."

"Good news?" I echoed, unable to keep the disbelief out of my voice.

"With any luck, College Sport is back on board."

"College Sport?" I gasped. Never in a million years would I have thought this deal could have been saved. As far as I'd been concerned, it had been over. Finished. But now, it seemed, there was hope on the horizon. Was this the second chance I'd prayed for?

"Look, I had a meeting with them yesterday," Dave continued. He cleared his throat. "I explained to them things hadn't been going well between us. That we'd had some problems recently. I told them that anybody can make a mistake…once."

"Once," I echoed. My mouth felt dry.

"That's it," Dave said. "The once. And I told them I forgive you. Which I do, Claire. It's taken some work, but I've reached that stage. They want reassurance that it won't happen again; so we're going to present a united public front and go for counseling. As an example, you see, to everyone else who loses the way. We could become role models. No marriage is perfect, right?"

"What?" I shouted out the word. "Jesus Christ, what's going on here? Dave, we're in the middle of a divorce!"

There was a short pause.

"Yeah," he said, and I thought he sounded abashed. "Look, it was premature, okay? But you know how upset I was."

"But what about me?"

"I'm sorry, babe," Dave said. He was misunderstanding me and I couldn't work out if he was doing so deliberately. "I know I shouldn't have rushed into the divorce without thinking everything through. But we can make things right."

"I don't think so," I said, but it was as if he hadn't heard me.

"I'll let you know more soon. But for now, you don't have to pay any money back. And they're considering renewing your contract, like they were going to do."

That news silenced me. After the scandal, I'd given up hope of having the contract renewed, and the truth was that this contract was absolutely essential to me financially. There was no other way I could earn enough to support my parents as well as myself.

My mother had been a quadriplegic for the past three years after a fall while she'd been doing the sport she loved—rock climbing. Her care, equipment, medical bills, and physical therapy costs were frighteningly expensive, and my dad, who was only a few years away from retirement age, had been laid off from his job last December and hadn't been able to find new employment.

"I've scheduled a meeting with the College Sport team for Tuesday. You'll need to be there, of course," Dave told me.

That was in four days' time.

"I'll be there," I said in a small voice.

"I'll send you a mail with the details. I assume you'll be home before then?"

"I'll be back on Monday," I said reluctantly, my stolen holiday shortening with every word we exchanged. What was the definition of stress? Saying yes when your brain was screaming no? That was the way I felt right then.

"And in the meantime, Claire, just make sure you look good, okay? I think maybe that's gonna swing it. Get your hair done, and make sure you're in shape, you know? They're gonna have to be sold on you all over again, as the face and body of the brand. We need to remind them that you're hot property. Not just a sportswoman, but a public figure. A model and a presenter who was marketable a while ago, and who could be again."

I thought guiltily of that thick cream I'd spooned into my coffee this morning. How rich and sweet it had tasted. I'd need to go for a run to make up for that. Or something.

"Oh, and you need to set their minds at rest that your injury is fully healed," Dave added. "When are you seeing your surgeon?"

"Um…" With a jolt, I realized I'd missed my appointment, which was supposed to have been yesterday. God knew when I'd get another appointment; he was very busy. Perhaps he could squeeze me in, or I could get another opinion. "I'll see what I can do by Monday," I promised.

"I'll be in touch again soon. Take care, okay?"

"I will," I said.

I disconnected, and for a while I sat on the bed, feeling utterly torn.

This was the answer to my dreams, the miracle I'd needed, the second chance that I should grab without hesitation. I could make a living once again by pursuing my passion. I could try to improve my rankings, to be included in future international teams. It wasn't enough to be a pretty face and a slim body… College Sport also required me to compete. I sometimes felt like I was their full-time employee, attending hundreds of meetings and functions, doing numerous photo shoots and interviews, and squeezing my gym time and training into every busy day. But ironically, the more I'd dieted and exercised, the less time and energy I'd had for training. My rankings had been slipping. I needed to get them back on track.

A new sponsorship deal would provide me with a nest egg of savings, while being able to support my parents.

I should be jumping up and down with excitement, and yet, I felt strangely deflated, as if life hadn't turned out the way I was hoping it would. I must be going crazy. Perhaps it was that, for the first time in ten years, I'd had a taste of another life, and I was reluctant to turn my back on it so soon.

But this wasn't just about me. It was about Dave, who'd worked so hard to get all the deals. It was about my parents, whose life was tough and grim right now through no fault of their own. And my sponsors—how could I say no if they were prepared to invest money in my brand, the fencing star Claire Harvey?

With a jolt, I realized it was a quarter to one. I'd been so preoccupied by the astonishing turn my life had taken that I'd forgotten about my lunch date. Now, I felt nervous, but without any of the earlier excitement. With so much at stake, it was vital, for the sake of my career, that there were no further scandals.

"Be sensible," I told my reflection in the brass-framed mirror on the wall. "Remember, your future is in the balance, and your family's, too."

After that stern warning, I changed into a pink top and the only skirt I'd brought, and went downstairs to wait for Patrick.

CHAPTER 7

Patrick arrived at 1:05, and as soon as I saw the sleek silver body of the Merc purr up the driveway, my heart jumped into my throat.

He climbed out and strode over to me.

God, but he was gorgeous—heart-stoppingly good-looking, and so confident in his own skin. So unlike the mess of doubts and regrets that I was right now. I wondered briefly, and with a stab of jealousy, how many lucky women had enjoyed his company in the past.

"I'm late. I'm sorry." He walked over to me, wrapped his arms around me, and I pressed my face into his neck so I would not be tempted to kiss him again. His skin felt soft against my lips, and I breathed in the faint spice of sandalwood.

"I wanted to be punctual." He opened the car door for me before getting in the driver's side. "Do you know, I shouldn't tell you this, but I've been driving round these lanes for twenty minutes, so that I could be exactly on time for you. And then, as I'm heading down this road at exactly five to one, what happens but I get stopped by a shepherd and have to wait while about two hundred sheep cross to another field."

"Oh, no!" I found myself laughing at the picture.

"Un-flocking-believable!" He grinned at me and I smiled back, unable to look away. I was utterly captivated by his charm. The rogue lock was flopping over his forehead, tempting me to smooth it back just for the sake of running my hand through his shiny, dark brown hair.

He drove out of the farm gate and up the lane, stopping briefly at the crest of the hill to point out the offending sheep, now wending their way down a narrow lane between two stone walls.

It struck me suddenly that I didn't know the first thing about this man, beyond the little he'd told me the first time we'd met and what Noreen had said the previous night. And here I was, in his car, being driven to an unknown destination. Not a soul in the world knew where I was going—not even me.

If I were sensible, I wouldn't have gotten myself into such a situation. But here I was…and I was enjoying it. It felt like my final taste of freedom. Behind the car's darkly tinted windows, I felt safe and anonymous. It was surely unlikely that I would be recognized by anyone on this one outing. And whatever restaurant we went to, I'd sit facing the wall and wear my shades.

"Where are we going?" I asked Patrick, but he shook his head at me and said, "We'll see."

"Well, tell me this, then," I said. "What are you doing here?"

"I sold my business a couple of years ago," he said. "As of now, I'm dividing my time between Ireland and the States, investing in a few ventures that I enjoy."

"Like the hotel?"

"Exactly."

"You weren't a hotelier by trade?"

Patrick shook his head. "I'm still not. I don't have a clue about the hospitality industry. Pouring a glass of champagne is about my limit. So my managers look after the running of it, and I make sure it stays in the black financially, and returns a profit."

We reached the main road and he turned right. Getting my bearings, I saw we were heading into town. Seeing as he'd told me he owned it, I suspected we might be going to the Park Hotel, but when we turned through its ornate wrought iron gateway, I found myself feeling nervous about the choice of venue. Okay, so as the owner, he would get top-class service, but what if any of the press from yesterday's event were still around?

"Don't worry," he reassured me, as if he'd read my mind. "We aren't going into the hotel itself."

Sure enough, he bypassed the parking lot and instead drove up to a boomed-off entrance which was marked "Private." He touched one of the buttons of the remote-control on his key ring, and the boom swung open.

The Mercedes purred up a narrow driveway, which led past a few stone outbuildings and then wound through a large, beautiful expanse of garden. He parked under a tree and we climbed out.

"Come this way," Patrick said.

I walked with him along a paved path that led up the hillside and curved its way toward a small pavilion. It was only when I got closer that I appreciated the building's amazing location. Its balcony offered a dramatic view over the cliffs and onto the sea. Fresh salty air filled my nostrils, and I could hear the breaking of waves far below as I leaned over the rail and stared down at the shimmering waves.

Patrick walked over to stand beside me. He slid an arm round my waist, his fingers moving down to stroke over my hip. Light as it was, the touch tempted me with the promise of more. I knew exactly where Patrick's skillful fingers desired to roam. I wanted to melt against him, but I resisted the temptation. This lunch was a chance for us to talk, and I intended to use it.

"Can I offer you a drink? Banqueting did a good job," I heard Patrick say in approval, and I turned to look properly at the quaint building.

A table for two had been set up on the shady balcony, covered with a starched white cloth and perfectly set with glassware and silverware. Bottles stood in an ice bucket, and a wicker picnic basket was on a stool nearby.

"Oh, that's wonderful!" I found myself smiling in delight at this idyllic setting.

"Would you like champagne?" Patrick asked. "There's wine if you prefer, or mineral water."

"Champagne sounds great," I said.

Patrick popped the cork and poured us each a glass.

"To meeting again." He touched his glass to mine. Our fingers brushed. I noticed his hands were broad, long-fingered, tough and capable looking. They spoke of a workman's heritage. He might be a business tycoon, but he had the hands of a horseman, I decided. I imagined them holding the reins with strength and sensitivity, restraining a powerful Irish hunter during the excitement of the chase.

"To meeting again," I echoed.

The dry champagne felt crisp and icy on my tongue.

I took a long sip of it, savoring the taste, feeling suddenly lightheaded, and not only from the bubbles.

Then Patrick's phone rang, its loud trill interrupting the serenity of the moment.

"Damn it all, and I was sure I'd turned it off." He took it out of the pocket of his grey chinos and checked the screen. "Actually, I do need to take this. Please, sit down."

I sat on the comfortably cushioned chair, looking out over the ocean as I listened to his one-sided conversation.

"I'm sorry, Kathy," he said. "I should have called you yesterday. I'm not traveling tonight. Last minute change of plans. Yes, please cancel the ticket. No, I don't need to rebook at this stage."

"Where were you going?" I asked him when he'd turned the phone off.

"I was flying to New Jersey," he said. "But I don't have to go anymore."

He'd been heading to my home state just after I'd left it? What a coincidence.

"Well, that's lucky," I said, and his mouth softened.

"It is indeed."

He sat down, pulling his chair closer so that our knees brushed.

"So, tell me, Claire, why did you travel here?" he asked.

I frowned, wondering if he knew about my recent circumstances. I didn't want to have to explain the whole embarrassing saga to him. He must have been sensitive to my dilemma, because he rephrased the question.

"I should say—why Castle Hill? Why did you choose to come here?"

I felt my cheeks grow red. So he did know, then.

"I've always wanted to visit this town," I explained. "It's

been at the top of my list, ever since a stranger on an airplane told me how beautiful it was." I glanced at him from under my lashes, feeling flirtatious and embarrassed all at the same time.

Now, his eyes sparkled.

"Are you serious? You came here because I told you about it?"

"The way you described it was poetry."

Actually, the way he'd done a lot of things was poetry… talking about his home town was only one of them.

"I've always wanted to visit since then," I said. "This was the first…"

I hesitated, realizing too late that I was saying more than I should. Oh, well, it wasn't as if he didn't already know. "This was the first chance I've really had to go anywhere on my own since we last met. To do what I want to do."

There it was…out in the open. The admission of why I was here, and what had gone wrong.

"I guess you know about me. I can tell when people do," I said, feeling my cheeks redden. "There can't be much you want to ask me, apart from the obvious questions, and I don't want to answer those."

He shook his head. "There are plenty of other questions I want to ask you. First one, how long are you here for?"

"Till Monday."

My eye was caught by a faraway glint—the sun on glass, perhaps? It was coming from the cliffs on the opposite side of the bay. I was attuned to such sights, because they often meant cameras. And cameras, now, meant trouble.

I gazed out over the cliffs again, but I didn't see the flash of light a second time. It must have been something else. I told myself not to be so jumpy; that nobody could possibly have seen me here, and I returned my attention to Patrick, who was now watching me curiously.

"Next question—favorite color?"

"Favorite color?" I could hear the surprise in my own voice.

"Well, I want to find out more about you. I have to start somewhere," he teased.

"Blue." I took another sip of champagne. "And yours?"

"Mine's green. Favorite food?"

"Um…" I did a mental run-through of everything on my forbidden list. "Roast chicken and gravy. With crispy skin, of course!"

"I'll second that," he grinned. "And another question… you've had the easy ones. Now let's move on to something different. Why did you start fencing?"

"I started because I read about sword fighting in a book when I was about twelve," I said, feeling rather embarrassed; I'd never told anyone about this before. "It was a fantasy novel. *Strands of Starlight*, I think it was called. I loved the heroine. She was so strong-willed, so courageous—and she learned how to use a sword. When I found out fencing was a real sport, and I could do it at school, I signed up."

"Did you find it easy from the start?" Patrick asked curiously.

"I started out using the epee," I explained. "My instructor saw I had some ability, but decided I would be more suited to fencing with the saber. Saber fencers need strong legs and gluteus muscles, which I have, and because the saber is shorter and lighter than the other swords, it's also a faster sport. Speed is important, which seemed to suit me."

Being left handed had helped me, too, because it was less common and therefore put my opponents at a slight disadvantage. And of course, my strange ability to see pictures had also played a part. When I was relaxed and confident, in the zone, I could occasionally read my opponent's moves before she made them. Knowing what was going to happen gave me a split-second advantage, and that was usually all that was needed to score a point. I wasn't going to tell Patrick that, though.

"I also liked its roots. I found them romantic," I continued.

"Why's that?"

"Because saber fencing originated on horseback. It was done by cavalry troops, which is why today, hits still have to be scored above the waist. The legs would have been hard to reach, and a pointless target, when riding a horse."

"How fascinating. I didn't know that."

"To most people, fencing is fencing. They don't even know that there are differences in the foil, epee, and saber categories. But I guess I don't know much about Ironman competitions. Do you still do them?" I asked, although from the way he looked, I was sure he was still in training. I couldn't see as much as an extra ounce of fat on his body.

"I enter two or three competitions a year, but try to train constantly," he said. "I'm turning thirty-five soon, which means I have a few years left at my peak, although I must admit competing never seems to get any easier. I'm an enthusiastic sportsman, but not a talented one. Not like you."

"Really?" I asked, surprised.

Patrick nodded ruefully. "I'm a hopeless swimmer," he said. "Way too slow. I always end up near the back of the field, and have to try and catch up during the cycle and the run. I do it for the personal challenge, and I choose the events where I can enjoy the travel. I realized long ago I'm never going to make the rankings."

"Probably more sensible. When you compete seriously, it can take a lot of the fun out of it. And you don't really see much of any of the places where you go."

I'd also visited many countries, but I had never had the chance to sightsee. There hadn't been time. But now, sitting with Patrick in this secluded pavilion overlooking a summer's ocean view, it suddenly felt as if we had all the hours we needed in the world. It was as if Patrick sensed my thinking, because he leaned over, slid his arm round my waist, and kissed me.

The touch of his lips made me feel dizzier than the champagne had done. Last night, our kiss had been rough and urgent. Now, his lips brushed over mine in a sensually light touch. He'd shaved—the pleasurable friction of his stubble against my skin was gone, and in its place, a voluptuous satin smoothness. His eyes stared into mine, capturing me in their smoldering, golden depths as the kiss deepened. His mouth tenderly parted my own, his fingers strayed to my waist, caressing the curve of my buttocks.

Unhurried as this leisurely exploration was, my body's

response to him was as intense as before. I felt breathless with desire; as if each deliberate caress was melting my core. The soft thrust of his tongue against my own made me turn liquid inside. My fingers, roaming along his thighs seemingly of their own accord, tightened in urgency. A pulse was beating hard in the pit of my stomach, its throbbing reaction begging for deeper penetration in other ways.

There seemed no way of stopping this rollercoaster response. This time, I was powerless to resist the flood of passion which overwhelmed us both. I let out a small cry of delight as his fingers brushed over my nipples, and my right hand moved up to the taut hardness at his groin, where my caress caused him to groan deeply.

His arms closed around my waist, his grip tightened, and then he stood, his firm grasp supporting me despite the languorous weakness at my knees.

He stared into my eyes, and I saw my own truth reflected there—the tumult of emotions, the undeniable honesty of our attraction.

"Inside," he whispered.

Inside? My heart quickened. I had thought this was an alfresco occasion, but as he moved with me to the door and pushed it open, I saw that I was wrong.

The pavilion's interior was softly lit by the sunshine that filtered in through the white blinds. I'd imagined this building would be a meeting room or function venue, but it was not. It was a bedroom. A four poster bed, decked out in ivory linen, was set against the back wall. On its right was a comfortable two-seater couch, and on its left, a dressing table.

Patrick pushed the door closed; the snick of the latch reassuring me that we were going to be private here.

This was crazy...too far, too fast, but there was no way I was stopping; not when the memories of what we'd done in the airplane were spurring me on. There was only one thing troubling me, and as we moved to the bed, locked in our embrace, I found the words to say it.

"Wait, Patrick," I whispered. I didn't want him to stop, not even for a second…but I had to make sure.

"What?" he breathed.

"I just…I just need to know…I'm worried about safety…"

"Claire." His hand cupped my face, the touch, warm in comparison to the scorching passion in his eyes. "I'll use a condom. But beyond that, I want you to know that I'm currently single. I'm not fooling around with you behind anyone's back. That's not something I would ever do. And I'm clean. My previous partner and I split up in March, and we were both tested for everything."

"I—I'm also clean," I stammered. "I've been tested recently, too. We do full blood-works with the physicals before we travel. I'm not on the pill…I haven't taken it for a couple of months."

I had a pack of pills in my luggage, and since I'd just finished my period, any time within the next five days would be safe to start taking them. That was not what was concerning me the most, though.

"It's just…are you sure it's private in here? No cameras or hidden recorders, or anything like that?" I knew Patrick would not have done such a thing—well, I was pretty sure—but what if one of his staff had taken a chance? These things happened, as I knew only too well.

"I'm totally sure. But in case you're worried…" Patrick tugged on a rope and the drapes surrounding the bed came loose from their ties. We were cocooned in the whispering hush of curtained privacy.

"Is that better?" he asked. His lips almost brushed mine as he spoke.

"Yes."

He lowered me down gently until I was sitting on the bed, and I gazed at him, watching the focused expression on his lean, sculpted face. He carefully undid the buttons on my top before letting it fall loose to expose the turquoise satin of my bra. He smoothed his fingers over the cups, and I gasped as he touched my erect nipples.

Lowering his head, he bit each nipple gently through the fabric. The light friction of his teeth on these hard, sensitive nubbins caused a spike of desire in my groin. I gasped, loving this teasing pleasure, but tormented by it, too.

He slipped a hand under my back and unsnapped my bra. Then he slipped my clothing off my shoulders. Laying me down on the bed, he loosened each of my sandals in turn, placed them on the rug, and then slid my skirt off.

Clad only in my white bikini panties, I was too aroused to feel self-conscious as he gazed down at me, the hunger evident in his eyes. I felt breathless with expectation…such a deliberate, sensual ravishment was something I had craved for what felt like forever. It felt as if the circle was completed; the desire that had smoldered in us when we'd first me had finally been able to blaze.

"You're so fucking gorgeous," he murmured. "For ten years, I've been imagining what your body would look like. I still remember how your skin felt. Smooth as satin."

I caught my breath as his fingers traced a deliberate line along my panties, from the white ribbon at their top, all the way down between my legs.

He was breathing fast; his attention entirely focused on the light circling of his fingertips, as they stroked their way along the crotch of my panties, brushing over the plumpness of the lips they covered. His mouth was slightly parted as he touched me, his eyes narrowed in desire. His white shirt hung open, revealing the strongly muscled torso beneath. I longed to run my hands over it, but the truth was I couldn't have moved while Patrick was doing this to me. I was enslaved by his teasingly erotic caresses.

"I can feel how wet you are, touching you through these," he murmured, his voice unsteady. "Christ, if you knew how often I've dreamed of doing this."

His fingers hooked into the sides of my panties and drew them down and I let out a shaky breath.

"Claire," he whispered. His hands felt warm as he smoothed my hair off my face. His mouth felt cool as he kissed my tingling nipples, but the touch of his tongue was warm and lush.

"I've been longing to make you come," he murmured,

turning his attention to my other breast.

"You…you've already made me come," I said. I'd never forgotten that orgasm on the plane—how, using only his skilful fingers, he'd been able to bring me to a shuddering, gasping climax. But, to be truthful, it hadn't been just that once on the plane. It had been a few times since then, when the memories of him had been too intense, and I'd been too frustrated, and I had found a breathless relief in pleasuring myself while fantasizing about the wicked Patrick Maguire.

"Not this way," he told me.

His lips trailed a sensual path down my stomach, his hands cupped gently over the jutting wings of my hipbones. My desire for him felt painfully intense, the throbbing between my legs was a delicious agony. I let out a soft moan as his exploring mouth reached the narrow strip of hair above my cleft, and his tongue pierced between my smoothly shaven lips. Oh, God, he was tasting me…sucking me…

I wondered again, in amazement, how it was possible that this man could have the measure of my body so completely. He seemed to know, instinctively, what would turn me on the most. He circled my clitoris with the tip of his tongue, the softly sensual friction causing me to arch my hips toward him. This fluttering, delicious sensation was melting me from within. I was loving it—craving it. Craving *him*.

He'd found the rhythm I needed to take me to orgasm with the play of his lips, tongue and the lightest graze of teeth on my pulsing flesh. Desire pooled inside me, the sensation becoming more intense as my body begged for release. I was breathing fast, the space inside this curtained four-poster suddenly far too warm. Oh, God, he had me on the brink.

Then, for a moment, fear held me back…my own doubts threatened to pull me out of the moment. How could I trust somebody I'd known for such a short time? Did I dare to let go and succumb, finally, to my body's needs?

Maybe it wasn't about trust, but rather about taking what I desired. In any case, there was no getting off this rollercoaster ride. How long had I waited for this orgasm? And the intensity of it was shocking. I cried out as I felt my core tighten and then spasm in a blissful, shuddering release. I thrust my hips toward him, gasping, unashamed and unafraid. Sweat sprang out on my body as the pleasure reached a crescendo.

Then I collapsed back onto the bed, breathless, feeling utterly undone, but at the same time, completely whole again.

Patrick lay beside me, and I turned my head to kiss him deeply, tasting myself on him, his breath warm on my face. I dared to look into his eyes and was relieved to see only the honesty of his own desire.

"Claire, you're always beautiful, but never more so than just after you've come," he said.

"That was…incredible." Strength was returning to my limbs. I lifted my hand and stroked his face, the tenderness of my own gesture taking me by surprise.

"It's only the start," he promised. "I want…God, Claire, it sounds raw, but I want to fuck you. It's all I've been able to think about since I saw you yesterday." His lips curved into a smile. "In fact, if I'm truthful, for a lot longer than that."

His words were a powerful turn-on; they echoed my own primal needs. I slipped my arm around him, under his shirt, allowed myself to run my hand over his sculpted abs before pulling him close.

Already, I could feel the attraction between us again. I could feel it sparking like electricity along my own nerve endings, and I could sense it in the involuntary movement of his hips toward me; so that the hot hardness of his groin pressed into my thigh. My hand moved, as if unbidden, to his belt buckle and I fumbled to release it. Why did I have such an insatiable desire to touch him? What was it about this man?

Self-doubt followed, and a need to explain this crazy chemistry.

"You must think I'm a slut," I breathed, unbuttoning his pants and drawing down the zipper to free the steely bulge of his arousal.

"No, Claire, I don't think that. Not for one minute. Not at all," he whispered, his voice serious, his breath tickling my ear.

SOARING

"It's just that…" Suddenly I realized I'd gone too far with my need to explain. I'd crossed a boundary. I knew this was a secret I should keep, but my resolve had been weakened by my earlier pleasuring.

"I haven't slept with anyone. Not for ages. My marriage has become a sham," I told him. Tears prickled my eyes and wet my cheeks. Liquid proof of the loneliness I'd felt as Dave and I became increasingly physically distant; of the humiliation and the horror during the championships in Portugal two Novembers ago, when I had realized what the noises were that I could hear in the adjoining hotel suite, where my husband had slept.

Patrick kissed them away.

"I know," he whispered.

"You know?" My eyes flew open and I was pinned in his gold-green gaze. "How do you know?"

He took a deep breath. "This isn't the best time and place to tell you. But I guess there's never going to be a right time. Claire, will you trust me after what I'm going to say? Please?"

My own confidence in him was ebbing with every word, being replaced by a cold fear and the feeling I'd made a terrible mistake.

"I don't know until you tell me."

"I used to own a big media company." Patrick looked into my eyes while I spoke. "That's how I made my money. I started off with magazines: niche interest publications, trade magazines, a few gossip rags in the U.K. Then I expanded into the U.S.—*National Sport*, *People Exposed*. And a few very successful journals for the medical and scientific professions."

His words clawed away the comfort I'd felt. *National Sport* and *People Exposed* were my most hated publications. They only existed to crucify the reputations of those unlucky enough to end up featured in their pages, and what they'd written about me in the past two weeks had been beyond painful to read.

"I acquired other magazines, websites, a radio station, and a TV company," he said. "I sold them all, Claire. Early last year, I got rid of my final shareholding. I'd had enough. I sold the lot of them."

But it was too late. I pushed him away, fighting my way out of the curtained drapes that had seemed so warm and safe.

"Claire, please…"

I knew Patrick would try to follow me, but he was still on the bed, tangled up in his half-removed pants, and I had adrenaline on my side. I grabbed my top and skirt and tugged them on. Who cared about underwear? I was only going as far as the hotel parking lot. I shoved my feet into the sandals, grabbed my purse, and unlatched the door.

Another flash, from across the cliffs. Fear filled me.

I didn't trust Patrick; didn't have any faith left in him at all.

I sprinted down the path, ran along the road we'd come in on, slipped past the Private sign even as I heard the sound of the Merc's engine starting up. I turned right, headed toward the hotel's parking lot, and yanked open the door of my rental car. I collapsed on the seat, breathing hard, before slamming it behind me.

I was safe now. He would not find me here and if he tried to come to the farm again, I knew that Noreen would be an effective protector.

Tears streamed down my face as I put on my dark glasses and navigated my way through the light afternoon traffic, heading for the quiet country lanes.

CHAPTER 8

The farmhouse kitchen smelled comforting, the rich aroma of chicken emanating from the pot on the stove which Noreen was stirring.

"How was lunch?" she asked, glancing round as I stomped inside.

"Lunch?" I echoed. "What lunch? I'm starving!"

I collapsed onto the wooden bench, buried my head in my hands, and started to sob.

I heard the clank of the pot lid being replaced. Then Noreen's hands were on my shoulders, warm and reassuring. Gently, she rubbed my back.

"I'm sorry," I got out between sobs. I couldn't seem to contain my misery—the floodgates had been well and truly opened.

"It's okay, Claire," she reassured me. "Just let it out. Sounds like you need to have a good cry."

She was right…the sadness I felt went beyond what had happened at lunch. The misery that spilled out of me now had its roots further back than that. It was the helplessness of defeat, the regret at not being fast or skilled enough to be the best. It was anger at the people who dictated my future, but who didn't even know who I really was. And it was raw, dreadful hurt at my husband's betrayal, the shame of having separate bedrooms whenever we traveled—*Claire's an athlete; she needs an uninterrupted night's rest*—and the agony of never knowing if he was alone in his room, or who was sharing it.

Noreen placed a box of tissues in front of me, and stayed with me until my sobs had finally abated. Then, while I was mopping up my swollen eyes and streaming nose, she made me a cup of tea, and placed a bowl of the chicken soup on the wooden table.

"You want to talk?" she asked. "If not, fine by me. But it can help to share."

I took a shaky breath. Where to start?

"Patrick told me he used to be in the media industry," I sniffed. "He said he owned newspapers, magazines, TV stations, radio stations. Including celebrity and gossip publications."

Noreen frowned slightly. "Yes, that's right. I remember the paper said something about that when they reported on him buying the Park Hotel. They called him a billionaire ex-media mogul."

"That's a problem for me. A big problem. Because…" What the hell. Noreen might as well know the truth, since her curious Women's Guild friend had probably already guessed my identity by now. "Because I'm a professional athlete, or was, until now. A fencer. And I'm here because I've just been involved in a huge media scandal, which has lost me my sponsorship."

"Are you a top fencer?" Noreen sounded genuinely amazed. "Good heavens, Claire. I'm sorry for my ignorance, but I had no idea. I never watch sport, apart from dressage, of course, because of my daughter. But I can see how that might complicate things between you and Patrick."

"I wanted to not be around anyone who knows me. I—I know him slightly from way back, and I was going to make an exception for him. And now I find out he was involved in the worst industry of all. The one that's just ruined my career."

Noreen pressed her lips together sympathetically. "Although he isn't involved in it any longer, I understand."

"I know. It's just…how can I trust him?"

"It's difficult in those circumstances. And it can't be easy being in the spotlight for all the wrong reasons. I guess the media's a double-edged sword, if you'll excuse the pun. It builds you up but it can also break you down."

"I guess so." I wanted to hug Noreen for not having asked about the scandal.

"Are you going to eat your soup?" she asked. "You look like you could use a few square meals. Having cheekbones you can tap-dance on can't be healthy for anyone, athlete or not."

SOARING

I took a spoonful of the rich chicken soup, which tasted every bit as good as it had smelled. By the time I was halfway through the bowl, I was beginning to see my situation in a different light.

"Do you think I might have overreacted?" I asked Noreen.

"Probably," she said. "But in the circumstances, I'm sure he would have expected you to."

I was starting to think I had overreacted, and badly so. I'd allowed my fear to get the better of me. I still felt angry toward Patrick, but now I was realizing I should not have run. I should have stayed, and talked it through. That would have been the adult approach. For a twenty-eight-year-old, I sure hadn't acted in a very adult way.

My soup was finished, and I drained my mug of tea, feeling suddenly better about life.

"Thank you so much for the meal, and the shoulder to cry on," I told Noreen. "If you'll excuse me, there's a call I have to make."

Gathering up my courage, I phoned the Park Hotel, and asked if I could speak to Patrick. I felt sick inside with fear. I felt like I needed to apologize, and that Patrick would have every right to be as angry over my behavior as I had been with him.

"I'm sorry, Mr. Maguire is not in," the receptionist said.

"Does he have a cellphone number I could try?" What did they call it, here in Ireland? "A mobile number?" I added.

"May I ask who's calling?"

"Claire Harvey."

"Please hold."

I waited, feeling ill, twisting the raffia mat on the desk in my fingers as I wondered whether my name would open doors or have them slammed in my face. After a minute, she came back on the line. I was in luck. She told me she would transfer me directly through to his cellphone.

I waited, feeling my meal sitting uneasily in my tight stomach.

It rang four times…five…What was I going to say to his voicemail? What message could I leave?

And then he answered, his voice brisker and colder than I

remembered it.

"Patrick Maguire."

"Patrick." My voice was so hoarse from nerves, I had to clear my throat and try again. "Patrick, it's Claire."

"Claire," he repeated. "I'm on my way…" The rest of his words were a scramble. Cell signal was not great here in the Irish hills. At any rate, he didn't sound like he wanted to talk. Well, if I never saw Patrick again, so be it, but at least I hadn't ended our acquaintance by childishly running away without trying to discuss the problem afterwards.

"You want me to call back later?" I asked.

He said something I couldn't hear.

"Sorry, signal is really bad. I'll call you again this evening," I said.

Finally, I could hear him again, and he sounded exasperated—with the poor connection, and not with me, I hoped. His voice came through the line, strong and confident and clear as a bell.

"I was trying to say I'm on my way to you. I'll be there in exactly two minutes. Or seven, if there are any sheep crossing the road."

My eyebrows just about hit my hairline.

He was coming here, to me?

If I stuck my head right out of the window and craned my neck, I could see where the gateway opened onto the road. And there he was, the silver Merc gleaming in the afternoon sun as it turned into the driveway.

I was red-eyed, swollen-faced, and I had hardly any time to do damage control. In a panic, I implemented a hasty triage system. I ran to the bathroom, grabbed my eye drops from my toiletry bag, squeezed one into each eye. I dragged a brush through my tangled hair and splashed some water on my face. Time for lip gloss? Not really, but I was going to put it on anyway. And a spritz of perfume.

I heard the car door slam even as I headed full-tilt down the stairs.

CHAPTER 9

I sprinted down the corridor and thundered through the farmhouse kitchen, causing the cat to raise his head curiously from his fridge-top eyrie.

"Good luck," Noreen called as I ran out the kitchen door, in time to meet Patrick by the mint bed.

I stopped dead, facing him, breathing fast from my headlong dash through the house.

He was holding a large bunch of long-stemmed red roses. He looked as gorgeous as ever, in a slightly tousled, just-out-of-bed way, and looking at his wayward bangs got me thinking all over again of what had happened between us in that private bedroom.

I didn't know what to say.

"Claire," he asked, his voice gentle, "do you ever stop running?"

Did I spy a glint of humor in his eyes?

"I just...look, I wanted to meet you at your car. I feel bad about what I did. I'm sorry I left you at lunch so suddenly, but I'm still angry!"

"Lunch? I don't recall having lunch," he said.

He was definitely smiling now. He handed me the flowers.

"These are an apology. I'm not sure at this stage what exactly I'm apologizing for. But that doesn't make it any less heartfelt."

"I don't think I deserve them. But thank you. They're gorgeous."

We walked together to the kitchen, where he and Noreen greeted each other, and she exclaimed over the beauty of the roses before fetching me a vase. I carried it up to my room and put it on the desk next to the bed. I spent just a few seconds admiring the beauty of this magnificent bouquet before hurrying back downstairs to where Patrick was waiting.

We walked back to the car together and climbed in. On the passenger seat was a small, white muslin bag tied with a red ribbon and printed with the hotel's logo. A quick peek inside, and the blood flooded to my face as I found my abandoned underwear, neatly folded and now discreetly returned to me.

"Thank you," I said, rather shamefacedly.

"I was sorely tempted to keep it," Patrick said, a comment which momentarily silenced me and didn't do anything to help get rid of my blush. We didn't speak again until we were on our way, heading in a different direction from town.

"So," I asked, "where are we going?"

In his company, my attraction was overriding the fury I'd felt. I didn't know if that was a good thing. Probably not. But now that the shock of his confession was over, all I could remember was the way I'd felt when I'd been with him. How he had brought me to orgasm, so swiftly, so expertly; how I'd come so hard to the slick caresses of his tongue.

I had to admit it…the thought of never seeing him again had terrified me.

"I'm going to show you a place I hope you'll like," Patrick said. "And while we're driving, you can tell me why you're so angry."

"It's because of what you told me about owning media companies," I snapped. "And not just any companies!" Finally, I could summon up the righteous indignation I needed. "Those publications…Patrick, those are the gutter press! They publish stories that are wrong, inaccurate, hurtful."

He was quiet for a while. Then he responded, "So what negative things did they publish about you?"

"Do you want a list?" I asked, outraged. "In the past two weeks, I've headlined…"

"No, not the past two weeks. What damaging stories did they publish about you in the past few years? In the days when I owned those magazines and websites?"

"Um…" I thought hard, staring out of the window at the emerald scenery. We were driving deeper into the hills. I racked my brain for specifics that I could quote to Patrick. Obviously, I'd have featured in those rags at some point. But now he was putting me on the spot, I couldn't name any one instance.

"There were none," Patrick stated, and I was taken aback by the confidence in his tone.

"None? No, that's not right. There must have been…"

"Claire, I was the boss," he explained patiently. "I used to review all content from my media before it went to press. You were featured once in a while in those publications—in a positive light only. And that was because I had the final say over what went into them."

"How do you mean?" I couldn't believe what I was hearing.

"I didn't ever run stories that could have damaged you. I either canned them before going to print, or requested a rewrite. I guess my old-timers got to know, after a while, the unspoken rule that nothing negative must appear about Claire Harvey."

I glanced at Patrick, astounded by his words.

"You can't be serious."

"I am."

"But why?"

"Because…" He let out a long breath. "I guess because… that night we shared on the airplane always stayed with me. I couldn't do it, Claire. I couldn't write badly about somebody that I had such a strong connection with, and I couldn't allow anyone else on my payroll to do that, either. It would have felt…I don't know. Like a betrayal."

I was shocked into silence. My mind raced as I made sense of his words. I had to acknowledge they were true. The media owned by Patrick Maguire had done me no damage—the opposite, in fact. Part of the reason that I'd received the College Sport sponsorship had been because of my squeaky clean public image, and my positive media profile.

"Thank you for that," I said. "I appreciate it. But Patrick, that's only because you knew me. What about all the other celebrities who've been exposed in those pages? What was written was cruel. Careers have been destroyed. Lives ruined. Marriages wrecked."

Patrick nodded. "I'm not proud of what I did. That's why I got out of it, in the end. But Claire, we never wrote anything inaccurate."

"Are you serious?" I asked, frowning.

"We had a few lawsuits come our way—not many—and they were usually settled out of court after we were able to prove what we had written was factually true. So, I don't believe any marriage was wrecked as a result of what we published, or any career destroyed. Not unless they were heading for wreckage in any case, and we simply exposed the cracks."

"Well, I…hey, why are you pulling over?" Patrick indicated left and eased the Mercedes to a stop in one of the wider sections of this narrow lane.

"Because there's a car that's been following us for a while now," he said grimly. "It's probably just an innocent local on his way somewhere; but I'd rather be sure."

I twisted round to look. The car behind us, a white Golf, slowed down, and then abruptly sped up, pulling right and accelerating past us, before disappearing around a bend in the road.

Like our car, this one had deeply tinted windows, and it was impossible to see more than the shadowy profile of the driver as he passed.

"You just held a media conference at your hotel." I tried to stay calm, and not to let my anxiety show. "Who attended it?"

Patrick sighed. "Representatives from major magazines, websites, newspapers, radio, and TV from all over the world. About fifty delegates from the States. The hotel has been making a good profit after its refurbishment, so I invited them as a P.R. exercise, to bring more business to the hotel as well as Castle Hill."

"How many of them are still here?"

"About half. I offered them a free weekend stay after the conference."

"Damn."

"I know. I'm sorry the timing was so bad, Claire."

I tried to reassure myself that the driver following us had just been a lost tourist. I told myself firmly not to panic; that even if they had known I was here, the journalists and photographers would have better things to do than hunt me down.

I tried to silence the worried voice inside me that said it would only take one. Just one determined reporter, just one compromising photo. Here I was, with another man after the fallout from this recent scandal, in a town where half the world's press was roaming around.

Could my predicament be any worse?

"I want you to trust me," Patrick said. "I know you don't have much trust in my profession—my ex-profession—but I want to try and prove that you can have faith in me. And I want to know who leaked your whereabouts to the media, the morning you were photographed with Hassan?"

I felt my face flame crimson at those words.

"I don't know," I said softly.

I knew who had taken the photos, but I had no idea who had tipped that determined paparazzi photographer off. How had he known? The event had been private. The pictures had shocked the readers, but there had been more to them than anyone knew. More than I could ever tell.

I had known before that night that I was being hounded by the paparazzi. For a few weeks now, a lean, dark-haired, bearded photographer who I knew only as Carlos had been taking a too-close interest in me. He'd managed to infiltrate a private party I'd attended with Monika. Under strict instruction from Dave and my dietitian, I'd been drinking water only.

"Come on! Live a little," Monika had pleaded. She was a self-confessed cheap date, who could get merry after just one drink and became the life and soul of the party after two. Watching her enjoying her Smirnoff Spin made me long for one myself. I could imagine how good it would taste, tart and sweet, how the alcohol would relax me and allow me to enjoy myself along with her.

"Stop tempting me!" I chastised her smilingly. "No, you can't buy me one. If you're having another, I'd love a sparkling water."

"Nobody loves a sparkling water." Monika made a face. "You have too many rules you're trying to obey, Claire. Deep down, I know you want to rebel. Life needs to be fun, not all about boring work."

I smiled at the accuracy of her perception.

"I'll have a sip of your drink, if that's okay," I'd said. "Nobody can complain about that."

"You'll love it. It's so cold and good. I won't tell Dave, or your dietitian."

Laughing, I'd accepted the bottle she'd handed me, and taken a small sip.

A minute later, all the fun had evaporated from the evening when I had seen Carlos, camera in hand, threading his way through the crowds toward the exit.

Two days later, the photo that I'd been dreading had been published in the *National Enquirer*. "Drowning her Sorrows: Party Girl Claire Harvey Necks the Bottle." The following day, a different photograph, taken at the same party, had appeared in the *Examiner*. In it, I'd been speaking to Hassan, who had also been there. The music had been loud and I'd had to lean close to him, but from the angle of the photo, it looked as if we were about to kiss. He'd had his hand on my shoulder, which had not helped. Worst of all, the camera had slyly caught the lacy cup of my bra peeking out from inside the deep V neck of my top.

I had to acknowledge the photographer's talent. That blouse was not nearly as revealing as that single image had made it out to be. And the papers and websites had a field day with it.

"Is Model Fencer Claire Harvey Tiring of Her Husband/Manager?" the caption had screamed.

As a result of those photos, College Sport had summoned me and Dave to their offices that very evening to do, as they called it, reputation management.

"What the hell's going on here?" Daniel, Dave's brother, had asked, tossing the offending magazines onto the boardroom table.

"Look, nothing at all. It's all innocent," Dave had protested. Now that we were confronting our sponsors, he was finally taking my side, after having reduced me to tears in the car on the way to the meeting with his angry accusations. "She went to a party, she had a drink, she spoke to a guy."

"But why's it in the *Enquirer*?" Daniel had asked, frowning. "We're trying to keep our brand image squeaky clean. We're a family company. One of the reasons we sponsored Claire is because she epitomizes clean, wholesome, healthy living." He looked at me doubtfully. "Or should I say, epitomized?"

I drew a deep breath and spoke up. "It was a private party," I told him. "I took a sip of a friend's drink because she offered it to me. I was talking to another friend while loud music was playing. I'm sorry about how the photographs look."

He considered my words for a while.

"Well, it's clear you have to be more careful," he said. "Please, Claire, be aware of what you're doing and how you're behaving at all times. These photographs actually could be construed as breach of contract."

I heard Dave draw in his breath sharply as Daniel continued. "If you remember, you signed with us that you would not be photographed drinking alcohol. This isn't just hearsay and gossip, made-up stories, trash like that. We could ignore that, of course, but you're shown to be behaving in these photos in a way that doesn't reflect well on our brand."

Inwardly, I found myself burning at the unfairness of the situation, and stewing over who could have been gunning for me, and why. This was no accident. The photo had been taken deliberately. I'd thought I'd been among friends, but somebody there had not been a friend. Had that person tipped off Carlos that I'd be there?

I forced myself to nod apologetically. "I understand that, Daniel. I can see how the photos have come across. I will be more careful in future."

"This is your final warning. We can't have this happen again, seriously, Claire. In the meantime, we'll try and organize a photo opportunity soon to make up for this. A charity event, something like that. Something to put you in a better light."

"Just let me know when and where, and I'll be there," I

promised, and saw Dave nodding approvingly at my words.

But it hadn't worked out that way. When we left College Sport's offices and climbed into Dave's new BMW, our argument had resumed. In fact, it had escalated. Dave had flung accusations, and in seeking to defend myself from the pain of his words, I had attacked him in turn. I'd shouted out that he was irresponsible with money, that he had spent recklessly on luxuries without asking me, and that he'd wasted our savings on stock market gambling. That had made Dave furious, but instead of taking his anger out on me, he'd vented it on the accelerator pedal.

Clamping his jaw in rage, he'd sent the car speeding down the road, racing toward the traffic light at well over the speed limit.

I had seen the picture of the crash an instant before it happened, and that instant might well have saved my life. A flash sparked in my mind: an image of an equally angry and distracted driver heading along the crossroad toward us, unaware that the light on his side was red. He had blond hair and was driving a blue car. Blond hair, blue car. I knew it, even thought it was fully dark. Such strange details to see so clearly, in the instant of approaching death.

"Car!" I screamed. "Stop, stop, hit the brakes, Dave. You're going to crash! You're going to crash!"

"Oh, fuck! Fuck!" Dave yelled. Headlights blazed to my right as he stamped on the brakes, swerving violently to try and avoid the collision. If he hadn't managed that evasive maneuver the other driver would have rammed straight into my door, most likely killing both of us. As it was, the blue Toyota SUV slammed into the BMW's bonnet and sent it spinning across the road until, with a sickening thud, it collided with a street pole.

I remember the window splintering and my head smashing against the side of the car just as I felt a searing pain in my left arm. I had gasped in shock, my vision starred from the impact. I'd cradled my injured wrist as the ruined engine billowed clouds of smoke and steam.

The car was a write-off; the engine destroyed. I suffered a compound fracture of my left wrist, and was rushed straight to hospital to undergo surgery. The other driver was badly concussed, with two broken legs. Dave was the only one who walked away unhurt, although he complained for days afterwards that he'd suffered whiplash.

The accident meant I was out of action for two months. The charity event intended to save my reputation was postponed, and my upcoming competitions were canceled. And then, just a few days after my cast came off, I'd gotten into more trouble involving Hassan.

CHAPTER 10

Fencing is an interesting sport in that it can be played by almost any age group, and you get a whole lot of different shapes and sizes succeeding in it. The only rule is that epee fencers tend to be taller—height gives you an advantage in that category—although having said that, the men's epee World Championships was won a few years back by a fencer who was much shorter than average.

But it's not a sport you have to be skinny to play. You can be normal weight, or even carry a few extra pounds—if you're not also required to model clothing for your sponsors, of course; in which case, welcome to a life of starvation.

Generally, fencers have to do their time practicing. Five to six hours a day with the sword is imperative to stay on top form, but beyond that, there's not much other training that is going to help you, because only fencing can make you better at fencing.

I, however, was in the unlucky situation of having to try and stay on top of my fencing game, and also remain underweight for the cameras. This meant that after I'd finished doing my hours of practice in the local sports hall, I had to spend another hour or two at gym. It didn't escape me that I was probably overtraining as a result of all of this, and that the more I worked out and the more weight I lost, the more my fencing performance suffered. It was a lose-lose situation, really, but my modeling commitments and appearances were happening so frequently that they had to take priority.

Hassan was based in Newark for most of the year, and trained at the same international sports and athletics center as I did. More than that, he was also fanatical about working out. All that training didn't seem to do him any harm, though—he was ranked third internationally in epee. He was tall and muscular, so iron-hard in appearance that the joke in competitive circles was he didn't even need a fencing suit. It was only when I got to know him better that I realized his bullet-proof physique concealed a gentle nature and a deep sensitivity.

"What gym do you go to?" I asked him one day, when we were side by side in the fencing hall, practicing our moves. "I go to the one on Dawson Road, but it's so badly ventilated, and always too full; I'm sure I've been picking up viruses as a result."

"I used to go there. I know a better place. It's a private gym where most of the Moroccan team train when they're here. It's further out of town, but very clean and never too full. I can give you the address if you like."

Grateful for the information, I wrote down the address, and from then on I became a regular at the gym, which was far better than the other one I'd used. I often saw Hassan there. Frequently, he trained with a fellow athlete, Ahmed. Ahmed was a tall, handsome professional sprinter with a flashing smile, who was the most famous sportsperson I knew—as an Olympic gold winner, he was well off financially, with a few lucrative big-name sponsorships.

When Ahmed was not there, Hassan would sometimes help me with my weight training. Once, when I told him about a shoulder muscle that was bothering me, he gave me a massage, his strong fingers skillfully finding the tight fibers and kneading the knots out of them so that I sighed with relief.

We had lots of opportunities to talk, and we became good friends. And yet, I felt that Hassan was holding something back; that despite our closeness, he was not telling me everything in his heart.

One evening after I'd trained late, I'd left the gym and headed home, exhausted. I was depressed that it felt familiar to be spent with weariness, flat-footed with physical tiredness, aching all over, worrying that I was coming down with yet another bout of flu.

And despite all this, despite the dieting and the gym and the religious adherence to my program, I was not gaining the crucial edge of speed I needed; my rankings were slipping, and I was consistently being bested by Monika in our matches.

Despondently, I'd trudged down the two flights of stairs to street level, where I walked a couple hundred yards to the grocery store to buy some essentials, before crossing to the other side and walking back to the parking lot. It was only when I was standing next to my car, holding my bags of low-fat milk, fruit and oats, that I'd realized my keys were not in my purse.

Where were they? With weary resignation, in the growing darkness, I retraced my steps. I hadn't dropped them anywhere I could see or left them in the grocery store. That meant they must be in my locker at the gym.

I was sure the gym would already be closed—the only two people there when I left had been Hassan and Ahmed—but I had no other choice. To my surprise, although most of the lights were off, the building's security door was unlocked, and the glass-paneled entrance door swung open when I keyed in the access code.

I tiptoed down the short passage way, past the door to the admin office, which was closed, and up to the gym's access door, which always stood open. I was aware of how dark it was, suddenly realizing that this gym felt spooky at night when it was empty. The machines looked like lurking monsters, and without the usual music playing, the room itself was creepily silent…or was it?

What was that noise? I could hear something coming from inside the main gym.

Where on earth was the light switch? I'd never had to turn the lights on. I felt around on the wall, my fingers moving over the smooth plaster and catching on the edge of a thumb-tack that held up a poster. No light switches on this side, nor on the other.

And I needed them. Especially since I could definitely hear a noise, and it sounded human. Sighs, and the soft, ragged sound of breathing, were coming from somewhere ahead. Oh, God, what if a psychopath had crept in here just before lights-off and was waiting in the shadows to pounce on me?

I caught my breath, freezing in position, because this was not just my imagination at work. There really was somebody there. I could see a shape silhouetted against the faint light from a street-side window opposite. Or was it really a human shape? Something didn't look quite right with it. Adrenaline surged through me, temporarily banishing my tiredness. And at that split-second, I remembered where the light switch was. It was behind the reception desk.

I edged toward it, my heart pounding, every muscle in my body tensed and ready to flee if I pressed it down only to reveal a raggedly dressed, snarling intruder, his upraised knife gleaming as he spun round toward me...

With my hand trembling, I located the large switch and pressed it.

The room flooded into light, illuminating the grey tiles, the shiny vinyl and chrome of the machines, the clean white window blinds—and my mouth literally fell open as I saw the couple near the window, who had been locked in a passionate kiss and who were even now separating hurriedly, guilt and fear written all over their faces.

Hassan and Ahmed, still dressed in the gym outfits they'd been wearing earlier. The picture I'd seen when the lights went on was etched on my mind. Their bronze, muscular arms had been intertwined, their sculpted bodies pressed together, their lips touching. There had been so much beauty in that moment of love I'd witnessed, but they were obviously mortified that I'd seen them, and that fact was making me embarrassed.

I should have known. I should have guessed that the two of them were lovers. Now, looking back, it all made perfect sense. I felt a little hurt that Hassan hadn't confided in me, but perhaps he'd been unsure about my views on gay relationships. Some people were prejudiced...maybe he hadn't wanted to risk spoiling our friendship.

"I'm sorry," I said. Their obvious discomfort was making the situation so awkward and I didn't know where to look. "I forgot my keys in the locker room, I think. I didn't know anyone was in here. I'm so sorry to not...uh...to not have knocked first."

I could sense they wanted me to leave, and as fast as possible. Well, I'd get my things and be off. We could talk about this another time, when all of us were less embarrassed. I started hurrying across the gym, but knocked a folder off the desk in my haste and had to stop to pick it up. Great, just great. Replacing it on the desk, I practically ran over to the locker room, relieved to see my keys were there. I grabbed them before heading for the door.

"Claire!" Hassan's voice, filled with stress, brought me to a standstill just before I made my escape.

I turned to see him striding across the floor toward me.

"Claire, I must apologize," he said. "I should have told you. I should have explained."

"No, no," I reassured him, smiling in an effort to dissolve his tension. "It's okay, really it is. I understand why you didn't. And you don't need to worry. I—I think it's wonderful, that the two of you…"

The expression in his face made my words dry up.

"Claire, it can never be wonderful," he said, his voice heavy with sadness. "It can never be anything but secret. Please, I beg of you, will you keep this to yourself? It's very important."

"Of course," I said, and I was going to reassure him further, but from near the window, Ahmed cut in. "Not just important. It's life or death."

"How do you mean?" I asked, confused.

"If we were seen together, like this, in our home country of Morocco, we would be imprisoned immediately, and detained for up to three years." Hassan's voice was hard. "It is an offense there. Against the law."

I felt the blood drain from my face.

"Oh, my God," I whispered. "You can't be serious."

But looking in his eyes, I could see the truth there, even before his nod confirmed it. Ahmed walked forward to stand beside his lover.

"It can never be made known, this love we share," he emphasized. "It must always be secret, even while we are training here in New York. It is too dangerous, otherwise."

"But can't you move permanently to the U.S.?" I asked. "Both of you—you're brilliant athletes. You would be able to emigrate if you wanted to. You live here for most of the year, anyway."

"It's not just us," Hassan explained, his voice sad. "We are working on it, Claire, believe me. But my family has to move, too, and that is a problem that is taking longer to solve."

"Oh," I said, understanding.

"We cannot make this public while my close family still live in Morocco. My younger brother and sister, they are still in school. We cannot risk it. Not the way things are there."

Hassan sighed, and standing next to him, Ahmed nodded solemnly. "If anything happened to them, we could never forgive ourselves," he added.

"I won't ever tell," I promised.

I left soon after that. There was nothing more we could say. I had trudged back down the stairs with a heavy heart, thinking of my two friends, and their love for each other that would have to remain secret, with each stolen assignation carrying a terrible risk.

CHAPTER 11

As the Mercedes crested a hill I blinked furiously, trying to clear the sad memories from my mind and returning my attention to my present circumstances. Where was Patrick taking me? The good news was that the driver who'd been following us seemed to have disappeared into the hills, and the road was quiet.

A little further along, Patrick indicated left, and turned into a narrow lane whose entrance was almost concealed from view by a large, sprouting hedge. We started climbing steeply up a wooded hill. I craned my neck, hoping to see what lay ahead as we rounded the bends, but each time, my view was blocked by trees.

"There's no fear of anyone following us up here," he reassured me. "This road leads directly into the place we're going."

So where were we going, I wondered. I could ask him, but from the teasing way he'd dropped that hint about the road, I had a suspicion the answer might only be, "Wait and see."

In any case, Patrick's attention was focused on the steep, winding route. I glanced at his profile, stealing a look at him while he drove. He had a straight nose, a strong chin. Classic features that would do justice to a nobleman or a lord. The rugged perfection of his profile was broken only by his luscious mouth creasing into that roguish half-smile. The expression was so charming that I was sure it had served him equally well in the boardroom and the bedroom.

And what did this handsome man want from me, I wondered—beyond the obvious, of course. Was this just about sex? If so, I had to admit, my own attraction for him was as strong as his for me; this was no one-sided pursuit. But what if his reasons were more complicated?

What if Patrick had another agenda, but was keeping me in

the dark about it?

Could I really trust him?

The road straightened out, flanked by vivid green trees, and Patrick glanced at me and caught me peeking. Hastily, I looked away, and glimpsed the shape of a tower through the trees. Was this where we were going?

The trees thinned as we crested the hill, and I caught my breath at the sight that lay ahead. Beyond the woods, green meadows stretched to the tall, battlemented walls of a castle, whose central feature was the high stone tower I'd spotted earlier. Its majestic height cut the skyline, the afternoon sun lending some warmth to its pale grey stone.

Colorful flags flew from its ramparts. I recognized the Irish flag, the Union Jack, and the stars and stripes of my own flag, together with a few others that were familiar to me because I'd traveled to those countries, or I'd seen athletes holding them in parades. Russia, Germany, France, Brazil…

"Wow, it's amazing," I breathed.

"I wanted to bring you here to see a part of the country I've always loved. And to show you the worst investment I've made in my life," Patrick explained.

"What investment?" I asked, confused.

As we neared the imposing tower, the trees gave way to short, immaculately trimmed hedges. A group of men in yellow safety vests were at work a short distance ahead. Two of them were trimming the hedges, the other three were cutting the grass. The buzz of their tools sounded loud in the otherwise still afternoon, and as Patrick wound his window down, the scent of fresh-cut grass filled the car.

"You mean—this *castle* is your investment?" I asked, incredulously.

"Give me a moment, please," Patrick said. "I've just got to speak to my maintenance team."

He stopped the car and climbed out, closing the door before walking over to the group. They switched off their machines when he approached, and I could hear their voices, interspersed with bird calls and the far-off bleats of sheep, but couldn't make out exactly what they were saying.

His castle?

I stared ahead at the tower, a bold, dramatic structure against the deep blue afternoon sky.

After a minute, Patrick climbed back in the car.

"Yes, it's mine," he said. "I own it. I bought it, and a hundred acres of the surrounding woodlands, five years ago."

"And why is it such a bad investment?"

"Well, the castle itself—Kelly Castle—was built in the late sixteenth century by the O'Kelly family, who were Irish nobility. They owned a huge tract of land going right the way down to the sea, but from all accounts, they were a hard-living, hard-fighting bunch. Drunkards. Fighters." He gave me a sidelong glance. "Adulterers."

"So what happened?"

"In the early 1700s, the heir to the castle was killed in a duel. It passed to his brother, who was an alcoholic, and allowed it to fall into disrepair before he cracked his skull out hunting. From there, it changed hands a few more times, each time ending up with more unsavory owners."

"Go on," I encouraged him. I was fascinated by the account of this place, so steeped in history.

"Well, over time, the woods began encroaching, and when it was up for sale the last time, the castle had been basically swallowed by the forest. Trees had taken over, and were growing all the way up to the moat, their roots starting to push under the foundations. The building itself had fallen into disrepair, and had become a hangout for vandals and drug users."

"Wow," I breathed, my eyes wide as I imagined its walls, dark in the shadows of the forest and sheltering ne'er-do-wells.

"An American investor put in an offer to buy it. He was planning to have it dismantled and shipped out to his ranch in Texas, stone by stone."

"No!"

"Yes. I found out about it. I had the money available, so I bought it and have spent the past few years restoring it to its former glory. We're not quite there yet, but almost."

SOARING

Patrick parked the car in a paved lot. I climbed out and walked with him to the imposing main gates, where a wooden drawbridge arched over a deep moat.

I followed him over the drawbridge, my footsteps muffled by the thick, heavy, wooden planks. Two enormous chains supported its weight, and a brightly shining steel grille protected the top section of the inner archway.

I glanced down into the moat as I passed. Its waters were very dark and absolutely still. I imagined how a warrior would have felt, fighting on the drawbridge, only to be shoved into those icy waters. The sides of the moat were completely sheer—there would be no way out. Wearing heavy armor, death by drowning would swiftly follow.

I shivered as we walked through the inner arch, passing under the steel grille and into a square courtyard. Perhaps sensing my discomfort, Patrick slipped his arm round my waist. It was the first time we'd touched since I'd run away, and I felt acutely aware of the strength of his arm, the warmth of his palm. His touch didn't feel comforting. It didn't offer me the reassurance I supposed he'd hoped it would. Instead, with his body now pressed against mine, I felt the familiar coil of lust inside me.

I couldn't help it. I slid my arm around him, tightening my grasp, so that I could feel the taut hardness of his body against mine.

As we reached the inner courtyard, we stopped, arm in arm, taking in the sight. The center of the courtyard was well-kept grass, with a few wooden benches. A wide, covered corridor ran all the way around its sides. Beyond that, the castle walls were separated, at intervals, by archways, which led to its interior. Scaffolding on the east side of the building, near the tower, told me that the work here was not yet complete, but to me, it looked pristine.

"It's gorgeous," I said. I stared, craning my neck to see every detail in the stonework that stretched high above me. "You said it was your worst investment. Why?"

"Because it will never do much more than pay for its upkeep. I'm planning to open it to the public next year, as a tourist destination and a venue for locals that can be enjoyed by everyone for a reasonable fee."

"Well, that sounds great," I said, "but why did you buy it, knowing that?"

That smile was back, hovering over his lips, daring me to kiss it away.

"It was an emotional decision," he admitted. "My heart won over my head."

"Why?" I asked, surprised. I hadn't thought him to be a heart-over-head person.

"I grew up here. This town deserves better. I'd hate to see the castle dismantled and transported to the States just because the global recession hit Ireland so hard, and nobody was willing to invest in it. It has the potential to be an incredible tourist attraction, and tourism will do a huge amount to uplift the area. It was throwing money away, but throwing it into a place that is part of my history, and my heart."

He turned to me while he spoke, and I nodded in response, thinking his words through carefully. They did show another aspect of him; a gentler side. A generous side, even though the cynic in me was wondering if the castle had also been a convenient tax write-off. At any rate, he must have put a huge amount of work into this place to transform it from the spooky ruin, engulfed by forest, that he had described. Nature had been tamed here now; the woods cut back, the surroundings carefully tended to create a setting that was both tranquil and beautiful.

Perhaps I should give Patrick the benefit of the doubt.

At that moment, his cellphone rang. Excusing himself, he slipped his arm from my waist—reluctantly, I thought, before walking a few steps away from me and answering. "Afternoon, Claude. No, it is afternoon here, because I'm still in Ireland. Plans changed. What's the latest regarding the Heathways deal in Dubai? Did you meet with Abdul?" He waited, listened. "No. I've got the info on my laptop. Give me a sec and I'll send it through to you."

Mouthing a, "Sorry," at me, he turned and walked briskly

out of the courtyard, heading toward his car.

I couldn't help but smile to myself. Once a businessman, always a businessman, I guessed. At any rate, while he was busy, it would be a good opportunity to wander around the castle and take a peek at what lay beyond those high stone archways.

Noticing a discreet brass sign for the restrooms, I decided to make that my first stop. I headed across the grass and under the shade of the walkway. I shivered, noticing how much cooler it felt as soon as I was out of the sun and close to those stone walls. How had they kept warm in the old days? I was imagining fur blankets and roaring fires—lots of both.

The Ladies' was beautifully decorated, with a pristine tiled floor and the fragrance of pot-pourri in the air. I used the toilet and washed my hands, impressed that rose-scented hand wash and moisturizer had been provided. There was still no sign of Patrick when I headed out, so I turned left and walked to the next huge archway.

"Dining Hall" read the brass sign near the tall wooden door. The door itself stood open and I stepped into the huge chamber. An enormous wooden table was the room's centerpiece, with rustic wooden benches placed along its length. This could not be the original table, surely, but I guessed it was a carefully made and costly replica.

I admired the wall hangings and tapestries, which depicted feasts and battle scenes. In contrast to the throngs depicted in these embroidered artworks, the silence of the place felt almost expectant. It was silly to think that ghosts might lurk here, but on my own in this empty hall meant for such crowds, I found myself feeling strangely uneasy.

I turned and left, crossing the courtyard in the bright, comforting rays of the sun, heading for the archway opposite. As I drew closer, I saw a brass sign that said "Armory."

Curious, I peeked around the half-open door to see that the armory was still a work in progress. It looked as if Patrick was going to make this room into a kind of museum, with the armor, shields, helmets, and weapons on display, but the exhibits were not yet complete. A long, polished table that was the room's centerpiece was empty, although displays covered the walls. My eyes were drawn to a display of swords on the far side of the room, just below a tall, narrow window that let in a bright beam of afternoon sun.

I walked across the room to take a closer look at the swords. Their shapes were at once familiar and foreign. That huge weapon must be a broadsword. It had a wide handle and a long, gleaming blade that looked thick and heavy. Surely it must have taken a two-handed grip to wield that behemoth? This one was the opposite. Its gilded handle and short, deadly sharp blade made it more of an ornamental weapon, but certainly one that could kill. Here was a scimitar, and my eyebrows rose as I recognized the distinct shape of an old-fashioned saber hanging next to it on the wall.

These two blades were the predecessors to the fencing tools I'd practiced with every day for as long as I could remember. Not since my early teens had I gone without my saber practice for such a long time. It gave me a strange feeling to look at a blade that was so familiar, and carried with it so many associations.

I remembered the way the sweat would pour off my body inside the suit so that I was gasping for breath…I always overheated badly in them. In summer, a fencing suit was suffocatingly hot, and in winter, I sweated almost as much and grew immediately cold when I stopped moving. Monika and I used to joke that nobody took up fencing in order to wear comfortable, fashionable gear.

And then another memory of Monika and me during a training match faded into my mind. The two of us were laughing together so hard that we were doubled over with mirth, after she'd mistimed a lunge and I'd flubbed the parry and we'd ended up staring at each other, each stupefied by our own incompetence, before beginning to giggle.

I remembered constantly massaging my left wrist and fingers, which took huge strain when I was practicing hard, because so much of what I did was controlled by fine coordination and fingertip pressure.

I had a sudden urge to pick up the saber, to hold it in my

SOARING

hand, just to see what it felt like. To see if, by holding it, I might somehow rekindle the old passion and fire that I had felt for my sport.

I checked behind me. Nobody was there. The sword itself looked sturdy enough. It was heavier than the ones I used, of course, but it seemed in pristine condition. I lifted it off its brackets and slipped the hilt into my left hand.

Heavy, yes, but beautifully balanced. It felt amazing to be holding a blade in my hand that carried so much history. Where had it been forged, and by whom? And where had it been used? Had this blade seen battle…had it killed?

My fingers automatically tightened around the grip, my index and middle fingers finding the places they needed to be to control the blade…but with the more solid weight of this weapon, fingers alone wouldn't do it. My wrist and elbow would have to come into play. How would my injury cope?

I moved to an open space, to where the beam of sun fell onto the bare floor, and turned my back on it so the light wasn't in my eyes. In front of me, I imagined an opponent. Perhaps one of the invaders from ancient times, clad in rustic armor and carrying a shield and wielding a short, heavy sword. How would I defend myself in a real battle? What would it feel like to fight for my life, instead of just for a medal on a ribbon?

I parried, thrust, parried again, and then I was off, shifting my weight, advancing and retreating while adjusting myself in perfect alignment with my dancing blade. This circular defense had always been one of my weaknesses, but it felt so easy here, in this quiet space. The light gleamed on my blade as I thrust it forward, hopefully to penetrate a weak spot in my invisible opponent's armor.

Although, this skirmish would not end in first blood. Swords were invented to fight to the death. Sometimes, I guessed, you might even have to take an injury deliberately to lure your opponent in, if it meant that you could then deliver the killing blow.

So the duel would continue, then. The swish of my blade in the air was the only sound as I moved, my left arm sore from the effort now, the muscles no longer as fit as they had been and the weight and length of the sword was more than I was used to. But who would allow their opponent to win just because of fatigue? I could push through that. I had done many times before. I had pressed through my own exhaustion to please Dave, and to please my coach, and to please my parents and my sponsors and all those who were invested in my success.

Now, with nothing left to lose, I was doing it only for myself.

The ache in my arm felt good; it meant I was pushing myself. My breath was coming fast, my heart pounding as I shifted and sprang. My muscles were taut, coiled, ready. My body felt like a spring, rather than leaden, which was how my last few practice sessions had left me. I could see my shadow in the splash of sunlight on the floor, and I imagined my opponent, blinking in the harsh rays which were blinding him.

What would I do? How would I try to finish this? Perhaps I could use the sixte position to protect my head from a downwards cut, and then riposte, aiming the blade not at my opponent's helmeted head or armored breastplate, but lower down, going for his vitals, sliding my blade into his stomach.

It was a difficult technique and one that could be clumsy; but I managed the sequence perfectly, ending with a low, deadly lunge. In my mind, I imagined myself ramming my blade into my opponent—his shriek of rage as he realized I had bested him.

Breathing hard, grinning in delight at having won my bloody fantasy battle, I lowered my blade. And it was only then that the words, "Well done," from the door behind me caused me to whirl around in alarm.

CHAPTER 12

Patrick stood in the doorway, his arms folded across his chest, and his eyes intent, although the expression on his face was one I couldn't read.

Guilt flooded through me as I stared down at the saber in my hand. What must he be thinking after seeing me prancing around in his armory with a sword I'd had no right to touch?

"I'm so sorry," I said. I was breathing hard. "I just...I decided I'd have a test fight. Just to...just to see if my left arm was in shape."

"You looked powerful," Patrick said, and at his words I felt something inside me soften, because I'd imagined he'd be angry, but his praise had disarmed me completely. "Watching you was incredible. You were like a machine. Beautiful and deadly. No, not like a machine. More like a warrior princess." He smiled wryly. "Did that last lunge destroy your imaginary opponent?"

"I got him under his breastplate," I admitted. My face was burning, and not just from the exercise. The saber's grip felt slippery in my hand; my palm was now damp.

"Good move."

"Hey, it was kill or be killed," I quipped, to emphasize the silliness of my pretend fight. It was crazy that I'd felt such joy wielding the sword, but deep down I knew it had been because there had been no pressure on me to succeed.

I had reveled in the simple delight of doing it for myself, without the weight of others' expectations, or having to face a masked opponent who was as hungry for that medal as I was.

Ashamed of my thoughts, I carried the sword over to the wall and replaced it carefully in its brackets.

"What about your arm? You said you were testing it out?" Patrick asked.

For some reason, in his presence, I was finding it difficult to get my breath back. Making an effort to slow my respiration down, I straightened my left arm, flexed it, then opened and closed my hand. It felt sore, but it was a healthy pain, rather than the knife-sharp agony which had stabbed through the muscle a few days ago when I'd tried a similar move.

"It feels really good," I said, with more enthusiasm than I felt. "I'll be ready for competition again before too long."

"And is that what you want?"

Patrick's question was neutrally worded, but his words struck a chill through me. Perhaps it was the tone in which they were spoken, or maybe because they hinted at an alternative.

And there was no such thing. Not for me, not now. I had only one future to strive toward, if my sponsors decided it was still open to me.

"It's definitely what I want!" My voice rang with false enthusiasm. "I can't wait to get back into training. The world championships are coming up soon. It's back to work next week for me."

"So you'll go home on Monday?" His words felt like ice shards, shearing off from the vaulted ceiling.

"I have to," I said, remembering the meeting I'd promised to attend.

I was filled with dread at the thought of returning to training. It wasn't the hours of practice that disheartened me, nor the rigorous diet—although that was discouraging. More than that, it was feeling as if I would be climbing back into a box that I'd just had the chance to escape from. A box closed firmly by other people's expectations of me.

And how could I live up to all of them?

I glanced again at the burnished steel blade, in its resting place on the wall, and wondered why the fight for life or death could seem so simple, while everything in between was not.

"As long as you're happy," Patrick said. I couldn't read the expression in his eyes, but his voice was cold. In my confusion, only one feeling was certain…it was over now, between us; it had run its course. Whatever spark had been there had burned itself out earlier that day. Now, my decision had cemented the fact that we would be going our separate ways.

"Oh, I'm happy," I reassured him. My voice sounded rather formal.

"Good."

He walked toward me, and as he came closer, my smile became wobbly and my mouth felt suddenly dry.

"Well, I guess it's been a great drive. Seeing the castle and all. Thank you," I said. My heart was racing. Bizarrely, I felt more nervous now than I had done when we'd been together outside the honeymoon suite, although I didn't know what I was afraid of.

He grasped my hands in his own and I sucked in a gasp of air involuntarily at this unexpected gesture. His hands felt warm and strong, his fingers twined through mine and then tightened.

His gaze pierced me and, looking into his eyes, I felt my own eyes widen, my mouth soften.

"It's not over yet," Patrick said softly, and I knew he wasn't just talking about the drive.

He lifted my left hand with his right, turned it palm up, and I looked away for a moment, not wanting to see the calluses on my palm that, despite my recent layoff from fencing, remained visible.

He caressed my palm with his thumb. The pressure was light, but sensual. He lifted my palm to his lips, as if he was going to kiss it, but at the last minute he squeezed my fingers hard, closed his eyes, and pressed my hand into his cheek, pushing his face against it.

My eyes widened, this strange and intimate gesture somehow affecting me more than a simple kiss would have done. And from my own response, the way I felt as my fingers touched his skin, I knew this was not over yet. How could I have thought so?

Releasing my hand, he enfolded me in his arms and pulled me close. I was surprised by his strength, the firmness of his grasp, even though I was clasping him just as hard. We kissed roughly, desperately. The desire he'd kindled in me earlier was now flaming again. God, I needed him. I needed to crush my mouth into his, to feel the heat of his breath on my face, to greedily taste him while he was plundering me.

Our tongues slid together and I closed my eyes, abandoning myself to the raw sensations of his kiss. But this wouldn't stop at kissing—it couldn't, not now. I sensed this, and knew he did, too. As the kiss deepened, I moaned, and he grasped me tighter. His erection, hot and hard, was pressing into my belly. The feel of it was driving me crazy with desire…this physical proof that his lust for me was as strong as mine for him.

I moved my hand down, touching his cock, feeling its length through the soft grey fabric of his chinos, reveling in his groan of pleasure.

Abruptly, his arms closed around me and he lifted me off the floor, carrying me for a few strides before placing me gently down again. The hard edge of the table bumped against my thighs, and then he was guiding me back, lowering me so that I lay on its flat, polished surface. He undid the buttons on my blouse, his fingers clumsy with haste, or perhaps with desire, because one of them snapped off and I heard it spinning away across the floor.

"Sorry," he murmured, and I let out a breathy laugh, that served to reduce the tension between us for just a moment. He opened my blouse, let out a ragged sigh as my bare breasts were revealed. He stroked his fingers over them, circling his thumb around my tautening nipples before pinching them, teasing them into pulsing peaks of desire.

"Wait," he said. He smoothed his hands over my breasts once more before he turned and strode away. I looked round, my gaze passing over an arrangement of spears and shields on the northern wall, as I watched him push the heavy wooden door closed and slide the bolt into place.

We were completely private now, and I shivered with expectation, resting my head on the table and looking up at the vaulted ceiling as I heard him return. Glancing to my right, I saw that dust motes, disturbed by our movement, were dancing in the golden ray of sun that now streamed through the narrow, arched window.

Patrick's hands smoothed over my knees, pushing my skirt up, easing my legs apart. I was acutely aware of my lack of panties as he slid his left hand under my bare buttocks to support me. If I hadn't been so turned on, I might have felt shy, but I was beyond shyness now. He leaned over me, his features taut with desire.

"You are so fucking gorgeous, Claire. Sexy beyond words," he murmured, and I let out a small cry as I felt the delicious caress of his fingertips over my cleft.

"So wet." His face was intent as he stroked between my swollen lips, massaging my clitoris before pushing two fingers deeper into me. He thrust them into my throbbing flesh to push on the hot erogenous zone of my G-spot, causing luscious warmth to pool inside me. Oh, God, this stimulation was so erotic, so intimate…all the more so because, while he fingered me, his gaze didn't leave mine, and I could not look away from him. My breath was coming fast, in shallow gasps, and so was his.

He gently withdrew his fingers, and I heard the click of his belt buckle and the whisper of fabric as he undid his pants. If there had ever been a time to say no, this was it, this was now. But I could not have uttered the word, not even if a posse of invaders had been battering at the door. My body was clamoring for him with an intensity that felt like a shout; I was consumed by a need more primal than anything I had experienced before.

I heard a rustling sound and realized he must be doing as he'd promised…he was putting a condom on. Then his arm underneath me flexed, lifting my hips higher so that I felt his cock touching my slit.

Transfixed by his gaze, I could only gasp, "Yes, oh, yes, please," as I felt the wide head of his cock push into me, stretching me open. He let out a groan as he entered me. This penetration felt so incredibly erotic, so perfectly right. My eyes were locked with his and I could see my sensations, my emotions, reflected in his face.

I could not believe he was finally taking me the way I'd

dreamed and fantasized about for so long. His thick shaft filled me up as he pushed deeper, inch by delicious inch, causing me to gasp as he thrust over nerve endings that were suddenly pulsing with delight. The stimulation felt so intense, it was almost painful. Sensations ripped through me, tendrils of fire flickering in my lower belly. His thighs were hard against my own, my legs wrapped around him, pulling him closer.

"God, you feel so good," he choked, but this felt more than good. It was as if, for the first time, I was truly experiencing being one with another person.

He slid his other hand under my buttocks, angling me to allow his shaft to push against the pulsing spot his fingers had stimulated earlier, so that I moaned in delight. This deeper pressure made me feel as if I was melting inside. As the tempo of his thrusts increased, my body began shuddering, the pleasure spiraling inward to create a tightening coil of sensation. Each powerful movement of his hips was pushing me closer to the brink... toward an edge that felt higher and steeper than any I'd encountered before.

"Oh, yes, Claire," he got out, his voice hoarse, as I abandoned control with a cry. My orgasm was so intense, it shook me, sweat springing out on my skin, and I closed my eyes as tight spasms of ecstasy tore through me. He rode the waves with me, deep inside me, and from the catches in his breathing, I knew he could feel every pulse from my climax.

He leaned forward, his arm reaching around my back to hold me against him tightly. His body radiated heat and his breathing was rapid as he slammed himself into my wetness, going hard and fast, knowing that I could take it now, that I was softened and ready for this deep, merciless ravishment.

His features were etched into the brutal honesty of lust. I could feel his skin, slippery with sweat, and the flex of the muscles underneath; then the moment when they tensed into steel. He groaned, crushing me to him, his hips pistoning into mine as he reached his own pinnacle.

His arms were tight around me as he held me, gasping, and I clung to him until our sweat had cooled. He kissed me once more, his lips lingering on mine, before withdrawing himself from me and helping me off the table. My legs felt weak and unsteady. I wanted nothing more than to stay where I was, in Patrick's arms, to keep kissing him. This desire was so intense, it frightened me.

Hurriedly, I stepped away, smoothing my skirt, now creased and crumpled, down over my thighs and locating my sandals on the floor. I couldn't even remember how or when they'd fallen off my feet.

"I'll be a minute," I said, not meeting Patrick's eyes before turning away.

Even though my hands were still trembling, the bolt moved smoothly back under my grasp and I pulled open the heavy door and hurried to the bathroom.

My reflection said it all. Swollen lips, smudged eyeliner, tangled hair, and the missing blouse button, which meant that my cleavage was now teasingly visible through the too-low neckline. This wasn't the carefully-groomed, innocent-looking reflection I was used to seeing. I looked sexy, as if I'd just been ravished. Just the expression in my eyes would be enough to get College Sport on the phone to their lawyers with instructions to cancel the contracts immediately.

I looked wanton, and at that moment, I loved it. I smiled back at my disheveled reflection, feeling a rush of pure happiness. I wished it could last forever, even though I knew that what we'd shared could be no more than a precious, fleeting moment in time.

CHAPTER 13

In the bathroom, I splashed water onto my face, smoothed my hair down, and spent a few minutes making myself presentable again. I was still tingling all over. Try as I might to feel regretful and ashamed about what I'd just done, my body had never felt better. It was as if every fiber of my being felt more intensely alive, and the glow in my cheeks was refusing to abate.

I left the bathroom and headed back toward the armory, but before I could reach it, I heard footsteps from a narrow staircase set into the back wall, and Patrick came down the steep flight of stairs.

"Claire. Come on up," he said, stepping aside so that I could walk ahead of him to the castle's upper level. As I climbed, I noticed that a "No Entry" sign on a chain was hanging down from the right hand wall. So this area must be out of bounds to the public.

"We can't allow visitors onto the gallery," Patrick explained, as if reading my mind. "The stairs are too steep. They were designed for defense."

I could understand that. No point in having a wide, sweeping stairway in a castle when you might one day have to defend the upper levels against invaders.

The stairway made one turn, and then light streamed in again from above. Arriving on the upper level, I stared around me in surprise. It was beautiful up here. The courtyard was a verdant, groomed square below, and through the huge archway behind me, I looked down onto a green ribbon of lawn with colorful bursts of flowers that stretched out to meet the bank of dark, forbidding-looking trees.

I looked ahead, and saw that a table had been set up in the corridor, complete with a white cloth and two leather office chairs. A large picnic basket was beside it. After a second look, I recognized it as the one that had been placed beside the table outside the hotel earlier that day.

"We never got to have lunch," Patrick explained, "so I brought it with me in the car. I thought it would be nice to eat it up here. Sorry about the chairs—they're the only ones available. I borrowed them from the admin office down the passage."

"That sounds wonderful," I said. "Thank you."

I was a bowl of chicken soup ahead of Patrick, but even so, I suddenly realized I was ravenous. And the afternoon shadows were lengthening, meaning it was actually closer to supper time.

We sat at our impromptu picnic table and I helped Patrick unpack the basket. Crystal wine glasses wrapped in cloths, glass bottles of water, silver cutlery, and a variety of warm and cold foods in insulated containers. Aromas mingled in the fresh, clean air as we removed the lids.

Patrick poured us each a glass of fruity, refreshingly dry white wine.

"You'll enjoy this, I think," he said, passing me a container. "Chicken liver pate. It's the hotel's specialty. The chickens are from a local free-range farm, and the pate is made with brandy and real butter."

He passed me a basket containing golden-brown wafers of Melba toast, and I took a piece and smeared it thickly with pate. The pate was topped with a thick, buttery layer. It looked rich, decadent, and delicious. I took a bite and flavor exploded in my mouth—layers of meaty goodness coated my tongue.

"Mmmm," I told Patrick, reaching for more before I'd even finished my first piece, and he grinned, enjoying my delight.

The chicken liver pate was followed by goblets of chilled tomato soup, a simple Caesar salad with shaved parmesan and creamy dressing, and warm skewers of fillet and roast onion with a peppercorn dipping sauce. We took our time over the feast, and I was surprised by how easily we conversed while we ate.

I had thought there would have been some tension, some

uneasiness between us, but Patrick left no room for that. I found myself laughing at some of the stories he told about his misadventures in the media world, and in return, telling him more than I probably should have done about my own life, although I didn't mention my parents' situation. That was a secret I wasn't willing to share. But I spoke about my desire to travel and have time to sightsee, and of course, I couldn't help but laugh with him as I compared my usual restrictive diet, which left me constantly hungry, with this bountiful feast of plenty.

By the time we'd each enjoyed one of the thickly iced petit fours that had been packed for our dessert, the shadows were deepening to dusk and the lights placed around the castle had automatically switched on.

I felt completely sated, and I'd finished my second glass of wine by the time we packed up. I wrapped the glasses in their cloths again and stacked the used cutlery into a container provided, while Patrick wheeled the office chairs to their original home down the passage and, finally, carried the table back.

We made our way carefully down the stairs and it seemed natural for Patrick and me to hold hands as we crossed the drawbridge and walked to the car.

"I know you're trying to stay away from the Park Hotel," he told me. "It's the only reason I haven't already asked you if you'd like to come back there with me tonight."

To spend the night with him…my stomach did a slow, lazy curl at that tantalizing thought.

"I was going to ask you," I said, my mouth feeling dry with anticipation, "if you might want to spend the night with me. Top floor, the farmhouse, somewhere in the deepest Irish countryside."

Patrick glanced at me. I expected him to be smiling, but his face was serious.

"I would love to take you up on that offer. More than I can tell you. But you're a paying guest in somebody's home. I don't want to get you in any trouble with your landlady, or to offend her," he said.

I nodded reluctantly, seeing his point. Noreen's anger was something to be reckoned with, and although I was torn apart at the thought of having to say goodbye to Patrick tonight, I was touched by his consideration and gentlemanly good manners.

"I'm sure Noreen wouldn't object to you coming in for a coffee," I ventured.

"Good idea," he said, sounding relieved, and I wondered if he, like me, did not want this magical day to end.

While Patrick was driving, I quickly checked the messages on my phone. I had three messages from numbers I did not recognize, two voicemails from Dave, and a text from Hassan. I didn't want to listen to any of the voice messages. But I did open Hassan's message.

"How are you doing?" the text read. "I wanted to say, again, how sorry I am this happened, Claire. I am so distressed. I wish there was something I could do to help—if there is, please, tell me. I owe you, more than I can ever say. Things are looking positive for Ahmed and me; the paperwork for our green cards has been submitted. My lawyer says it should take another year at most. When we are safely in the States, we're going to tell the truth; we are going to come out as a couple. Till then, thank you, and thank you again. H. xx"

I sighed, but discreetly, because I didn't want to attract Patrick's attention, or have him ask what had provoked it.

And, as we wound our way down the narrow lanes, I found myself thinking back to that private function, and the events that had taken place there.

I had agreed to go with Hassan. Why not? Dave was out of town, I was on my own, and this party promised to be a fun event. It was being held by a wealthy friend of Monika's to celebrate the opening of his gorgeous, new Long Island guesthouse—a converted mansion. No members of the press were allowed; this was a private party, with the media opening taking place the following week. And Ahmed would also be there, which I knew meant a lot to Hassan. Perhaps, if we were discreet and careful, they would be able to spend the night together.

We all had room keys allocated, but Hassan didn't take his key. Ahmed and I had neighboring rooms, which were large and beautifully decorated in rich, bright colors. Sliding glass doors opened onto secluded balconies, with a shared garden beyond. In the end, we decided I should use Ahmed's room because the balcony in the other room, right at the end of the corridor, was more private. This would be better for the two men, so we swapped keys.

The party was held in sumptuous style. A buffet groaning with food, an open bar, a live band. I'd expected to party into the small hours, but ended up exhausted long before midnight. My two neighbors retired at about the same time. I'd climbed into bed feeling happy at the thought of them spending the night together in this opulent setting, hoping that before too long, they could live in love, without fear of repercussions.

I woke suddenly, early in the morning, with gray light filtering through the curtains. I sat bolt upright, my heart pounding, sweat chilling my body. I realized I'd just wrenched myself from out of a terrible nightmare. The residue of fear still lingered, prickling my skin. What had my bad dream been about? At first, I couldn't remember. Breathing hard, I turned the bedside light on to banish my fears, knowing I wasn't going to get back to sleep.

And then it hit me…a vivid picture, spine-chilling in its detail.

I saw a man I recognized, using a flashlight to sort through the room keys. The beam shone onto the list, lighting up Hassan's name, which was next to an unclaimed key. The man smiled at the sight of it, quickly photographing this evidence before checking for my name on the list of occupied rooms and searching for a spare key…

I let out a moan of terror. The man I saw in the picture was Carlos, the paparazzi photographer.

Was my vision for real? I jumped out of bed and then stood, indecisive, the tiles cold under my feet.

Was it true, or just a nightmare? Had Carlos somehow infiltrated this event? I felt cold all over. I tiptoed to the door, listening, and dread filled me as I heard the faint sound of footsteps, quietly approaching down the long, tiled corridor.

I sprinted to the glass doors at the back of the room, wrenched them open, and in a few seconds I was tapping urgently on the glass doors of the neighboring room.

"Hassan!" I hissed. "Quickly!"

It was Ahmed who appeared at the door a moment later, naked apart from a pair of boxer shorts, his hair tousled from sleep and confusion in his eyes.

No time for a proper explanation.

"Out!" I whispered, pushing the sliding door open and shoving him through it. "Someone's coming!"

Carlos was trying to be quiet in order to surprise us, and that fact bought me an extra few seconds; just long enough for Hassan to jump out of bed, grabbing the white duvet in his hands as an afterthought, and pulling it with him to conceal his nakedness.

Then the door swung open and we turned to face it, standing side by side; victims of the merciless flash and click of the camera as Carlos triumphantly captured the shots of Hassan and me together. We both started shouting, screaming…I flung up my hand defensively, if too late; bunching the duvet in front of him, Hassan leaped forward, but not fast enough. The door slammed, and running footsteps vanished down the corridor.

Carlos had done his job. He had gotten the pictures which would potentially end my career, and my marriage.

All I could cling to, in the hellish days that followed, was the knowledge that Carlos hadn't found Ahmed and Hassan together, had never suspected that they were lovers. He had not taken shots which would have destroyed not only my friend's career, but also, potentially, his life.

CHAPTER 14

The flicking of the car's indicator pulled me out of my somber thoughts. We'd arrived back at the farmhouse, and Patrick had agreed to come in for coffee. How long could I stretch coffee out for, I wondered, as he parked next to my hired car. I didn't want to say goodbye to him tonight.

I could only hope that Noreen's kettle would take forever to heat up.

"Where is your landlady?" Patrick asked, as if reading my mind.

"I don't know," I said. Her car wasn't outside the barn where I was used to seeing it. Perhaps she was at a meeting or a knitting evening with the Women's Guild. Or else, I hoped, she was out having fun.

"Guinness isn't here, either," I observed. She must have taken the collie with her. I glanced up and saw that the cat was on his usual perch atop the fridge, washing his face with his left paw.

I let us into the kitchen and filled the kettle with cold water before putting it on. To my relief, it took a minute or two before I even heard it start to simmer. With any luck, boiling would take much longer. Years, preferably. And, in the meantime, Patrick had seated himself at the kitchen table and pulled out the chair next to him, ready for me.

I sat down, close enough that our legs brushed. I loved that I could see the creases in his shirt from the passion we'd shared earlier, and his hair was rumpled in a way that made me long to run my fingers through it to neaten its disarray—seeing as, after all, I'd been the one to cause it.

Having our legs brushing wasn't enough. He turned to face me and moved his left leg in between mine, his thigh warm against my own. He laced his fingers through my own, his thumbs caressing my palms. It felt so good to be physically close to him like this…the touch of his skin on mine felt so exactly right. Already, I could feel desire welling inside me again. He leaned toward me and our lips touched, the kiss quickly deepening.

And then the noise of Noreen's Isuzu truck rattling up to the farmhouse caused us to break apart like two guilty teenagers. We moved away, out of that intimate closeness, although his knees still touched mine. I heard the tread of Noreen's shoes walking quickly up to the door, and then she was in, and Guinness was trotting over, tail wagging, to greet us.

"Evening, evening," Noreen said, but I thought she sounded stressed, and she was frowning. "Hi Claire, hi Patrick. Did you have a good day?"

"Evening, Noreen," Patrick replied, standing up and greeting her with a handshake. After shaking his hand, Noreen drew the curtains tightly over the kitchen window, and pulled the latch across the inside of the door.

"Our day's been wonderful, thanks," I said. "Is everything okay here?"

"Well, I think so, now," Noreen said. "There was an intruder prowling outside the farmhouse earlier, though. Guinness started barking and alerted me."

A cold feeling settled in my stomach. "What happened?"

"He was hiding in the bushes. It looked like one man, on his own. When I let Guinness out, the prowler ran down the driveway, with my dog chasing him. He climbed into a car parked outside, near the hedge. Then he sped off. I jumped into my truck and tried to follow him, but he drove like the devil was after him, and I lost him on the back roads."

"What car was it?" Patrick asked.

"Some sort of smallish white sedan. A Golf, if I had to guess," Noreen said.

Patrick and I exchanged a worried glance, and I thought again about the car that had followed us up the hill in the direction of the castle, before Patrick had noticed it and pulled over. That had been a white Golf.

Was it a paparazzi photographer?

Worse still, could it be Carlos?

The shrill whistle of the kettle made us all jump.

"Shall I drive around and have another look?" Patrick asked, after turning it off.

"I think he's well gone now, but I phoned the neighbors just to let them know," Noreen said. "I guess we'll have to be careful for the next while, that's all. Anyway, I'm off to get some sleep. Got an early start in the morning. Somebody's coming to look at the farm for sale, fingers crossed."

Before leaving the kitchen, she paused and turned back. "Please, before you go to bed, will you make sure the door is locked? Just in case?"

"We'll make sure," Patrick promised.

Noreen left the room, followed closely by Guinness, his paws clicking on the tiles as he trotted along the corridor behind her.

"The intruder who was here is the same person who was driving behind us today, I'm sure of it," I said to Patrick in a low voice. Suddenly, I didn't feel safe in the farmhouse anymore. I was glad the kitchen curtains were drawn, hiding Patrick and me from the prying eyes of cameras. Imagine if Guinness hadn't been alerted. We could have been photographed through the window. A published image of our kiss would be dynamite.

Patrick nodded, his face serious. "There's a good chance it is the same person. I'm going to call up my old contacts tomorrow morning. If you're being hounded by the media, I want to know who's behind it and why. Who's paying Carlos? Your scandal has blown over by now. You shouldn't be a story anymore. Who's trying to make sure that you stay in the spotlight for all the wrong reasons?"

I shook my head. I didn't know, but it made me fearful to think that somebody might be targeting me that way. What chance did I have, if that were the case?

"Anyway, coffee time," Patrick said.

He got the cups together while I opened the fridge and removed the bowl of clotted cream.

"This seems to be an Irish tradition," I told him. "Maybe it's just a Noreen tradition. Either way, it's delicious."

Patrick grinned, and with his smile, I felt the tension inside me dissolve just a little. "I think it's an excellent idea," he said, topping each of the cups with a large dollop of cream.

The coffee was finished all too fast. For a moment, I felt a sense of panic—how could this day be over so quickly? I wished I could stop time, or hold it back, so that we could sit here for longer.

And then I replayed Noreen's words in my mind.

"Before you go to bed…"

She hadn't spoken them to me. She'd addressed both of us, but she had been looking directly at Patrick while she'd said that. And if that was the case, then she was expecting him to stay—or at least, accepting that he might.

Patrick was obviously thinking along the same lines, because he pushed his cup aside, put his arms round me, and said softly, with his lips tickling my hair, "I think your landlady might have given me permission to sleep over. Do you agree?"

I could hear the hint of a smile in his voice. As for me, I was filled with a heart-pounding excitement at the thought of this dream becoming reality.

"I would agree," I whispered back. "And you'd be doing us a favor. If the intruder came back, you could chase him away."

"I could." He brushed his lips down my cheek. "Let's lock up and go to bed, then. But first, I want to take a last look outside. I'm going to walk down to the gate and check the road. I'll be back in ten minutes, if all's clear."

He strode outside, closing the door carefully behind him.

CHAPTER 15

I washed the mugs and put the cream away, and then checked the messages on my phone. If there was anything important from Dave, it was best I listen to it now, before Patrick came back.

"Hi, Claire. You seem to be hard to get hold of at the moment." There was an edge of annoyance in Dave's tone. "Please call me urgently. I need to discuss things with you."

I grimaced in frustration, pulling back the curtain and looking outside before I dialed, but there was no sign of Patrick. He'd told me ten minutes and I guessed he might even take longer while doing a thorough check. I would just have to keep my conversation with Dave short.

Of course, Dave didn't answer, and I had to leave a message and sit watching my phone, willing him to call back quickly. It felt as if more than ten minutes had passed by the time my phone rang, and I snatched it up immediately, not wanting to waste a moment.

"Hi, Claire. Have you sorted out that medical report?"

"No, I haven't had time," I said. In fact, I hadn't even thought about it. But the fencing I'd done at the castle had convinced me there was no permanent damage to my arm.

"Well, get it done. Now, listen. Things are looking very positive for this meeting. Daniel has been able to convince the other shareholders that you're a bankable prospect in spite of this hiccup. Obviously, your rankings need to improve, but we can work on that."

"Yes," I said, trying to sound more optimistic than I felt.

"We'll also need to present a united front in our marriage. Family values, that's what the brand is all about. Healthy activity, family time. We need to try again, Claire. We've drifted apart recently, and this must change. I'm willing to do it if you are."

Drifted apart? I couldn't believe what I was hearing. Dave had been unfaithful for years! Why was he not willing to acknowledge it?

He wanted to try again…but did I? Could I?

I didn't think I could. In that case, we would carry on as before. Living a lie, for the sake of my sponsorship, our lifestyle, my parents.

"We can talk about that," I said diplomatically.

"What did you say? This connection is terrible and it's noisy here."

I could hear the background noise. He sounded as if he was in a shopping mall. I could pick up the clatter of carts.

"I said we can talk about that," I repeated more loudly. "But Dave, do you really mean it? The sponsorship is on again? I won't have to pay anything back for breach of contract?"

"Not a cent, the way things are looking now. In fact, we can put in a swimming pool for the…"

"No!" I interrupted. "No pool, Dave! Damn it, you know I didn't even want us to buy the house. It's far too big for the two of us, and too expensive. We didn't have to live in Montclair, in a home with five bedrooms and two entertainment areas."

"You think I want to be cooped up in a condo somewhere? Besides, the house is a great investment. It's in a safe, up-market neighborhood, and it's close to your training center and to the airports."

Not as close as a small apartment in Newark itself would have been, like the one where Monika lived. But Newark wasn't good enough for Dave; he needed a better address.

"I wanted to put my money toward looking after my mother. And I couldn't do that because of the decisions you've been making without consulting me. So no more home improvements until my folks are taken care of."

"We'll talk about that," Dave said, echoing my words, although in a much sulkier tone.

"Well, at least it's good news about the sponsorship." Now I was trying to placate him.

"I've been working hard on this." He sounded aggrieved. "You'd lose pretty much everything if it fell through. A thank-you would be nice, if you can spare it."

"I'm sorry, Dave," I said, humbled by his words. Whatever his faults, he had saved this deal for me, and given me a chance at a future. "I really do appreciate what you've done. Thank you."

"Oh, and there's a function at the Park Hyatt in New York City on Tuesday night. College Sport wants you to be there. Don't know if you've received the invite, but I'll forward it to you just in case."

"A function on Tuesday night? What function is this?" I asked.

"Sports Stars Achievement Awards. College Sport is the major sponsor so you need to be seen there. You'll have to go on your own. I have other plans that night."

I wondered briefly what those plans were

"I'll put it on my calendar," I told him.

"I gotta go," he said brusquely. "We'll speak on Monday, then."

"Okay."

I thought he was going to disconnect, but then he said, "Oh, and Claire, I'll email you a link. Check it out when you have time. Monika sent it to me a half-hour ago. She was worried about it. Said she forwarded it to you earlier today, but you didn't respond."

I really needed to check my emails. I'd have a look first thing tomorrow morning, I decided.

"I'll get back to you on that," I promised.

"Speak soon."

Dave rang off, and a moment later, the kitchen door opened and Patrick walked in.

"Nothing to be seen," he told me. "I went all the way down to the crossroads. Not a car in sight, not a sound. It's very quiet out."

He turned and carefully locked the door.

"Let me show you where my bedroom is," I said. I felt like a naughty teenager smuggling a boyfriend in. "You'll need to be quiet. Some of the stairs creak, and the wooden floorboards are very noisy."

"I'll be right behind you." His hands smoothed through my hair.

I turned and tiptoed out of the kitchen, stopping as I passed the fridge to rub the cat's head. Unimpressed with my attempts at affection, he yawned mightily before settling himself down again.

Behind me, Patrick clicked off the kitchen light and we crept upstairs.

The creak of a board behind me made me stop.

"Sssh," I warned.

"Sorry," he hissed, brushing his hand over my backside by way of apology.

I felt giggles erupting, and controlled them with an effort. This was fun…I'd never dreamed I'd be sneaking up this squeaky staircase, closely followed by the sexiest man in the world. Never mind that this afternoon we'd made love on the premises of his magnificent castle…here we were now, trying our utmost to be quiet as we crept up to my simple rented room.

"The bedroom is here," I whispered, stepping carefully over the floorboard that always moved when I stood on it. "And the bathroom is down the hall."

"We must have a shower together." Patrick stood on the floorboard, which let out a sharp cracking sound. "Oops."

I clapped a hand over my mouth to stifle an outburst of laughter.

"There's no proper shower," I told him when I could speak again. "Just a claw-footed tub."

"Even better."

I snapped the bedroom light on. It shone directly over the vase on the desk, crammed with the deep red roses he'd given me, illuminating their petals to a bright ruby. Their rich scent flavored the air. With the thick curtains closed, it felt safe, warm, and private.

Patrick's arms enfolded me and eagerly I met his kiss. Just one step in this small room took us to the bed, and we sprawled onto it, locked in each other's arms, our bodies pressed together. This attraction, this lust between us felt so real, so intense. It dizzied me to know how strongly we both felt it. He couldn't keep his hands off me any more than I could keep mine away from him. Where we touched, I felt heat spreading through me.

"Oh, Christ," he groaned, cupping his hands over my buttocks, his fingers warm on my flesh as he pulled me closer. I ran my fingers over his wide shoulders, feeling the power in them, the way his strongly muscled back tapered to the tautness of his waist.

Under that sexy exterior, inside the tailored broadcloth of those expensive shirts, he was all raw masculinity. His skin smelled faintly spicy, the subtle fragrance of sandalwood. I didn't know if it was soap, cologne, or just him. Whichever, I wanted to press my face close to him and breathe it in.

A heady excitement filled me at the thought of having my way with this gorgeous man while he lay on his back, sprawled so enticingly on my rented bed. I wanted to see him in all his glorious nakedness, to appreciate that taut, toned body that he pushed to the limits of his endurance in the Ironmans.

I unbuttoned his shirt—carefully, unlike the way he'd ripped mine off my body earlier. All his buttons were intact when I opened it to reveal his lightly tanned midriff—his bulky pectorals and defined abs. I eased the shirt off his arms, over those broad shoulders, and he twisted to help me. Placing the shirt on the room's only chair, I turned my attention to his pants. I unbelted and unzipped him, tugged them off, the dark gold hairs on his legs tickling my fingers as I did so.

The pants joined his shirt on the chair and, a moment later, so did his silk boxers. Removing them was a challenge, because he was already so hard, his cock thick and erect, arching upwards toward his navel, its root buried in a soft profusion of deep brown hair. God, I could have feasted my eyes on him for hours…his body was so taut, so ripped, so starkly powerful. But he was watching me, his expression both quizzical and aroused, and suddenly, wickedness overcame me .

Leaning forward, I blew a stream of air softly along the engorged length of his shaft. My lips were so close that I could sense the heat coming from him, but not quite close enough to touch.

I buried my fingertips in the softness of his hair, gently caressing the heaviness of his testicles, and this time, I allowed the tip of my tongue to meet his skin in a feather-light caress.

I heard him groan; half in pleasure, half in frustration, because I knew these teasing touches were whetting his appetite for more, but I decided to prolong his agony just a little, and stroked ever so lightly down his shaft with my left hand, letting my fingertips flutter over him, so that he writhed beneath me, pushing himself up into my hand.

I took him in my left hand, wrapping my fingers around his length, moving my hand up and down in a way I hoped he would enjoy. From his gasping response, I knew the feelings went beyond enjoyment; and when I took his engorged head in my mouth, he let out a moan, then clapped his own hand over his lips in an attempt to stifle the sounds of delight that he could not stop himself from making.

I felt as if the sensations storming through his body were rushing into mine as well. I felt emboldened by the power of what I was doing to him, the joy of being able to turn this powerful, self-willed man into a groaning slave, held captive by my actions and his own throbbing desire. I loved the sensation of his cock in my mouth. I stretched my lips wide around it, taking it as deep as it would go. I curled my tongue along his shaft, caressing him, feeling his skin slick and soft, wet from my saliva.

Gently, I pumped him with my fist, clasped around his root, and it was not long before he tensed, tautened, thrusting his hips into my grasp, his breath sobbing out from between his fingers.

I felt him come, warm semen pumping into my mouth. My body was tingling all over; I felt dizzied, elated that I'd been able to repay some of the incredible sensory pleasure he had given me.

"Ah, God, Claire, you don't know…how good…that was." His whisper was breathless; his arms locked around me, pulling me to him.

"My heart is racing," he breathed in my ear. "I think I may be about to die happy."

He kissed me long and deeply, so that my heart, too, began to pound, and I could feel from his hardness against my belly that he was already becoming aroused again.

Finally, we ended the kiss, and he propped himself on his elbow to stare down at me as he smoothed my hair away from my face.

"Come on, gorgeous," he said. "If we don't take that bath now, we never will."

"I'll get it started," I told him.

I tiptoed to the bathroom and removed my make-up while the water began trickling into the deep tub. Watching it was hypnotic, and I found myself having to wrench my eyes away from the flowing stream. The quiet, soothing sound was making me realize how tired I was. After the passion the day had brought, the rich food, the wine… I suddenly wanted to sleep for an eternity, and if I could do so in Patrick's arms, so much the better.

I woke in quiet darkness, disoriented after the deepest sleep I could remember, still tangled in the tendrils of half-remembered dreams as I tried to puzzle out where I was.

I breathed in the heavy, rich scent of the roses, and remembered. I was in the comfortable bed in my lodgings, with the faraway crowing of a rooster signaling that the sun would soon be rising. And I was not alone. Patrick's sleeping form was cupped behind mine, his arm curled over my waist. His body fitted mine perfectly; my buttocks pressed into his thighs, his breath moving through my hair.

I'd spent the night with Patrick, but my memory of it was hazy. All I could recall was lying in a deep bath while he sponged my shoulders, sending warm water cascading over my breasts.

SOARING

And then, nothing but dreams. I could recall only fragments, but they had been tender and intensely erotic.

Patrick moved his hand, lightly caressing my stomach, and I moved my fingers to brush against his. In my state of deep relaxation, I realized I was incredibly turned on, acutely aware of the sensation of his skin on mine, of every place where we touched. My body had responded to his closeness through the night. It had awoken long before I had.

"Good morning, sleeping beauty," he whispered, his lips nuzzling my neck.

Sleeping beauty? I wanted to ask him why he'd used those words, but the question was forgotten as he cupped his hand over my breast. My nipple responded instantly, tightening and hardening to become almost painfully sensitive. Desire rushed through me, causing my skin to tingle and a melting warmth to pool in the pit of my belly.

He must have heard the soft sigh of pleasure I gave, because his fingertips circled my nipple before gently pinching its engorged tip so that I drew in a sharper breath. This teasing stimulation was triggering a desire that pulsed in my core. I was hungry for him...no, what I felt went beyond hunger. I was desperate to feel his touch where I needed it the most.

I arched my body closer to his, hearing his own breathing quicken as the thick hardness of his erection brushed my inner thigh. He released my nipple, trailing his fingers down my belly to brush lightly over my cleft.

My heart was pounding—I could not breathe as they pushed between my delicate flesh. He groaned as he discovered the wetness there.

"Christ, Claire, you're so ready."

"Your fault," I managed to get out in an unsteady whisper. I didn't trust myself to say any more, not while his fingers were gliding over my clitoris, sending shivers of delight through me. Oh, I wanted him so badly, I needed him inside me...now.

"Please." My voice caught on the word as he moved his hips and I felt the head of his cock parting my sodden lips, stroking over flesh that was trembling in anticipation. I could feel the heat of him, the powerful hardness contained in that engorged shaft.

"I don't have a condom on," he murmured.

Was this why he felt so good? Because it was his smooth, naked skin touching mine? I didn't know. The craving for him filled my mind. It scared me how badly I desired this connection.

"That's…that's okay."

"I'll be careful, I promise."

He pushed into me, his thick shaft stretching me with a sense of delicious fullness as I accepted him. It felt amazingly good to be taken like this, raw, naked, his chest against my back, his thighs on my buttocks, so that I could feel his skin's silken heat. Slick and wet, this was flesh on flesh, a primal connection that was as satisfying as it was dangerous. I would have to trust him…I wasn't on the pill…but I couldn't think past the sensations he was offering me.

His right hand pressed into my pubic bone, his fingers sliding over my clitoris and stroking the tender skin around it; I gasped. These soft caresses stroked over my sensitive outer lips, while his strong thrusts angled directly into my throbbing G-spot. God, this was too good…the sensations were all-consuming, and they were intensified by the emotional closeness, the sense of oneness, I'd never felt so strongly before.

How was this possible, with a man who was still so much a stranger to me? I couldn't say. This was fucking in a way I had not experienced before, the intense physical pleasures of the act an embodiment of a far deeper need that was being fulfilled.

At this thought, I felt myself relax, softening to him, giving over my trust and my body to him completely, and it was as if he sensed my submission. He slid his left arm around me, pulling me toward him more firmly as his tempo increased. He took me hard and fast, gasping as he drove his cock into me while the sensual caresses of his fingertips on my clitoris drew me to my climax.

We couldn't make a noise, but I could not remain silent. I grabbed his left hand in my own, pressing it to my lips, tasting his skin as I muffled my sounds in his broad, strong palm. This felt incredible; the deep stimulation of my G-spot with the softer fingertip pressure, but as I felt myself tense and tauten, he pushed more firmly into my clitoris. The delight of this stronger touch was so intense, it was bordering on pain, but how could I resist when the pain itself felt so voluptuously good?

I came hard, crushing my lips and teeth into his hand so that my cries became whimpers. I bucked my body violently into his and he held me tight as I spasmed around him. He buried his mouth into my shoulder as he choked out his gasps of delight. A few more thrusts into my tight, quivering depths and he pulled abruptly out. He'd taken himself to the brink, perilously close to his own orgasm. His hips jerked against my own and I felt the pulses of his semen, hot and wet against my back.

I was trembling, my breathing rough. I let go of his hand, ran my tongue over my lips. I'd bruised them in my effort to remain silent, but the soreness felt good. His arms around me felt even better. He was holding me like he never wanted to let go.

Eventually, he kissed my shoulder softly before moving away. Reaching behind him, he grabbed a wad of tissues from the box on the bedside table and used them to wipe me off. I blinked, realizing that daylight was filtering through the curtains, turning the darkness of the room to muted sepia shades. I rolled over so that I could look into his eyes. He lay down beside me, his hand resting on my thigh, his eyes looking into mine.

"Why sleeping beauty?" I asked.

He gave a soft laugh.

"You were out for the count last night," he said. "You practically fell asleep in the bath. I had to hold your head above the water." His smile made me think this must be an exaggeration, but even so, it explained my memory lapse.

"I half carried you back to the bedroom, and you were asleep before your head reached the pillow," he said. "And you slept for…" He checked his watch. "It's a quarter to six. You slept for nine solid hours. How tired have you been?"

"I guess I've been under a lot of stress the past few weeks," I admitted. More like the past few months, but no need to tell

Patrick that.

"And you're going back to it again?"

My future felt like a trap, but what option did I have but to walk into it with as much courage as I could?

"Tomorrow," I confirmed. "I've got a meeting with my sponsors. And I have to be at an event on Tuesday night—the Sports Stars Achievement Awards."

His heavy sigh told me that he was as eager about me leaving as I was.

"We need to talk," he said.

"Okay," I agreed, feeling a thread of nervousness pull tight inside me at what he might say.

"Not now. It's too early for serious conversation. What are your plans for today?"

"I don't really have any plans," I said. There was no way I was going to go into town and hunt down a doctor to examine my arm. Even if it were possible to find one, it would take the best part of the day. I'd just have to schedule the appointment for when I was back in the States.

"I have meetings from ten-thirty onwards. I'm free until then, and I'm free tonight."

"I'd love to spend that time with you. Now, and tonight." My heart lifted, and the jaws of the waiting trap seemed suddenly less intimidating. "I have to make a few calls quickly, though, and answer some emails."

"I should go for a run, then." He grinned at my surprise. "I've got my gear in the car. I always keep it there. I'm used to snatching opportunities for training in between work."

Patrick fetched his gym bag from the car before going into the bathroom to change.

"See you in an hour," he told me. His body looked incredible in the running clothes. I couldn't help but admire his toned legs and muscular calves, the taut definition in every inch of his body. It was the sculpted evidence of his own single-minded efforts—a man who pushed himself to his limits in every direction, whether it was work, sport or play. I wasn't quite sure how he did it. After the intensity of the sex we'd had, I thought

SOARING

I might find it difficult to stand, let alone run.

After he'd gone, I stayed in bed for another luxurious half-hour before getting up to have a quick bath and change into jeans and a white short-sleeved top. I went downstairs with my iPad to sit in the kitchen. What had Dave said last night? That there was a website I needed to go to, and he'd sent the link? Monika had told him about it...she'd been worried.

I glanced up at the fridge, noticing that the cat was not in his usual position. In fact, there he was, strolling into the kitchen to eat a few kibbles from a bowl near the door.

"Why aren't you on the fridge?" I asked him, bending to scratch him near his tail.

He glanced up at me disdainfully as if to say, "The fridge? Why would I go there?" His meal finished, he leaped gracefully out of the window and disappeared.

Sitting down at the kitchen table, I checked through my emails. Dave had sent a copy of the revised contract with College Sport. I would have to look at that, see whether any of the terms had changed. And there was the email with the link he'd mentioned.

I frowned when I saw it, because it was one of my least favorite gossip sites. A link here was never going to be good news, sandwiched in between such salacious headlines as "Woman's Oral Sex Selfie with German Shepherd" and "Why This Bachelorette Needs to Go Underwear Shopping." This site claimed 22 million monthly visitors. If I was on here, it was bad, bad news. I took a deep breath and clicked on the link, waiting for it to upload, praying that this would be no more than a rerun of the shocking images that had been published last week.

I opened the page and said, aloud, "Huh?"

"Who's Going to Run Half Naked Through This Vista?" the headline announced. The photo, which looked to have been taken from far away, showed only a sea of greenery with a small building in its center.

"This might look like a simple landscape," the caption read. "But keep watching...because tomorrow, we're going to zoom in on it and show you one of our favorite athletes and sports presenters, running through this greenery. What's she doing? Where is she going? Is she wearing underwear? We're wondering too! Don't miss tomorrow's photos, where you'll be able to see for yourself. All we'll give you in the meantime is this hint…running isn't her usual sport!"

Was this something to do with me? Monika must have thought so, or she wouldn't have sent it. I peered down at the photo, wondering why it looked familiar. I clicked on it to see if it would enlarge, and when it did, I clapped a hand over my mouth.

The photo was of the hotel pavilion where I'd had lunch with Patrick the previous day.

CHAPTER 16

"Oh, my God," I said aloud, staring at the photo on the screen, feeling suddenly sick.

Somebody had indeed been waiting for me, hiding in those cliffs on the far side of the bay. Somehow, someone had been tipped off and had managed to get a lucky shot. Those flashes I had seen had not been my imagination. They had been the real thing—the sun reflecting off a large zoom lens.

I remembered my headlong dash out of that private place and along the drive. My blouse half-unbuttoned, my hair in a mess, my underwear abandoned. My breasts might have been visible through my blouse. A lucky shot could have shown a glimpse.

Cold settled in me as I wondered whether the photographer had also got a shot of Patrick. He hadn't been mentioned—there had been no hints dropped about anybody else.

Why? Was this still to come?

Or was he in on this? Had it been a set-up?

It was a grim possibility, but one which I had to face.

"Morning!" Noreen's cheerful greeting tore me away from my broodings.

"Good morning."

"Sleep well?" She gave me a conspiratorial grin as she opened the fridge, removing a small bottle of orange juice.

"Yes, thank you," I managed to smile back at her, even though I felt stressed and panicky inside. "Patrick stayed over. He's gone out for a run."

"Feel free to make some breakfast when he gets back. I don't have time to do any of that this morning. Got to go and show the farm to this buyer." She paused before leaving the kitchen. "I'm bringing the horses up to the barn later this morning. If you want to have a ride, meet me there at about ten."

"Thanks," I said. "I will."

After Noreen left, I spent the time alternately fretting over the photo and reading my other emails. The terms of the sponsorship contract were strict, and it made me feel sick to think that this new photo could already have jeopardized them.

According to the contract, I would basically be employed by College Sport for the next three years. I would need to compete in all the major tournaments, as well as appear at numerous events and participate in several photo shoots. There were several clauses relating to negative publicity. It was not allowed. During my term, I was to do my best to promote and uphold the family values that the company embodied.

Harsh as these conditions were, they were paying me generously to be the face of the brand.

I could not think of this as a trap. It was an amazing opportunity. Hardly any fencers received such generous sponsorships. Monika was far more skilled than I was, and she had never had an opportunity like this. From time to time, she complained about battling to pay the rent, and when she persuaded me to go out dancing with her, I always insisted on paying. Fencers didn't earn the same income that models or presenters did, although I had a horrible feeling that I had not truly managed to succeed in any of my careers. If I had, surely I would be wealthy by now and wouldn't have to worry?

The new sponsorship was an offer I could not refuse. Just three more disciplined years, and I could provide for my parents' retirement, assuming Dave didn't gamble on the stock market again, or get any more ideas about big houses and fast cars.

It was an opportunity which I had to protect, whatever the cost.

Reading down the list of mails, I saw I'd received one from my mother yesterday—which would have been typed and sent by my father. It filled me with guilt that I hadn't replied to it already, because I was sure she was worrying about me.

"Hey, Claire! I hope you're okay. Dad and I just wanted to say how much we love you and how we hope your problems will blow over soon. We know how amazing you are and we're sure there is another side to this story. Hope your arm is feeling good. Lots and lots of love."

I was busy with a reply to this when Patrick came back from his run. When he opened the door, a cool breeze blew in, lifting the edges of the tablecloth. It looked like it was going to rain later today. Deep grey clouds were gathering on the skyline, blotting out the sun.

After giving me a quick kiss on the lips, Patrick went upstairs to bathe and change, giving me time to finish off the email to my mother and to think about what I was going to say to him about the photographer who had been hidden, waiting on the cliffs.

Of course, my carefully thought out words remained unsaid. When he walked downstairs again, his hair still damp, looking sleek and groomed in a black polo-neck jersey, I blurted out, "There was somebody taking photos yesterday, when we were at that supposedly private pavilion."

Patrick frowned, looking confused and surprised. Genuine emotions? I could not think otherwise.

"What do you mean?"

I pushed the iPad toward him, link open.

"Take a look at this." I could hear the anger in my voice.

Patrick picked up the iPad. He looked carefully at the link for a long time, and while he did so, I saw his face change. A frown appeared, his mouth tightened, his jaw tensed. Suddenly, although he looked as handsome as he'd done before, he came across as darkly intimidating—ruthless, even. I wouldn't have wanted to go head-to-head with this man across a boardroom table. I didn't even feel comfortable facing him across the kitchen table.

"How did you hear about this?" he asked in carefully neutral tones. I had a feeling he was struggling to keep the fury out of his voice.

"My best friend Monika sent it to me. She was worried…she knows I'm here."

"Who else knows you're here?"

"Well, my husband. That's all. Except…obviously somebody else does know."

"Any ideas?"

"There was somebody here at the farm the day before yesterday, talking to Noreen from the Women's Guild. She said she recognized me but couldn't place me, and she was going to find out. And I might have been noticed by one of your guests at the hotel." I shrugged, trying not to sound accusing as I added, "You've got enough media there."

Patrick nodded.

"I know what you must be thinking…that, somehow, my invitation to the pavilion was a setup."

"No," I said, but even I could hear the doubt in my voice.

"From those cliffs, there's a good view of the hotel's main entrance further down. Somebody could have been waiting to spot you, and just got lucky when you appeared higher up."

"I suppose so."

"I need you to trust me on this." His voice was low and compelling. "I'm going to find out who's behind it. And I'm going to get that second photo, and any others, pulled. I know the owner of the site. He owes me a favor. He'll do it if I ask."

"Are you serious?" His words were lifting a huge weight of dread from my shoulders.

"Of course. It's not…" He stopped himself.

"Not what?" I asked, curious to know what he'd been going to say. Not difficult? Not a problem? When he spoke, after a pause, his words were shocking and nothing like what I'd expected.

"I shouldn't tell you this, but I don't think we should have secrets from each other." He pulled out a chair and sat opposite me, stretching across to take my hands in his. His grasp felt warm—or, more likely, my hands were cold.

"Go on. Tell me."

"I've bought photos before now, that could have compromised you. Two sets, one a year ago, the other further back. I purchased the full rights to them, but I never published them."

"Wh-what do you mean?" I swallowed. "A year ago, and further back? What photos could have been so damaging back then?"

"They weren't of you," Patrick told me, his voice hard, and it took me a few astonished moments to work out the truth.

"They were of my husband? Of Dave?" My voice was high with shock. So Dave hadn't always been careful…on two occasions, my womanizing husband had been captured on camera.

Patrick nodded.

"Who was he with?"

"Do you really want to know? If you do, I'll tell you."

His question made me feel cold. I thought for a while, and then said, "No, I don't. I don't want to know. Please don't tell me."

"All right."

"Why did you buy them but not publish them?"

He gave a hard smile that never reached his eyes. "I guess, when it came down to it, I couldn't bring myself to be that much of a bastard. He deserved it…but you didn't."

I was quiet for a long while after hearing that. I didn't know what to say. I felt furious that Dave had been indiscreet. And I felt ashamed. Patrick must believe me to be weak, having stayed with a man who cheated on me, but I could never explain the full truth. My parents remained firmly out of the media spotlight. Nobody outside of my immediate family knew about my mother's injury, which she had begged me to keep private. It was hard enough coming to terms with never being able to walk again without the world knowing, she'd said.

And, of course, nobody knew about my parents' financial situation.

"Thank you for not publishing them," I said in a soft voice.

Patrick shrugged, frowning. I got the feeling that holding onto those photos was a decision he regretted. It made me nervous to think they existed. He could change his mind—or they could fall into the wrong hands.

"I guess I didn't want to be the bad guy. Not where you were concerned. I wasn't even sure at the time if you knew what he was up to. But you did know."

"Yes," I admitted.

"Why did you stay married to a guy who screws you around like that? Why didn't you leave? Over the years, I've seen the photos. I've watched you on TV. I've seen how you've changed—becoming blonder, thinner, more unhappy looking." I could hear the frustration in his voice.

I shrugged. "Dave and I are good friends. And I'm very focused on my career. I guess...staying with him was more convenient."

"I can see that, with him being your manager. But there are other managers out there. Better ones."

What could I say? I was close to telling him the truth—so close—but I held back. I couldn't. Telling Patrick my own secrets was one thing, but confessing my parents' situation would be another.

"The reason I'm asking you this," Patrick continued, "is that I want to keep on seeing you, Claire." His fingers twined through mine and despite the stress of my dilemma, I felt a shiver of desire at this intimate contact. His words took longer to register.

He wanted to keep on seeing me?

The prospect of having an actual relationship with Patrick was everything I'd longed for and fantasized about. But how could it happen? My sponsorship would be jeopardized by a messy divorce, and I knew there was no way it would end up being anything but messy. And my contract was all I had. It was my lifeline, and my family's salvation.

Three more years, and I would no longer be bound by it. I would be financially independent, able to do what I wanted to do, and date whomever I desired. But how could I ask Patrick to wait for three years? I couldn't. It would be totally unfair.

What to tell him? My mouth felt numb. Then he spoke again.

"I need to know that you're single," he said. "That your divorce is finalized. That's important to me."

"It's not finalized," I told him, my voice sounding very small, and I saw him frown in concern.

"You don't know what your words mean to me, Patrick," I

continued. "What you want…I want it too, more than I can tell you. But I can't leave my husband now. I know our marriage is a sham, but he's just stopped the divorce proceedings and I'm not going to push for it. Not for the next while…another three years, maybe. While I focus on my career."

Did he even believe me? To myself, my words sounded empty and totally unconvincing. Anyone who'd been following my rankings could see that my performance had peaked in my early twenties; my best results were behind me.

And I felt ill when I thought about what I had turned down. This connection—emotional, physical, sexual—was more powerful than any I'd experienced before. I'd waited ten years to meet Patrick again, and now, just as he offered what I wanted most in the world, I was going to lose him.

"Are you telling me everything?" he asked. His voice sounded sharply suspicious.

Unable to meet his eyes, I nodded.

His hands released mine. Looking up, I saw his face was unreadable.

"I guess we all have to make choices," he said.

I nodded.

"I can't transgress the boundaries of a marriage, Claire—not anymore than I've already done," he said. "Not even if that marriage is a sham."

My breath was shaky. I bit the inside of my lip, hoping it would help me control my tears, because I couldn't cry in front of him.

"I understand that," I said.

"I hope you and Dave can make it work properly, second time 'round," he told me. "You're an amazing, passionate woman. You deserve to have some love in your life."

I blinked fast and stared down at the table, looking at the warm grain of the wood, the knots in it, the faint marks and scars it carried from a lifetime of use by a family.

When I looked up again, Patrick was gone.

CHAPTER 17

I buried my head in my hands. Now Patrick had left, I could let my tears flow, but despite the emotions raging through me, they did not want to come. Instead of grief, I felt a terrible sense of foreboding, as if, by not telling him the truth, I had made a dreadful, life-altering mistake.

What to do? I got up, walked to the kitchen door and looked out, wondering if I could catch a glimpse of him on the road. I wanted to call him back, but the Mercedes was gone. I looked at the space where it had been, the marks of the tires in the damp soil, and felt something approaching panic.

I had made an unforgivable error, and yet, I'd had no choice.

The weather reflected the darkness of my mood. Clouds covered the sky, grim and forbidding, and the wind had grown stronger, bending the trees and sending golden leaves scudding over the grass. The wind caught the door, blowing it wide open, so that I had to fight to get it closed.

"Don't be stupid," I told myself, trying to toughen up as I turned back to the comfort of the kitchen. "You knew him for how long? Two days?"

But it hadn't been just two days. Patrick Maguire had been with me for ten years. The thoughts of him, the memories, the fantasies of what might happen if we were to meet again one day. Now, I could no longer dream or hope. He was firmly, forever, in the past. I would have to rewrite my life without him.

I put the kettle on to give me something to do. The sound of the element heating up filled the silent room. Glancing at my iPad to distract myself from my despairing thoughts, I saw another email had come through.

"Just been told the sponsor meeting's postponed," Dave had written. "Daniel and Toby are in London until Thursday, so it'll be then. See you Monday."

"Monday?" I blurted out. Dave had told me to be back on Monday because of the sponsor meeting. I wasn't going to hurry back for no reason, if the meeting date had been changed.

Suddenly a light switched on in my mind. Daniel and Toby, the president of College Sport, were in London. I reread the email and realized how I could use this information. London was just a short plane ride away. I could meet with them, without Dave there. I could ask to renegotiate the terms of my contract. I could request that the sponsorship income be split fairly between me and Dave as two separate entities. Even though I did the vast majority of the work, Dave was still my manager. This way, we would both benefit, but we would not be locked into it as one. I would be free to make my own decisions in my personal life.

Hope brightened up an otherwise bleak future.

I dialed Daniel's cell, and within a minute, was saying good morning to him.

"Morning, Claire," he replied. He sounded surprised, and not in a good way.

I got straight to the point.

"I hear you're in London."

"Yeah, it was a last-minute decision. We've been offered a great deal on a location for a new superstore in Mayfair, so we're checking it out. Our meeting's on Thursday now. Didn't Dave tell you?"

"He did. That's why I'm calling you."

"How do you mean?" Surprise had been replaced by suspicion.

"I'm going to be in London tomorrow," I said. "I'd like to come and see you. I want to discuss something with you, personally. Confidentially."

There was a short silence. Then:

"Okay. I've got a gap in my schedule at eleven-thirty. I'm staying in one of the Park suites at the Dorchester. You can meet us there."

"Thank you," I said, but he'd already disconnected. Still,

he'd agreed to see me. I was sure he'd listen to what I had to say.

And then I could call Patrick and apologize, and explain that I was going ahead with the divorce. That the only commitment I had was my sponsorship, but that he and I were free to see each other.

My thoughts were interrupted by the kitchen door opening, letting in a gust of wind.

"Blown into my own house," Noreen complained, turning and, like I had done, struggling to close it again. She had a scarf over her hair, but even so, it had been tugged into disarray. Despite that, she looked the happiest that I'd seen her.

"Good news," she told me. "I've just had a firm offer on the other land, and accepted it. Signed and sealed. It's a cash deal, so no worries about it falling through. The buyer is going to run an organic farm, and open a gourmet restaurant and up-market lodge. He's got a similar setup in a neighboring county, and he says he can't keep up with demand. With the castle opening soon, and town becoming so busy, he says this area is the next big tourist destination."

"Oh, that's such great news," I said, forgetting my own sorrows as I thought of what this would mean to Noreen.

"It is such perfect timing because Connor's assignment in the Middle East is ending next week. He won't have to stay on there. He'll be able to come home."

Joy shone in her face. I was delighted for her.

"Well, I'd better get on and exercise the horses," she said. "I must fitten them up now. I'm sure he'll be keen to do some hunting when he's home. Do you want a ride, Claire?"

"I'd love one," I said.

Half an hour later, I was dressed in jodhpurs, boots and a hard hat. These various items belonged to Noreen and her daughter, but they fit me surprisingly well. The jodhpurs were slightly short in the leg, but Noreen provided me with a pair of knee-length leather gaiters which fastened snugly round my calves.

I helped Noreen brush the horses; the pleasant ache in my arms familiar to me from many happy hours at summer camp long ago, doing the same. Then Noreen saddled them up. An upturned plastic bucket served as a mounting block, and then I was atop Titan, staring down at his muscular gray neck while Noreen adjusted my stirrup leathers and girth before swinging into her own saddle.

We set off, walking the horses through the stable yard and along the cobbled path that led down to the gate. I felt very high up. Titan was far taller than the horses I had ridden at camp, but he felt steady and solid under me, walking quietly alongside Murphy, who was jogging excitedly, snatching at his bridle and shying dramatically at the blowing trees.

"You sit beautifully," Noreen complimented me, and I felt a glow of pride.

"We'll ride quietly on the road today, but if you're up for it, we can have a canter across the big field to end off. Let's see how it goes."

As we made our way down to the gate, I shortened my reins enough so I could feel a gentle contact on Titan's mouth. He arched his neck in response, gracefully yielding to me, and I felt him softly mouthing the bit. I tried my best to remember what my teachers had told me, so long ago. Keep heels down. Head high. Shoulders, hips, and heels in balance. So much to remember, and all with the added challenge of having an animal moving underneath me.

"That's great," Noreen said approvingly. "Good seat and good hands. You should do some dressage."

We walked out along the quiet road, and I realized how much better the view was from horseback, high enough to see over the bushy hedges and allowing me a full panorama of this exquisite countryside. How enjoyable it would be to go riding more often, to have some lessons back home and learn how to do dressage.

But even if money allowed, the demands of my training program would not. And I could imagine Dave apoplectic with rage at the idea of me riding a horse. What if I was injured? Where would Team Harvey be then?

We walked the horses for about twenty minutes and then had

a short trot. After a momentary loss of balance, I remembered how to post to the trot. Titan's muscles flexed underneath me, his forward movement was contained through my feel on the supple leather reins. He felt safe and strong, like a Rolls Royce.

"Well, you certainly look capable enough for a canter if you'd like to have one," Noreen said, when we'd slowed to a walk again. "That gate over there leads into the big field. Titan will know the way to the top gate up the hill, and I'll hold Murphy well back so they don't end up racing."

"All right," I said, excited and a little nervous at the thought of asking this enormous horse for more speed. I hoped I wouldn't let him down—or myself. As I turned Titan toward the gate, he pricked his ears, gathered himself together, and I felt his muscles bunch under me.

I moved my hands forward and he launched onto the grass in a bound. I'd expected to be unseated, but his stride was long and smooth; it covered the distance in surges that felt like waves. This sensation of controlled speed was incredible. The wind whipped my face, my eyes were watering from the cold air, and I found myself laughing in delight at the exhilaration of letting him go.

Near the top of the hill he slowed, collecting to a bouncy stride before dropping back to a walk, snorting out his pleasure at having been allowed to have some fun. Hoof beats behind me signaled that Noreen was catching up. Once she'd reined Murphy in, we walked them on a long rein round the field, heading back to the barn.

My heart was as light as a feather. The worries that had weighed me down seemed to have been blown away. This ride had given me confidence. It had made me feel that anything was possible, that a new and different future might lie ahead.

"Well done," Noreen praised me. "I'd hire you as a work rider any day, if I were a hunt stable owner."

"It was amazing," I told her. "Thank you for this. I wish I could do it again."

"You heading back?"

"Tomorrow. I don't want to leave, but I need to go to London and try to sort my life out. Look on the bright side, though, at least you won't have any more intruders lurking around your farm."

"You think he was a photographer?" Noreen asked, frowning.

"I'm sure of it."

She shook her head, looking annoyed. "On my land, and all. Should have called the police. Would have, if he'd hung around for longer. At least you know that it wasn't Geraldine from the Women's Institute who gave you away."

"Oh, why?" I asked. She'd been first on my list of suspects.

"She got it totally wrong. She told me yesterday she'd figured out who you were—that you were an actress. She's convinced she's seen you in an advert on the telly."

That was perplexing. I'd been sure it had been Geraldine who'd recognized me. At any rate, from tomorrow, I wouldn't have to worry about it and more importantly, nor would Noreen.

Back at the farmhouse, I booked my tickets to London. I started to feel nervous about the meeting the next day. I'd only ever met with these two men in Dave's company. What would I say to them? Would they be sympathetic? I hoped so, because I knew I wasn't much of a negotiator when things turned bad. For somebody who was prepared to fight until first blood with a sword in her hand, my phobia of aggressive confrontations didn't make sense at all.

I booked my flight back to the States for later that afternoon. There was no reason to spend more time in London on my own. It would be better to go and see my parents, who'd recently moved into a cheaper place and now lived in a run-down neighborhood in south Camden. It was a two-hour drive, and a world away, from the leafy, up-market suburb of Montclair. I hadn't seen them for far too long. I needed to touch base with them, to spend some time in their home and find out how they were doing.

I called my dad to tell him about my plans. After checking my watch and working out the time zones, I realized he'd be in the middle of my mother's morning routine, and would probably leave the call to ring through to voicemail. But to my surprise, he answered, sounding stressed.

"Hey, Dad. It's me. Is everything OK?"

"Yes, honey. Everything's fine. Good to hear your voice."

"I didn't expect you to pick up the call."

"I've been applying for a few part time jobs, so I keep my phone near me all the time now in case I'm asked to go and work. Don't want to lose the chance, and have them contact the next guy on the list."

"But...how are you finding the time to work, as well as care for Mom?"

Coldness settled in my belly. I had a bad feeling that his financial predicament was worse than he'd been telling me. The money I had been sending couldn't have been enough. He must have downplayed the extent of their medical expenses.

"Hey, it keeps me out of trouble," Dad laughed, although the sound was somewhat forced.

"I'm going to come for a short visit. I'll be there late tonight. I'm flying back from London this afternoon."

"That'll be great. I'll tell your mother. She'll be so pleased. We're missing you."

"I'm sorry. I've been so busy. Trying to keep out of trouble and failing," I joked. Dad's laugh sounded more genuine this time.

"We're looking forward to seeing you. Do you need a ride from the airport?"

"No, I'll take a cab." My dad's old Dodge was on its last legs, and I wanted to save him the trip.

I needed to tell my parents about my decision. They would have to understand why I was divorcing Dave. Perhaps I'd have to confess everything. I didn't want to share the sordid details of Dave's affairs, but it was important that they knew.

Suddenly, my life seemed to be filled with scary meetings. It was a welcome distraction to turn off my iPad. Walking through to the bathroom, I noticed the pack of contraceptive pills in my toiletry bag.

Should I?

Why not. It would be responsible to start on them again, and, who knew...if I was lucky, I'd be needing them soon.

I took a pill out of the plastic and swallowed it with a gulp of water from the bathroom tap. Then, feeling like I'd taken another positive step toward the future I wanted, I went downstairs to help Noreen get lunch together.

Half an hour later, we sat down to a simple meal of chicken and bacon sandwiches on warm, crusty bread. I smeared butter thickly on the bread, not looking forward to going back to the low-fat margarine in the fridge at home. It occurred to me that despite the fatty foods I'd enjoyed since I'd been here, I had not put on weight and had, in fact, felt more energetic. It would never be allowed at home, though. The nutritionist that Dave had hired for me was militantly anti-fat. I'd have to go back to my old diet, and being constantly hungry and exhausted.

The small television in the kitchen was on, and I was grateful for its background chatter and for Noreen's conversation, because whenever I thought about Patrick, my stomach twisted with a mix of nervousness and doom.

After lunch, I went up to my room, noticing the roses were in full bloom now. The buds were all opened, the petals a rich, inky red. The roses had lasted longer than the romance had, if you could call it a romance. Perhaps it had just been a fling for him. Had he been relieved to say goodbye?

"No," I said aloud. I would not allow self-doubt to taint my memories, or to erase my hope.

All the same, I realized I didn't have any contact details for Patrick. The hotel had put me straight through to his cellphone from their switchboard, so he might not have my number either. Perhaps I should call the hotel and get an email address for him.

A minute later I was dialing the hotel reception.

"Could I have Patrick Maguire's email address, please?" I said, when the receptionist answered.

"What's it in connection with?" she asked, her tone more curious than suspicious.

"I met with him earlier today, and I'd like to follow up," I prevaricated.

"Oh," she said, sounding reassured, before reading the address out to me.

At least I had a way of contacting him now. That fact offered me some comfort.

I filled the time in the afternoon by taking Guinness for a walk, packing my bag, and catching up on my admin. After supper, I hugged Noreen goodbye, taking down her contact details and promising to stay in touch. I paid her more than she had charged me and refused to take any money back. No price could be put on the companionship and support she'd offered me at a time when I really needed it.

Back upstairs, I checked the gossip website that had published the picture of the hotel view. To my relief, there was no follow-up photo of me there. Patrick must have kept his word and contacted the site owner, and I was filled with gratitude for this. Then, as I flopped onto the bed, gratitude was obliterated by the memories that flooded me.

God…what he had done to me, and how he had done it. The passion that we'd shared, and the way his face had looked when…

"No!" I said aloud. I couldn't let myself remember this now. It was making me feel incredibly alone. Instead, I turned my thoughts to my ride. The power in Titan's body. The long, sure strides he had taken, carrying me safely up that green hill.

The thudding of hoof beats on turf resonated in my dreams.

CHAPTER 18

The following day I left for Cork airport before sunrise. Not that there was a sunrise to see, because a thick, gray blanket of cloud covered the sky. A car drive, plane flight, and taxi ride later, I reached the imposing main entrance of the Dorchester. London was as gloomy as Ireland had been; the rain that had set in when we'd landed showed no sign of letting up. I didn't even have an umbrella. Although the doorman hurried forward to assist me with his own, the wind was gusting strongly and by the time I was inside, my hair felt damp and disordered, and I worried that my mascara had smudged.

With my limited wardrobe, I hadn't been able to dress as I would have liked. Jeans and a black top seemed inadequate for this meeting; a Christian Dior suit would have been more suitable and given me more confidence. I needed every scrap of assurance I could get. Daniel and Toby had a knack of being able to make me feel second-rate, as if I was never trying hard enough, or doing a good enough job, to meet their expectations. I was used to walking into meetings brimming with happy confidence and walking out again feeling totally inadequate and shredded by disappointment. It had reached the point where I became anxious and defensive right at the start. That didn't seem to work either. Eventually, I figured out that the meetings went most smoothly when I didn't try to argue, but humbly acknowledged that whatever they said was correct.

That didn't come easy to me, and I always felt angry afterwards. I had complained to Dave many times before that I found their attitude critical and disrespectful. He'd laughed. "Try working in any corporate," he'd told me. "Ninety percent of the guys at the top are like that, including Toby and my brother. It takes a killer instinct to succeed. Maybe you should focus on getting that mindset yourself, instead of complaining about other people's. It might improve your rankings."

And then, as if in apology, he'd leaned over and pinched my cheek. "If you weren't doing a good job, they wouldn't keep on sponsoring you," he added.

In the elevator to the suite, I glanced into the mirror. I would have liked to have seen a calm, self-assured woman staring back at me, but my bedraggled reflection looked haunted, with scared eyes. So much hinged on this meeting, and at this moment, my thoughts felt as windswept as my hair did. I had to remember Dave's words. I was doing a good job, no matter how Daniel and Toby made me feel. I had worked hard to promote their brand. Why should my marital status make a difference?

I tapped on the door to the suite five minutes before the appointment time, feeling sick with nervousness. It seemed to take forever until it opened, but finally, Toby showed me inside. He wasn't dressed for the occasion either. He was wearing a T-shirt and jeans that were three times as shabby, although probably ten times as expensive, as mine.

"Daniel's still in his room," he said. "He's resting. We had back to back meetings this morning. You can sit in the lounge until he gets here."

"Thank you," I said humbly, immediately slotting into the behavioral role I had molded for myself in their presence. Obviously, Daniel was too tired to be woken just because I'd arrived on time for a meeting. Or perhaps it was just that I was not important enough. I saw a black suit jacket had been flung onto one of the large, leather-covered couches in the living room. Toby picked it up and walked through the doorway opposite to the bedroom, and out of my sight.

He hadn't offered me a seat, but I perched on the nearest couch, feeling awkward and uncomfortable and annoyed with myself for not coming across more strongly. But how was I going to do that when Daniel and Toby could only be satisfied with groveling humility?

To distract me from my worries, I glanced out of the window, which had a view over the wrought-iron balcony and out onto

SOARING

the greenery of Hyde Park. A beautiful vista, although the colors were somewhat muted in the gray downpour.

There was a tray with coffee mugs and a teapot on the coffee table and a plate of chocolate-dipped shortbread biscuits on the sideboard. I looked at them longingly, realizing that I hadn't eaten all day. A quick sugar hit would give me energy, but I didn't want Daniel to walk in and see me stuffing my face with sweet treats. And I hadn't been offered coffee, so it seemed rude to help myself. I guessed I would just have to sit and wait, and hope that Toby hadn't also settled down for a nap in the bedroom.

The minutes passed, punctuated by nothing happening at all. With no sounds coming from the bedroom, I grew braver. I sneaked over to the cookie plate, snatched one, and crunched it down in seconds before resuming my seat on the couch. I reapplied my lipstick with the help of my compact mirror, and used a Kleenex to carefully clean away a small smudge of mascara from under my right eye.

Then I got up again and stole another cookie. This one, I ate more slowly before checking the time on my phone.

I had a shock when I saw it was already noon. How long was I going to wait here? I didn't have much more time because I needed to get to Heathrow. My flight back home was at four-thirty.

I was tempted to write Patrick an email while I waited. Why not? Thinking of what to say to him would help pass the time. Probably, the minute I started composing it, Daniel and Toby would walk in. And I didn't have to send it. I could save it…or simply delete it.

My hands started to shake badly as I typed in his email address.

"Hey, Patrick," I wrote. "I'm sitting here in London, waiting to go into a meeting, trying to sort my life out. I've been feeling terrible ever since we said goodbye. I know it sounds weird, but you've been in my thoughts, way too often, ever since we first met. I can't stop thinking about you now. I feel sick inside, like I've made the wrongest decision of my life."

Was "wrongest" a word? My spell check didn't seem to like it, but at that point I couldn't think of a better one. This letter was way too honest. I could never send it. In which case, I might as well finish pouring my heart out before deleting it.

"There are things I can't tell you about my current situation. But I'm working to change it. That's why I'm in London now. I want to be able to see you again. I really want to give us a chance. I need you to know that."

How should I end it? I obviously couldn't use the word "love." "Yours" sounded silly, because I was not his—not yet. Maybe I should write "Sincerely." That would be safer; polite.

But when I thought of what we'd shared, where he had taken me, there was only one word that would be honest enough.

"Love, Claire," I ended it.

At that moment, there was a tap on the door and I heard Toby shout, "Be there now," from the bedroom. I sat bolt upright. This was it…Daniel was here. Time to delete the message.

But I didn't. Instead, with adrenaline surging through me, I pressed Send before snapping the iPad's cover shut.

"Hey, Claire," Daniel said, strolling into the lounge after Toby had opened the door. He, too, was dressed casually—designer tracksuit pants which I supposed were from one of his own lines, paired with an Armani sweater.

He sat himself down on the other couch. Looking at him, I could see the family resemblance to Dave. Both men were tall, both dark-haired, both physically self-assured. Dave would have sprawled over the couch in just the way Daniel was doing now. I wondered if Daniel also liked to live beyond his means, like Dave did. Certainly, his Guiseppe Zanotti trainers looked expensive, and his gold watch must have cost a fortune.

I had a feeling that Daniel thought he was better than most other people, just the same way Dave did. Watching his body language now, I knew that he thought he was better than me.

Toby was not as arrogant. His confidence was quieter, but yet, of the two, he made me more uneasy. Perhaps it was because, as company president, he was the main decision maker. Or perhaps it was that he was less easy to read. I had no idea what he really thought of me; I never had.

"Coffee?" Toby asked.

"Yeah, I'll have a cup, with cream," Daniel said. "And a cookie."

"I'm okay, thanks," I said.

"So, Claire, how's the training going?" Toby asked, handing Daniel his coffee. I had the feeling this was obligatory small talk, a formality to be followed before the men got down to the real purpose of the meeting.

"I'm just getting back into it." The plastic smile that stayed pasted on my face during the College Sport management meetings was automatically in place. "My shoulder's feeling good. Back to normal, I think."

"You got the doctor's report?" Daniel asked.

"Not yet," I smiled. "It should be ready by Thursday."

Give or take a few hours of begging to get an appointment with somebody—anybody—who could give me the all clear.

I guessed that concluded the personal interest section of the get-together, because Toby leaned forward, his hands on his knees, and said, "So, why this meeting?"

I swallowed, wishing I'd asked for a glass of water.

"First," I said, "I want you to know that I am one hundred percent loyal to your brand. I've always tried to do my best for you and I will continue to do so. And I'm very grateful to you for giving me this chance."

Last year, a busy one, had included participating in eighteen tournaments, attending twenty-five corporate functions, and too many meetings to count. In addition, I'd demonstrated new gear in an exhausting five-week countrywide tour. I'd given numerous talks, I'd done three charity training days and appeared in four photo shoots, which had each taken days to complete.

This year had been even busier, up until my injury. So they couldn't argue I hadn't been working hard.

"Yeah?" Daniel said, slurping his coffee.

"I would like to discuss the terms of my new contract," I said.

Now, Daniel sat straighter, his face intent and his casual attitude gone. Toby's face didn't change. It remained unreadable, inscrutable.

"Please explain," Toby said, glancing at Daniel.

"I need the sponsorship income to be split fairly between myself and my husband. As you know, the money goes into our joint account as a lump sum. At the moment, my parents are having serious financial problems and I need to set money aside to help them. I would prefer the security, and the flexibility, of having my own money be paid into a separate account, and I'd like that to be included in the contract."

"But…" Daniel interjected. "Have you spoken to Dave about this?"

I shook my head.

"Dave has a lot of expenses, you know. There's your house, his new car. I don't want to include any terms that will end up with you screwing my brother over. I'm sure he'll organize to send your parents some money if you need it."

"So far, he hasn't been able to…" I began, but Toby held up a hand to silence me. Before speaking, he stared at me for a long while. I became aware how silent this hotel room was. We were sequestered within its plush, well-insulated walls.

"I don't think you understand how things are, Claire," Toby said finally.

I forced myself to draw in a shaky gulp of air.

"How do you mean?" I asked, my voice sounding very small.

"Like everyone else in the world, we've heard rumors about your divorce. I get the feeling that, from your side, they might be more than just rumors. Before you make any decisions, I'd like to remind you that your sponsorship is dependent on your husband's goodwill," he told me in measured tones. "Dave is the reason we did this deal with you. And he's the only reason we've reconsidered your contract and come back with a new offer."

He gave me a meaningful stare and I knew then that the compromising photos of me might be history in the real world, but they would never be forgotten by him; he would always use them against me.

"I hope that answers your question," Toby said.

Daniel drained his coffee and stood up. He looked angry, and spoke sharply. "This has been a waste of time. Toby, I'll meet you downstairs in a half-hour."

"Call a cab," Toby told him.

Daniel strode over to the door and left the room without a backward glance.

"I don't get it," I said. I could hear the anger in my voice. I was no longer prepared to humbly back down. I was fighting for my career and my parents' welfare. I had nothing to lose now, so to hell with the consequences. "Dave got me the sponsorship, sure. But I'm the one who's put in all the work. What's wrong with requesting that we split the money fairly between us? That way, we're both taken care of no matter what the future brings. And what's the decision got to do with Dave?"

Toby smiled. It was not a pleasant expression.

"Claire," he said. "Sometimes you can be very naïve."

He stood up and walked over to the door. Clearly, I was being invited to leave. But when I picked up my carry-on and marched over to him, he didn't open it immediately. Instead, he grasped my shoulder with a firm hand. He leaned forward and whispered into my ear, his breath hot on my cheek.

"I'm never going to say this in public, and if you accuse me of saying it, I'm going to sue you for every dollar you own."

I stood statue-still, imprisoned by him, my mind reeling at the terrible turn this meeting had taken.

"You're stupid not to have realized this isn't about you at all," he hissed. "It never was. There are hundreds of good athletes with pretty faces. It's about your husband. Daniel wanted to channel some of the profits to Dave, and the sponsorship was a handy way of doing it. It gained us some PR, and we could write it off as an expense. You owe your husband, more than you realize. If I were you I'd be very, very nice to him. Because the day he decides he doesn't need you," he drew his finger across his throat in an expressive gesture, "your sponsorship ends."

He released my shoulder and I stumbled out of the suite, hearing the door slam behind me.

I managed to wait until I was in the elevator before breaking down. I leaned against its mirrored wall, racked by savage sobs. I cried from heartbreak, from shock, and most of all, from humiliation. I felt completely disempowered. I'd been such an innocent fool, believing it was my talent that had landed me this deal when instead it was only nepotism at work.

This was a marriage of convenience for Dave, one that allowed him to be financially comfortable and enjoy semi-celebrity status, while having the freedom to consort with whomever he fancied. No wonder he'd reconsidered the divorce, when being married to me was such a win-win for him.

If I signed another contract, which would provide money I desperately needed, it meant I'd have to play by Dave's rules and accept it on his terms.

Toby had, in the cruelest way possible, explained to me that I was wholly dependent on Dave for my income.

"Ma'am?" A polite voice from behind me pierced my agony. "Ma'am, are you all right?"

I turned, rubbing tears away, my eyes swollen and stinging from the mascara that had run into them.

I'd reached the ground floor without even knowing it, and now a Chinese couple was waiting to enter the elevator. The person who was speaking to me was the male receptionist I'd seen in the lobby earlier. He'd obviously been called over to handle the unexpected problem of a woman delirious with grief.

With an effort, I pulled myself together enough to say, between sobs, "I'm fine thanks. I need to get to Heathrow urgently. Could you call me a cab?"

Tears consumed me once again. Pushing past the watchers, I fled to the ladies' room.

CHAPTER 19

I kept my sunglasses on the entire flight, and only took them off when I was in the rental car in the airport parking lot, ready for the drive to Camden.

My parents' new home, where they'd lived for the last few months, was a tiny ground floor apartment in a part of town where ranks of low-cost housing stood shoulder to shoulder with decaying high-rises. It wasn't the safest of areas to drive alone at night. I'd only been there once before and that had been in daytime. But when I opened my iPad to program the address into the GPS, my heart stopped as I saw that Patrick had replied.

Snatching off the sunglasses, I clicked on the message with fingers that were clumsy from haste.

"Claire, I haven't stopped thinking about you," his mail began. "Walking away from you was one of the hardest things I've ever done, and one of the stupidest. I believe in second chances—in third chances, even—and I believe in fighting for what I want. I want you more than I can explain. I need to see you again, and I'm more than prepared to wait while you sort your life out. I miss you. I feel like an idiot for leaving and I want to make it up to you as soon as I can. Love, Patrick."

His words sent a rush of warmth through me. I read and reread them. I wanted to keep on looking at that last word, "love," wondering what he'd been thinking while he typed it.

At the same time, though, I felt a huge sadness. Entering into a relationship with Patrick was not in the cards for now; not when I needed to spend three more years working to promote a brand I now loathed, in order to have any chance of supporting my parents.

If only I'd taken charge of the family finances earlier, put a tight rein on Dave's spending. No wonder he'd been so profligate with the funds in our joint account—he had known they were only there thanks to him. I'd believed that because we were married, my money was also our money. Dave had spent so recklessly because he'd believed our money was his money.

We were still deeply in debt. The fancy house was a millstone around my neck, the cars weren't paid for yet, and I didn't know how I was going to stop Dave spending money on a whim, when he and I both had access to the same accounts. I didn't know what I should write back to Patrick. There was nothing I could say. I looked one last time at that word, "Love," before closing my emails and activating the GPS.

My mother was in bed by the time I arrived, but my dad told me she was awake and eager to see me.

"I hope the car will be okay," he said. "We've had a couple of break-ins near here recently."

"It has an alarm," I reassured him, hoping that the rental would be fine overnight and I wouldn't have to return it with a smashed window and missing radio.

I walked through to the master bedroom, where my mother's special bed dominated the small space. The single futon where my father slept was squeezed into a corner. Last time I'd visited them I had been distracted and rushed, and I hadn't noticed much. This time, I saw how meager the furnishings were, and how cramped the living area was. There were a few treasured ornaments missing that should have been on display, as well as a large cuckoo clock that had been mounted in the hallway of the old house. Perhaps these valuables were in storage because of the smaller space, but I feared that they had been sold.

"Claire!" my mother greeted me, beaming, and I hugged her tightly, knowing how much she longed to be able to hug me back. "So good to see you! How's Dave? And how's your arm feeling?"

I smiled down at her, loving her for her courage, the inner beauty that shone through even with the gray growing into her hair and the weight she'd lost. My father was also looking gaunt, as if the strain of caring for her singlehandedly had taken a toll he would never, ever admit to.

"I'll tell you everything tomorrow, over breakfast," I promised. "My treat."

They'd prepared the sleeper couch in the living room, and I passed a restless night listening to the noise of traffic from the main road outside. Once, the sound of smashing glass had me on my feet and peering out of the window, but luckily it hadn't come from the rental.

In the morning, I drove to the nearest good supermarket, a Fine Fare twenty minutes away, and bought bags of groceries for my parents, as well as some freshly made bacon and cheese croissants. On impulse, I added a carton of cream to the shopping cart. When I got back, we sat down to breakfast in the kitchen, my mother propped up in her wheelchair while Dad fed her sips of cream-topped coffee.

"This is delicious!" she exclaimed. "Mike, do I have a cream mustache? You'd better wipe it away if I do. I can't talk to my daughter if all she's seeing is my cream mustache!" Turning her head to me, she said, proudly, "Your dad's been for three job interviews this week."

"I'm trying to get a half-day position somewhere," my father explained. "I'll be able to fit that in as well as look after your mom. So far, no success, but you know, the jobs are out there. If I don't keep applying, I'll never find one, right?"

I didn't share his optimistic attitude. At his age, in this economic climate, and in this depressed neighborhood, his chances weren't so good. And any salary he earned would be spent on nurses' fees because somebody would have to stay at home with my mom if he was out.

"How about you, Claire?" my mom asked. "You're looking healthier than you did the last time I saw you. You've gotten some color into your cheeks, but you're not looking happy. Tell me, what's up?"

"I feel as if I'm at a crossroads," I explained. "But I want to go in one direction while I'm being forced into another."

My mother frowned. "Explain?" She opened her mouth for

my dad to feed her a forkful of croissant.

I took a deep breath. And then it all came pouring out. My unhappiness in the marriage, Dave's unfaithfulness. I even told my parents about Hassan and Ahmed, knowing I could trust them not to say a word.

My mother pressed her lips together and nodded sympathetically. Although I knew she couldn't feel it, I leaned forward and squeezed her hand.

"Hassan is very lucky to have a friend like you," she said. She paused for a minute. "So, who else is there in your life?"

My eyes widened.

"Um...how do you know there's anyone?"

"Call it instinct," she said, smiling.

My father excused himself to make a fresh pot of coffee, mumbling something about needing to leave us girls to our girl talk.

"There is someone," I said. "But it's not going to work out between us. Financially, I have to stay with Dave. I'm going to be forced to. Because the sponsorship is due to him, not me; he holds all the aces."

I swallowed. It was painful to have to admit I'd fooled myself into believing I'd deserved the money when College Sport had simply wanted to channel surplus profits to a family member.

"It's so unfair," my mother sympathized. "What College Sport has done is unethical and entirely wrong. The only person who's conducted themselves with total integrity here is you, Claire. You've stood up for your friend at great personal cost, and now you're having to make a difficult decision. I want you to promise you won't think about us. With your dad looking for work, we'll be okay. And once this bit of bad press has blown over, you can do other things. You could get a job teaching fencing, coaching juniors..."

"You're right," I said, with a confidence I didn't feel. A teacher's salary wouldn't allow me to give my parents the support they required. They needed to move to a safer neighborhood. My dad had to take some time off; a part time nurse would make an enormous difference. What would happen if he fell sick? Right now, they were walking a tightrope with no contingency plans.

"You don't want to end up trapped in a loveless relationship," my mother warned me. "You never know what will happen in the future. Look at us. If your father and I didn't love each other, where would we be now?" She sighed, her normally cheerful expression slipping to reveal tiredness and sorrow. "Sometimes, love is all that keeps me going."

CHAPTER 20

I left my parents' place feeling sobered. The time spent with them had given me a lot of food for thought. Why couldn't life be simple? But it wasn't, and I now had to deal with complications that were beyond my power to put right.

Dave's brand new Audi RS5 cabriolet was in the driveway of our five-bedroom home. He'd bought it the day after the BMW had crashed, while I was still in hospital. I saw it was parked at its usual careless angle, as if he'd come home in a hurry and was heading out again.

A couple of unopened letters addressed to me lay on the hall table. A quick glance told me they were not important and could wait. There was also a colorful brochure for a new nightclub in Chelsea—the Bohemian Ballroom. I glanced at it, remembering the carefree time when a night out had meant dancing until the small hours.

"Hi there," I called, replacing the brochure on the table. "Dave?"

"Hey, Claire! You're back! Thought I was going to have to get in my car and come find you!" Filled with hearty humor, Dave's voice boomed from the lounge.

Putting my bag down in the hallway, I walked through the double doors of the main entertainment area and into the lounge beyond. Dave had his feet up on one of the long leather couches. Remote in hand, he was surfing sport channels on the flat-screen TV that dominated the wall.

When I walked toward him, he stood up and gave me a quick hug.

Dave was nine years older than me, but only an inch taller; a fact that annoyed him and meant I was forbidden to wear high heels when we were out together. He was a broad, muscular man with a big personality; loud and outspoken, sometimes aggressive. It made him seem larger than he was. It occurred to me that during our marriage, his extroverted demeanor had ruled us both. I'd become quieter than I had been. His voice had silenced mine.

I made an effort to hug him back, not wanting to be close to him at all. His arms were not the ones I longed to have around me.

"So, Claire-bear, you had a little holiday? Come sit." Resuming his relaxed position on the couch, he patted the seat beside him.

I sat, but further away from him than he'd indicated. He noticed the distance, I could tell; his eyes narrowed slightly.

Dave had started losing his hair in his mid-twenties and now kept his head shaved smooth, with a short goatee that added definition to his round face. It made him look older than his current age of thirty-seven, and it made him look more good-natured than he actually was. Many people had, in the past, been shocked by Dave's outbursts of temper. Right then, I couldn't tell what mood he was in.

"We got some talking to do, Claire-bear," he said.

"I know," I told him with a nod. I wished he'd put the remote down while he was speaking. I guess he found the flickering series of screens relaxing, as the picture shifted from motor racing to wrestling to football. Why couldn't he find one channel he liked and stick to it?

With some bitterness, I realized I could ask a similar question about Dave and women.

"So, this divorce," he said, finally leaving the remote alone and muting the volume. It was on some kind of ocean race. Blue sea filled the huge screen.

"Yes," I said. My mouth felt dry.

"Claire, I rushed into it. I was angry. I was…" He sighed. "I guess I wasn't thinking of the implications for you. What it would mean."

"Oh," I said. I sensed Dave hadn't finished, that there was more to come. Sure enough, after a pause, he continued.

"We're a team, you and me. I thought about this a long time and I figured if College Sport can forgive you, then so can I. If they're prepared to renew your contract, it would be wrong of me to walk away. After all, we're in this together, aren't we?"

He gave me one of his trademark lightning grins. The smile didn't warm his eyes. I became suddenly convinced that Dave knew all about the meeting I'd had with Daniel and Toby.

Did Dave really, in his way, still love me? Was this why he'd pushed for a second chance with College Sport? Or was another contract simply the easiest, most convenient way of guaranteeing his future income?

"You look worried," he observed, his voice surprisingly gentle.

"I guess I'm unsure about the future."

"Nothing to be unsure about," he stated. "I've put a hold on divorce proceedings. We'll finalize the new contract on Thursday. And I think we need to take a vacation together, before you go back into training."

"A vacation?" I repeated, stunned. Dave and I hadn't taken a non work-related trip together in years. Why now?

"Taking a week off won't hurt your training program. We can fly out to the Setai; you know, that exclusive hotel in Miami Beach. Celebrate the contract renewal. Get some sunshine before winter. A second honeymoon."

A week at the Setai…I didn't know of the place, but guessed it would be very expensive. Once again, he was spending money before it had even landed in our account; but as his words sank in I realized that wasn't even the main issue here.

A second honeymoon?

Did he seriously want our marriage to continue for real? Or was this just another one of his good intentions, like saving money every month, which would fall by the wayside like all the others?

Either way, it wasn't what I wanted. As my resolve crystallized, I sensed that he could read my decision in my face.

"You don't look happy, Claire." Now he sounded accusing.

"I'm not happy." My voice was so quiet he leaned forward,

frowning.

"Why's that?"

"Because marriage isn't a business decision."

"What? Of course it isn't. That's why…"

"I married you because I was in love with you. But I don't think we looked after the marriage, Dave. It became—well, I guess it became like a business relationship. We looked after the Claire Harvey brand. But in between my training and competing and all the sponsorship events, we didn't look after us. It was partly my fault, I know. I was so tired so much of the time. But we ended up with no intimacy. No closeness…and I know you looked for it elsewhere."

I was going to explain more, but Dave interrupted me, his voice loud; the vein in his forehead, always a sign of his temper, becoming visible.

"What the hell d'you mean by that?"

"You know what I mean."

"Claire, I've never cheated on you! Ever. How the hell can you say such a thing? How can you think…?" The vein in his forehead was raised now, his face flushed. "I can't believe you're saying this, seriously. You're the one who's had half-naked photo's plastered all over the media, and I'm the one who's cheated?" He was shouting now, his words battering me.

"Dave, I…"

"Show me the goddamned proof!"

What proof did I have? Only the noises that I'd heard that night, in his hotel suite. At the time I'd been sure. Those soft cries, the sounds of rapid breathing, had ripped my heart apart. They had been the sound of betrayal, confirmed by the fact that Dave had no longer wanted to be physically close to me… that for the last year, the closest we'd been was when he put his arm around me in public.

But now, his vehement denial was causing doubt to creep in. What if I had misheard, or been wrong? All I had was my own memories. Oh, and there were the photos Patrick had mentioned…but they could have been innocent shots simply taken at the wrong time. I could sympathize with that.

For a minute, the only sound in the room was Dave's rough breathing. Then, in a more controlled voice, he said, "Look, Claire, let's not fight about this. Let's just admit we both made mistakes. You had this incident with the Saudi guy…"

"He's Moroccan!"

"Yeah, whatever. And I didn't pay you enough attention. I guess we both put your career first. But that's gonna change, starting with our second honeymoon. So. What do you say?"

I stared back at him as silence fell again. I knew Dave didn't want the silence. He couldn't understand it.

"I need to think this over," I told him eventually. "I—I can't see a second honeymoon working out, Dave. Why this, and why now?"

"It just seems like the right time…" he began, defensively, but I overrode him.

"Where were you when my mother had her accident and I had to deal with it all on my own? And when my parents moved and needed help packing and unpacking, all you could do was complain that it was cutting into my training time. It would have taken less time if you'd been there to help me when I asked you, Dave, instead of making excuses that you had to go out of town with Daniel. And where were you on my last birthday, and the one before? There have been so many times when I needed you—really needed you—and you weren't there for me. So why is it important to you now?"

Dave's face was like thunder, and I couldn't help but notice the strong family resemblance he had to Daniel, which showed so clearly when they were angry.

"You're making a stupid mistake!" Dave shouted.

"Why is asking questions a mistake?"

"You're not asking questions; you're assuming the worst. You've just called me an adulterer and a user. I can't talk to you when you're like this. You're being so goddamned critical and judgmental. I'll see you tomorrow."

Leaping up, Dave stormed out of the living room, slamming the door so hard that the ornaments on a nearby shelf rattled. He banged the front door behind him, too, and a few moments later I heard the growl of the Audi's engine and the squeal of tires as he sped away.

CHAPTER 21

I found I was shaking. I hated these confrontations, and I realized that as good as it had felt to stand up to Dave and win the argument, it wouldn't get me anywhere long-term. Like Toby had said, I should be behaving very, very nicely to him, because my financial future was in his hands. I should be playing along with him, agreeing to what he said. Once the money was in our bank account, I could try to lay down the law.

I still had not replied to Patrick, and I was torn with guilt about it. What could I say to him, though? I needed to think about all of this, and hard.

A knocking at the front door made me wonder if Dave had forgotten his house keys when he stormed out, and he'd come back for them. Seething at the knowledge I would have to grovel and apologize to him, I opened it to find Monika there.

She stared at me, and for a moment I saw blank shock in her face.

Did I look that bad, I wondered.

The next moment, she had her arms around me.

"Hey there, bestie! You're looking great! So much less stressed than you were a week ago. I almost didn't recognize you!"

Relieved, I hugged her back. "It's wonderful to see you, too." Why was she here? Oh, yes, she said I might have accidentally taken her scarf home.

"I've only just got back," I said. "I haven't had a chance to look for your scarf."

"There it is!" She pointed to the chair in the hallway, and I saw it, neatly folded. Dave must have found it when he did the laundry, and realized it was hers.

Closing the door behind her, I walked with her to the kitchen to fix a glass of her favorite drink, Diet Coke.

Monika was four years younger than me and extremely slim—a feisty redhead with a sharp wit that was as quick and dangerous as her fencing skills. She was a far better athlete than I was. She'd been the youngest team member when we'd won the medal in London, not just the reserve. She was ranked number two in saber in the country, and eighth in the world.

"So, welcome home," she said after we'd sat down in the lounge. The memory of the argument I'd just had with Dave seemed to linger in the room. It felt as if his shouted words were still reverberating in the air.

"It's good to be back," I told her.

"What did you do in Ireland?"

"I had a holiday, I guess. I met…" I was going to tell her about Patrick, but at the last minute, I decided not to. My feelings for him were so intense, the situation so impossibly conflicted. I'd discussed it with my mother, but I found I couldn't share it with my best friend.

"You met who?" Monika repeated, eyes sparkling. Clearly, she was eager for some salacious details.

"I met a crazy Irishwoman who lives on one of the most beautiful farms you've ever seen," I said. "I stayed in the farmhouse with her. I ate really good food, and slept like you can't believe, and went for walks in the countryside, along paved lanes that had strips of grass growing down their center. I even rode a horse. First time since summer camp!" I told her proudly.

Monika looked disappointed. I guessed she'd been hoping for something more salacious.

"What's happening with you and Dave?" she asked.

"I don't know."

She rolled her eyes. "You need to leave him. He's a jerk."

"I wish it was that simple but it's not. It…"

Thinking of my sponsorship contract, I remembered with a jolt about the evening's commitments.

"Oh, my God, what's the time?" I asked her.

She checked her phone. "It's quarter to six."

"I'm so sorry. I have to get ready in a big hurry for an awards function. I'll be going on my own. Dave—er—went out a few minutes ago."

"Which function is that?"

"At the Park Hyatt. It's the Sports Stars Achievement Awards. College Sport is the major sponsor, so it's important that I'm seen there."

"I'll let you get ready then. Great to have you back. We must train together on Friday. I'll let you know what time." She drained her Diet Coke and I hurried with her to the front door, closing it before she'd even climbed into her small Ford.

I was used to getting ready at short notice, but this was cutting it even finer than usual.

I ran upstairs, where I put a hasty triage system into place. Shower, make-up, hair, dress, shoes, nails. I did my make-up while my hair air-dried, before blowing it to a glossy finish and adding a few diamante hairpins. I chose a red evening gown with a chiffon skirt that I'd worn only twice before. Probably not the best color for a scarlet woman to wear, but still. I slipped on high heeled court shoes—since Dave wasn't coming along, I could at least flaunt my stilettos—and only then applied a coat of varnish to my fingernails in a nude color, so that any slips or smudges wouldn't be too obvious. A hair dryer on the nails to set the polish, and a spritz of perfume on my wrists and neck. I slung my beige coat over my shoulders before hurrying downstairs to where another cab had just arrived.

The Park Hyatt in New York City was a forty-minute drive away, and to my relief, traffic heading into town was light. At seven o'clock exactly, I walked into the Hyatt, following the signs for the awards, which were being held in the ballroom on the third floor. I reached the elevator just before the doors closed, joining a group of formally dressed people who were obviously headed for the same function.

"Evening, Claire!"

I turned to greet the woman who'd called my name. She was standing behind me, her arm linked through her partner's. It took me a moment to remember that she was a product manager at College Sport. She'd been appointed less than a year ago, and even back then, we hadn't been friends. Now, from the obviously fake smile she gave me, I suspected she had been reveling in my public disgrace. As soon as I turned my back, I could imagine her whispering all the scurrilous details to her dark-suited consort.

"Evening, Maddie," I responded politely.

"Are you sure you're on the guest list for tonight?" she asked, in a way that made me think she knew more about that list than I did.

This comment drew the attention of the four other occupants of the elevator, who turned to regard me with interest and curiosity…a gatecrasher in their midst?

"I assume so," I said. "I've been away, but I was told I have to attend."

My face was burning under the fascinated stares from the strangers. When, oh, when, would we reach the ballroom level? The elevator pinged, and I glanced hopefully toward the buttons, but saw we were only at the second floor. The doors opened to admit yet another formally dressed man, and seemed to take forever before they closed again.

Maddie's smile widened.

"Your husband said he wasn't going to attend. I don't recall receiving an RSVP from you."

She put a meaningful emphasis on the word "husband," and suddenly I wondered whether she might be one of Dave's conquests. Either way, it was clear, she was making life difficult for me.

Well, if the people in the elevator hadn't signed up for the equivalent of *Days of Our Lives*, they were going to get it regardless.

"Dave and I are separated, pending a divorce," I told her. "However, I'm still the brand ambassador, and I was told I have to be here tonight."

Now Maddie's smile was positively saccharine.

"What a pity about the misunderstanding. I'm sure I can get you back onto the list."

"It's very kind of you," I thanked her, while smoldering

inside.

I was the first to leave the elevator, walking toward the reception table with everybody's stares burning into my back.

"Your name?" the uniformed attendant asked. I noticed she was flanked by two smartly dressed security guards.

"Claire Harvey, from College Sport," I said with a confidence I did not feel.

She ran her finger down the list.

I could sense the expectation building.

"I'm sorry, Ms. Harvey, the only guests from College Sport are Madeleine Butcher and partner."

Maddie stepped forward.

"I'll be able to add Ms. Harvey, but I'll have to call the organizers first." She glanced at me. "Until then, I'm afraid you'll have to wait."

Wait in reception? For how long? Anxiety filled me as I wondered whether Maddie was going to make sure I missed the event altogether.

There was no empathy in the smile she gave me.

"I'll call as soon as I'm inside," she said, waiting for me to move aside before stepping forward to receive her own name tag. Without a backward glance, she and her partner headed through the security cordon and disappeared into the venue.

"If you could please wait somewhere else, ma'am." The uniformed woman at the registration desk was obviously as much at a loss for what to do as I was. But there were other guests arriving, and I was holding up the line. Embarrassed, I stepped aside to allow another couple to pass. I would have to stand near the elevator and wait for Maddie to reappear.

If she reappeared.

"No need to wait anywhere," a deep and familiar voice said from behind me. "Luckily, I have a spare ticket, and Ms. Harvey is welcome to use it, as a guest of Maguire Media."

No! It couldn't be!

My heart literally stopped as I spun round and found myself staring straight into Patrick's eyes.

CHAPTER 22

I couldn't believe what I was seeing. Patrick was here? At this event? Standing within arm's reach?

He clasped my hand in his own, a formal handshake that somehow didn't feel that way at all. If it hadn't been for that supportive grasp, I might have fallen over from shock. What on earth was he doing here? Had my imagination conjured him up? But no, he was real...the touch of his fingers warm on mine, his willful bangs for once tamed sleekly into place. His black suit was perfectly cut, the fine wool weave hugging the breadth of his shoulders. The formal outfit brought out his stern, powerful demeanor...a side of him that I was not used to seeing.

His eyes narrowed ever so slightly as he stared down at me. That tiny change in his expression was like a caress, and I felt something deep inside me melt.

"Your name again, please, ma'am?" the uniformed woman asked, and I turned to face her in confusion, because for that moment I'd forgotten that anything else in the world existed.

Patrick spelled it out for her and the printer whirred.

Behind me, from the watching guests, I could have sworn I heard a collective sigh of relief.

A minute later, I had my name tag, and was heading past security and into the function hall, accompanied by Patrick. I was desperate to find a private corner, to ask him what on earth he was doing here...to turn toward him again so that I could see the expression in his green-gold eyes.

But Maddie was standing nearby, watching the door, and as we entered the opulent ballroom, I caught a glimpse of her face. Confusion warred with fury as she watched me walk in. She wasn't even on her phone, trying to sort out my entrance pass...she had a glass of champagne in her hand, which was already half finished.

I smiled at her, hoping it was as obviously artificial as hers. "Thank you for your help," I told her, "but, luckily, I met up with a friend."

"Patrick Maguire," Patrick said, extending his right hand to Maddie and her partner. His left palm rested on the small of my back, in a gesture that could, to an outsider, have looked like simple friendship. The caress of his thumb through the thin fabric of the bodice convinced me it was not.

"Good to meet you," Maddie's partner said, while she mumbled something in response. I hoped we could move away, because her angry gaze was drilling straight through me, but Patrick seemed to be enjoying the confrontation and he clearly wasn't done with the pleasantries.

"Congratulations on your third quarter financial results," he said. I didn't know what he was talking about, but Maddie obviously did, because her expression changed from furious to furtive.

"I heard from a connection that you've seen twenty percent growth in this quarter. I guess that proves the old saying that any publicity is good publicity." I didn't dare look at Patrick's face, but suspected there was a smile in his voice. "You can thank Ms. Harvey for that."

Maddie was silent for a while and I noted she was turning crimson. I couldn't take in Patrick's words. College Sport had shown an uptick in profit...and he was implying it was as a result of all the media attention?

"Who leaked that information to you?" Maddie's voice was high and unsteady.

Now I could definitely hear the smile in Patrick's voice. "I'm afraid I cannot reveal my sources. It would go against all my ethics. Now, if you'll excuse us, we must go and greet our hosts."

"Why are you here?" I whispered to him as we turned away.

"I came to see you," he told me in a low voice. "I'm still on the mailing lists for these events. You told me you'd be here. How could I stay away?"

SOARING

The next hour passed by in a whirl as we circulated among the guests. Patrick was a consummate professional at the art of working a room. We moved from group to group, identifying key people and speaking briefly to each one. I smiled serenely for photo opportunities while, inside, I was still reeling from the surprise and excitement of his arrival. Patrick kept a discreet distance from me, with no trace of anything but courteous friendship in the way he spoke to me. He gave no signs away that we had ever been intimate.

"You're...you're so good at this," I murmured to him as we approached the final cluster of people.

"Years of practice. Haven't done it for a while, now, but old skills die hard. And present company makes it a pleasure," he whispered back.

Ten minutes later, just as the opening speeches began, we were done. We stood near the back of the ballroom as the lights were dimmed and the MC walked onto the stage to a smattering of applause. Patrick moved behind me and I breathed in sharply as I felt his hands, under cover of the semi-darkness, clasp my waist and move down to caress my buttocks.

"You look so gorgeously beautiful in that gown," he whispered. "And so incredibly sexy, the way it hugs your body. It's almost a shame to say this...but all I can think of is how much I want to take it off."

I leaned against him, turning my head so that his lips could brush mine. His hands roamed to the front of my gown to press briefly, lusciously, into the folds of chiffon, stroking over the lace of my panties and the soft, plump flesh beneath. Desire welled inside me, the clamoring of my own body far louder than the booming from the microphone and the recorded music that filled the hall. In that breathless instant, it was easy to forget we were in a public place; that at any moment, the lights could be turned up again.

"We don't need to overstay our welcome," he murmured. "Let's go."

Clasping my waist, he walked with me, guiding me sideways, and in the gloom I saw he was heading for an exit door. Except this didn't lead into the large hallway we'd come from. It led into a smaller annex, where a couple of sofas were pushed against the wall, and chairs stacked into piles. It was warm and smelled slightly musty. Beyond, through another open doorway, I glimpsed a staircase, but as the door we'd come through swung soundlessly shut, the room was plunged into almost total darkness.

"Give it a minute," Patrick advised. He was facing me now, his breath warm on my face. "Our eyes will adjust. Then we can take the stairs."

I didn't want to take the stairs anywhere, though; not when the alternative was to stand in this quiet, dark place, with my body pressed against Patrick's, his arms locked around me, the feel of his body under my fingers and the smell of him—warm, spicy, incredibly masculine. The physical need between us was so intense, so all-consuming, that the flames seemed to burn stronger after every separation we endured.

"I still can't believe you're really here. I have so many questions to ask you," I whispered.

"You do?" His voice caught on the words. "Because I only have one for you."

I knew what that question was…it was the most important one of all. Perhaps the most important I'd ever been asked. I drew in a shuddery breath, blinking fast as a rush of emotion overwhelmed me.

"Hey," he murmured. "Hey, it's okay, Claire. Don't cry."

His fingers smoothed under my eyes, the tenderness of the gesture prompting more tears to flow.

"All I want to do is to ruin your lipstick." Now his fingertips traced the outline of my mouth. "Not your mascara…not ever."

I pressed my face into Patrick's dark jacket, the fabric soft and smooth on my cheek, and felt him stroking my hair.

"Come. Sit down."

I couldn't see a thing in the dark, but he guided me over to one of the sofas and helped me onto the firm cushions. We sat close, his arms tight around me. It felt surreal, being together with him in this cluttered little cubicle, close to the main event but entirely separated from it.

I felt so safe in his arms, as if his grasp kept away the chaos of my own confused thoughts. Patrick believed that the connection between us was something special, and always had been. And that raised another question.

"Did you ever think of contacting me after we first met…of getting in touch?"

His breath tickled my hair in a sigh.

"Of course I did," he said. "I thought about nothing else, some days. But, remember, you'd said no when I asked. And I was based in London, starting up a company, working eighteen-hour days. I was worried that you would be a distraction. I was stupid, Claire…I let my head rule my heart. By the time I relocated to the States, you'd already gotten married. And that put you out of the running." Now it sounded as if he was smiling. "You know, I wouldn't be surprised if I still have the bruises from kicking myself over that dumb decision."

"I thought about getting in touch with you," I admitted. Funny, it was easier to talk about these things here, in the darkness, in this stolen instant of time. Perhaps that was where we'd shared the most honesty—in these unexpected, transient moments.

"You did?" He sounded pleased, if surprised.

"Of course. I fantasized about it, so many times, but I had no idea where to start. I didn't even know your last name. I didn't have an army of investigative journalists to help me. And I was ridiculously scared of rejection. To me, you were this rich, successful businessman. Why would you look twice at a teenager whose only claim to fame was winning a fencing competition? And…"

I stopped, embarrassed about what I was going to say, and fumbling for the words I needed to explain it properly.

"Go on?" he encouraged gently.

"And I was still in my teens. I didn't know how—how rare, how special the connection we shared was. I thought I could find it again. I assumed I would…but I never did."

"Don't worry," he said. "I was twenty-four. Old enough to

know better, but I didn't know either. I also thought it would happen again. But it never did; not until I saw you walk out of that elevator at the Park Hotel. But about getting in touch…"

Now it was his turn to fall silent, although I had no idea why.

"What about it?"

"When we met up in Ireland, I was about to fly to New York to see you," he told me, and I frowned, totally confused.

"How do you mean, to see me?"

"Your photos were all over the tabloids. Your marriage was over. A reliable source told me your husband had filed for divorce. You were the reason I was booked on a plane to New York as soon as that damned media conference ended. I was going to arrive on your doorstep with a bunch of flowers. What I'd do after that, I didn't know…I hadn't thought that far."

I was stunned by what he'd just said.

He'd booked a flight to New York to see me?

At that crisis point in my life, we'd ended up seeking each other out.

That knowledge made my heart feel very full.

"We've got to stop taking advantage of these crazy coincidences," I told him, and now I found that I was smiling. "Maybe we should start planning better."

"That's what we need to do," Patrick said. "I want to be in your future, Claire. Not just an erotic memory, but in the here and now, a part of your life. I don't want to walk away from you again, ever."

The tenderness in his voice was making my tears prickle. I couldn't end up crying. If I did, he really would think that he was better at ruining my mascara than my lipstick. So, instead, I let myself do what I wanted to do every time I set eyes on this gorgeous man. I leaned toward him, my lips touching his cheek and then a moment later, as he turned his head, meeting his own in a kiss that swiftly deepened. His tongue slid against mine, sending tendrils of lust deep inside me as he groaned with pleasure.

We'd have to get away from here soon, because this was never going to stop at kissing…not the way I felt right then. I needed desperately for us to make love, and I could tell he felt the same.

In fact, Patrick wasn't going to wait another moment.

Grasping my waist, he lifted me onto his lap, tugging my skirts gently out of the way before resting my thighs on his own hard-muscled ones. I clasped my hands around his back, pulling myself closer to him as he eased his hand under my dress. I could feel the brutal power in his broad shoulders, the tough ridges of muscle that flanked his spine. Perfectly contained in the immaculate lines of this designer suit, his body was a raw and rugged work of art, honed by his own pain and sweat through the ordeal of training that I knew all too well.

He touched me with the most exquisite gentleness, his fingers trailing tantalizingly over the lacy crotch of my panties, as he teased a gasping response out of me. Then he eased the lace aside to stroke me, fingertips on flesh, a delicate caress that quickly became more urgent as he felt how ready I was.

He slipped two fingers inside me, his thumb circling my clitoris. I was paralyzed by lust, my mind whirling at the audacity of what we were doing…that just a few yards away, a group of elegantly dressed guests were standing in the ballroom. And I was hiding away in a darkened annex packed with spare furniture, on the lap of the most desirable man in the world, grasping his broad shoulders tightly while he sensually fingered me.

I could only pray that none of the guests suddenly came over all faint and needed a chair.

My hand moved unbidden to his crotch, feeling the bulky hardness that bulged under the soft woolen fabric. God, he was as turned on as I was, and now it was my chance to take what I wanted from him. He let out a shuddering groan as I fumbled with his pants buttons, pulling them open, my fingers brushing over his silken boxer shorts before I freed him. I cupped my hand around his shaft, stroking it, amazed by its thickness and power, the silken softness of his skin contrasting with the virile strength it contained.

His hips thrust toward me as I touched him, and from his rapid breathing, I knew that my teasing caresses had robbed him of any self-control he might have retained. He shifted me on his lap, lifting me easily, pulling me onto him as, from outside, the microphone boomed again.

He eased me downward, and, straddling him, I felt the kiss of his engorged head as it touched the lips of my sex. We were both gasping as he lowered me slowly, pushing me wide as he entered me, filling me up with his length. I could feel the heat of him, the tautness, could sense the primal need that throbbed in his manhood.

This was dangerous in every way. It was reckless beyond wildness to unleash our passion here and now. The lights could come up. Somebody—a waiter, a guest, one of the organizers—could walk in and find us here. But, driven by my own desire, I could not stop or resist, and neither could he. He groaned as he thrust up into me, reaching flesh deep inside of me that was quivering with the delight of feeling him again.

"Claire," he whispered. "God, you don't know how sexy you are…how addictive you feel."

If I'd been able to speak at that moment, I would have agreed with him. But I was temporarily without a voice, engulfed by the waves of sensation as he drove deeply, voluptuously into me. With every thrust, his shaft caressed my throbbing G-spot while the thick base of his cock pressed hard into my clitoris. The stimulation was so strong, it skimmed my threshold of pain, turning my breaths to sobs. If I'd had a voice to use, I would have uttered just one word: *More!*

"I want to know you, every last inch of you." His voice was soft, husky. His warm hands grasped my buttocks, squeezing my flesh in time with the powerful movements of his hips.

I gave a soft moan, and his lips met mine, devouring the sound, his tongue licking my own while his fingers strayed again to the tender lips of my sex, stroking over flesh that was slick and wet with desire. Then he began lightly massaging his moistened fingertip over my anus. I tensed in surprise at this, momentarily shy and worried about what he was doing, knowing he could feel my hesitation.

And then I decided to trust him, to allow him to explore my

body in its totality, even in this most private area. I found myself relaxing into him; began to love the deeply pleasurable feelings he was giving me as he softly caressed this puckered flesh.

"Don't hold back, Claire, please." His mouth brushed mine as he murmured the words. For a moment they confused me… how could he think I would do that, when he was making it so impossible for me to resist?

Or…was he not talking about the secrets of my body, but rather the ones I was keeping hidden away in my mind?

I suspected he might be. I wanted so badly to tell him all my truths, but how could I risk that confession, with so much at stake? Perhaps it was better they remained locked up. I was not afraid of the physical honesty between us. I was willing to open myself to him completely, to let him into my body, any way he wanted to take me. Surely that would be enough?

In answer, I kissed him again, hungrily, devouring his mouth with my own as I slid my tongue between his lips. This action drove him wild. He thrust inside me faster, more strongly, ramming his cock so deep and hard that I found myself, once again, swaying on a tightrope between pleasure and pain.

I wanted more…needed him to take me all the way. I felt so hungry, so greedy for the sensations he was giving me. Shuddering on the brink of orgasm, it was only when he slid his fingertip into my anus that the unexpected delight of the double penetration triggered a strong, sudden climax.

I crushed my mouth against his, stifling a scream and swallowing his own cry as I felt myself tightly convulse around his pulsing cock and gently pumping finger. Ecstasy suffused me, weakening my limbs and choking up my lungs so that all I could do was cling to him.

"Are you…are you safe?" he rasped breathlessly, and I knew he was asking if I'd gone back onto the pill.

Unable to speak, I managed to nod.

He must have been holding himself on the edge, because immediately, I felt him release. His groan of pleasure breathed into my lips. I felt each brutal jerk of his hips as he came inside me. I was flooded with hot jets of semen, the sensation causing me to clench around him again, milking him of every drop as the aftershocks of my own climax rippled through my spent, panting body.

His arms cradled me, holding me tight against his heaving chest, the hot, wet length of his cock still spearing me. My cheek against his was damp with sweat. In the dim light, I could see his handsome face, framed by hair now in mussed disarray as he stared into my eyes.

He kissed me again, gently, before withdrawing from me, moving the lacy crotch of my panties back into place, and helping me to my feet while he straightened my skirts. My legs were quivering; I stepped unsteadily back on the stiletto heels. I could feel his semen inside me still, making me feel lush and wet and filled with desire for him again.

"That was, by far, the best cocktail function I ever attended," he murmured in my ear, causing me to let out a breathy giggle. "But I think it's time to leave now."

Patrick appeared to have catlike vision in the dark—or maybe he'd used this exit to leave functions early before. Arm in arm, we walked across the room, and his whispered directions and strong support helped me safely down the three flights of stairs, despite my treacherously high heels and the lack of light. Patrick must have used this as a handy escape route from other, boring functions in the past, I decided, as he guided me unerringly through a maze of corridors until we reached a door that led into the main lobby, and a minute later, we had made our escape.

CHAPTER 23

Traffic in the city was heavy, the headlights of the passing cars merging into pathways of brightness. There was a party feel in the air. Music throbbed from a nightclub nearby; the air was rich with spicy aromas from the restaurants across the road, and I turned my head as a screech of laughter cut the air—a group of young women were climbing out of a minivan. From their color-coded outfits and matching fancy hats, I guessed they must be out on a girls' night.

Patrick hailed a cab and we climbed inside. I had no idea where we were heading. All I knew was that this night felt like an amazing, unexpected adventure. This time was ours…this city was our playground.

"You look gorgeous," he told me, lifting a wayward lock of my hair back into place as I raked my fingers through his unruly bangs, trying my best to do damage control. I wasn't sure if I believed his definition of "gorgeous," and took out my compact mirror to check.

Surprisingly, I didn't look too bad. My hair was tousled, my cheeks were flushed, and every speck of lipstick had been kissed off my swollen lips—but my mascara was good to go. I rearranged my hairpins and put on a fresh coat of lipstick.

Meanwhile, Patrick told the driver to go to an address on Central Park South. The location was unfamiliar to me, but the destination proved to be a small, exquisite seafood restaurant. It was packed full, with only one empty table for two—which turned out to be the table Patrick had reserved earlier that day.

"I'm an optimist," he confessed as the waiter pulled my chair out. "And sometimes, it's good to plan ahead."

"What would you have done if I hadn't come with you?" I asked. "Or if I hadn't been at the function at all?"

"I'd have gone to your house and picked you up," he told me, and I suspected he was only half joking.

"You don't know where I live," I said, but even as I spoke the words, I realized they probably weren't true. My address would be in the public record somewhere. If he didn't already know where I stayed, it would be an easy job for him to find out.

In response to my statement, Patrick simply smiled, confirming my suspicions. I guessed I should feel angry, but I didn't. I did think it was unfair that I knew comparatively little about him. But then, all I had to do was ask.

"Where do you live?"

"I've got an apartment in Manhattan," he told me. "Nothing fancy, a comfortable three-bedroom place where I stay when I do business here. And I have a home in Orange County, on a large piece of land. The house is surrounded by big fields and trees; it's quiet, apart from birdsong. It feels like I can breathe when I'm there. I'm never sure which my favorite is, though—the country house or the one amid the energy of the city."

The waiter poured champagne for us and we clinked glasses. I studied the menu without really taking it in. Everything looked mouthwatering, but most delicious of all was the man who sat across the table from me, his left hand clasping my right, his thumb caressing my palm.

We ate divine plates of food, sharing from each other's forks so that we could try more of everything. Sharp, flavorsome Sicilian anchovies, tender grilled octopus, seared sea scallops and rich, butter-poached halibut. We shared a bottle of French Riesling that danced on my tongue. When we weren't savoring the food in companionable silence, we talked about a hundred different things. It was astonishing how much we had in common—the important things, at any rate. And Patrick was an entertaining dinner partner. His wry observations and witty humor had me laughing out loud several times.

I even found the courage to ask him about his previous girlfriends. He told me he'd played the field in his teens and early twenties, seeking out relationships that were long on passion and excitement, short on commitment. "You wouldn't have wanted to know me then," he admitted ruefully. During his mid-twenties he'd focused mainly on his business, dating occasionally. Since then, he'd been in a number of more serious relationships, but had never felt ready to take them that important step further.

"There was always something missing," he told me, stroking my hand. Then, smiling, he added, "Or perhaps, not something, but someone."

Coffees concluded our meal, and ten minutes later, we were collecting our coats.

"So, where to now?" Patrick asked. "What do you want to do, Claire?"

Going back to his apartment and making love again sounded like the best option. I was so tempted to suggest it, but then I thought of something else we could do first; something I was suddenly longing to do with him.

"Let's go dancing," I said.

"Good idea." That quirky grin hovered over his delicious mouth. "Although, I must confess, I'm not a great dancer. Not even a good dancer. But for you, I'll be happy to try."

"Well, I'm a pretty useless dancer, too," I told him. "So we can pool our inexpertise. Perhaps we can learn some moves from each other. Or learn what moves to avoid."

Now his smile widened. "Let's get onto that dance floor then. Where do you want to go?"

My knowledge of nightclubs was sketchy these days, but then I remembered the brochure I'd seen on the hall table at home.

"There's a new club in Chelsea called the Bohemian Ballroom," I said. "I saw it advertised today."

I had no idea of its address, but the cab driver knew, and a short while later, we were standing outside its colorfully lit entrance, waiting in the short queue, listening to the throb of bass notes emanating from within. I was excited to be walking into its sumptuous, semi-dark interior, with its red and gold décor. My heels trod on soft carpet, and colored lights sparkled on the walls. I was stoked at the chance to be spending an hour or two dancing with a man who I suspected I was falling in love with. Or maybe it was too late…maybe I had already fallen.

Dancing with Patrick was an extension of what being with him was like. Close, intimate, sensual, and with an element of fun. He had said he was not a great dancer, but he made me feel like one in the way he moved with me. Time flew by as we gave ourselves over to the rhythm, until I felt my face glowing and my shoes starting to hurt, and then as the music slowed, I moved gratefully into his arms.

This was where I belonged. I could feel it. I was certain of it. We swayed together, our hips pressed close. My hands caressed his back; his own were locked around my waist, and it felt as if there was nobody else on that busy dance floor except us two.

Except…the crowds to my right parted, giving me a glimpse of a woman's red hair and pale limbs, an image etched in my mind that left me blinking in surprise, certain that I'd recognized her.

Intrigued, I looked again, trying to make out what I had seen between the swaying bodies.

"What's up?" Patrick bent forward to ask me, his breath tickling my hair and cooling my face.

"I thought I saw someone I know."

He looked too, and as we stared, the dancers shifted again, and I saw who it was.

I found myself smiling. How could I ever have mistaken that hair, that strong, sharp profile, those lean, toned arms. It was Monika, wearing a spangled halter top and a leather mini skirt. She was dancing suggestively, flirting, tossing her russet locks back and thrusting her hips at her partner.

Who was he? The lights swung away just as I looked. I was suddenly curious, because I'd never known Monika to have a steady boyfriend. Had she met someone? If so, why hadn't she told me?

The crimson light moved round again, bathing Monika in its glow, and there he was, staring down at her before bending forward to kiss her.

I stifled a cry, the dance floor suddenly unsteady under my feet, my fingers digging hard into Patrick's arms as I saw what

SOARING

I saw.

It was impossible, unthinkable.

The man slow dancing with my best friend was my husband, Dave.

CHAPTER 24

I was aware of Patrick's hands grasping me firmly round my waist, supporting me as he turned and guided me out of the club, weaving our way through the swaying throngs. I couldn't even see where we were going. Tears blinded me; I stumbled forward, twisting my ankle as I took a misstep which would have been more serious had he not been holding me so tight.

I was sobbing with hurt. I couldn't think past the pain. My husband and my best friend...how long had this been going on while I had been oblivious?

Nausea clenched my stomach as we left the club, exchanging the vibrating beat of the music for the sounds of cars and horns—lighter traffic now, but moving faster.

"I'm going to be sick," I told Patrick, who now had our coats under his arm, carrying them as well as half-carrying me.

"That's okay," he soothed me, slinging the coats over his shoulder and holding my hair back as I doubled over, staring down at the pavement beneath me, taking deep gulps of the cold night air. I didn't vomit. Slowly, the feeling passed, leaving me weak, my skin damp with sweat.

I stood upright again. My arms were pimpled with gooseflesh, and my eyes were streaming. Patrick helped me put my coat on before donning his jacket. He passed me a tissue, and I crumpled it in my hand before burying my face in his shoulder and sobbing my heart out.

Patrick simply stood, with his arms tight around me, letting me cry into the soft fabric of his jacket as he protected me from the curious gazes of passersby. I wept for grief, for the pain of loss, for the tearing agony of betrayal. He didn't try to get me somewhere private or hustle me into a taxi. He just held me, supporting me until I was ready to step back, take a deep breath, and finally wipe the worst of the damage away with the now shredded tissue.

Only then did he hail a cab.

"I should go home," I said, my voice trembling, as he helped me in.

"No," Patrick countered. "I'm not letting you go home tonight. Not in this state; not to be there alone."

He gave the driver an address that turned out to be his apartment.

Patrick had called it comfortable, but I would have described it as luxurious—a penthouse in a fifteen-storey building with three large bedrooms, two entertainment areas, a kitchen that any chef would have been proud to cook in, and a rooftop garden.

I had only a fleeting glimpse of these rooms on our way to the main bedroom. This room was decorated in taupe and whites—a neutral, comforting space. The bathroom had a deep, sunken bath and twin basins with a mirrored wall above them. I did my best to remove my mascara from under my eyes with a make-up removal pad. The woman who stared back at me from the glass had a pale face and haunted eyes. I couldn't seem to dry the tears which trickled down my cheeks.

When I returned to the bedroom, the lights had been dimmed and my side of the bed turned down. A glass of water and a cup of cocoa had been placed on the bedside table. Patrick was in bed, and when he saw me, he put down the magazine he'd been reading and climbed out.

He was wearing only the silk boxers I'd brushed my fingers over earlier. His body was taut, ripped, an athletic masterpiece. Carefully, he helped me out of my dress and undid my bra. Then he waited until I'd climbed into bed and pulled the covers up over me.

If I'd imagined what my first-ever night in Patrick's Manhattan apartment would be like, I would have been totally wrong. Cushioned by the soft pillows, the downy coverlet, and his care, I felt safe. My breathing was still ragged, my eyes felt sore and swollen. I put my head on his shoulder, and he encircled me with his arms.

Within a surprisingly short time, I was fast asleep.

When I woke, golden light was streaming in through the pale blinds. Patrick was asleep, lying on his side facing me, his left arm outstretched toward me, his right clasped under his head.

I was amazed by how innocent he looked when he was sleeping. With his eyes closed and his luscious mouth relaxed, it was as if a decade had rolled back and I was staring once again at the man in his mid-twenties whom I'd met in business class. I had the opportunity to examine his face closely, smiling as I saw how long his eyelashes were. No wonder he could charm his way through life so easily.

His tousled hair fell onto the pillow and a shadow of stubble darkened his strong jaw. My gaze roamed to his forearms; thick, strong, and sinewy, with a tan that spoke of hours outdoors and a dusting of pale golden hair a few shades lighter than his velvety-smooth skin.

With so much wrong in my world, I was fortunate to be able to wake up next to the one person who, through his presence alone, seemed to be able to make it all feel right. That didn't mean the problems had disappeared, though.

I thought of my betrayal; tested the pain.

It was still there, although it hurt less, but my deep sigh awoke Patrick. His gold-green eyes flickered open, and when he saw me watching him, he smiled.

"Waking up next to you in this apartment…something I've dreamed of doing ever since I bought it," he said. "Come here, beautiful." His arms wrapped round me, pulled me toward him, into the warmth of his body.

"How are you feeling?" he asked me a while later, propping himself on an elbow so he could look into my eyes.

"Not so bad," I whispered. I stretched up, kissed his stubbled jaw. I ran my fingers down his shoulder, tracing the line of his bicep. His body felt as sexy as it looked…every inch of it. And speaking of inches, I could feel his hardness pushing into the curve of my waist. He'd woken up aroused, and at that moment, I realized I had, too.

He nuzzled his lips into my shoulder, kissing his way up my neck.

He stroked his hand over my breast, took the nipple in his mouth and began massaging it with his tongue. I could feel it hardening, becoming instantly responsive, the skilled tip of his tongue offering a pulsing pleasure that suffused my body.

"I'm feeling a little better now," I told him. I was teasing him, but there was truth behind it, because when I was with him, all the problems and pain seemed to melt away.

His hand roamed lower, smoothing over my hip, traveling round my thigh before touching and gently parting the lips of my sex. My legs seemed to melt open, inviting him in between them, and his expert touch moved deeper, a finger—two fingers, penetrating me in a way that made me moan. I was so wet, so ready for him, my body begging for the ravishment it craved.

"And now?" he murmured.

"Even better," I whispered.

"I think I see the way forward," he said. His voice was husky. The pumping of his fingers inside me was awakening a flood of lust. I was dizzy with longing; the rawness of the emotions inside me at odds with the calm, neutral surroundings of the bedroom.

A flashback to that airplane seat so long ago…he'd sprawled beside me, his body pressed to mine, those skilled fingers working their wicked magic in a way that had brought me to a fast, intense, utterly amazed orgasm. I'd buried my face in his neck to stifle the sounds I couldn't help making. For the first time ever, I had not held back; I'd opened myself—my body, my innermost emotions, maybe even my soul, to him…I'd trusted Patrick, that stranger, to take me all the way so that I came undone, gasping in delight, grazing my teeth over his skin.

It had been electric between us then, and it was now…I guessed it would always be. He kissed me deeply, the sensual plundering of his tongue mirroring the thrusts of his fingers. This was what I needed…to taste him, to feel him, to let him consume me, in every way that he wanted and sensed I needed. I knew from his uneven breathing that for him, my response was the most incredible turn-on.

The desire inside me was tautening into an almost painful tension. Lightly, his thumb caressed my clitoris, the touch melting me, so that I uttered a breathy groan. He was going to do it again, to make me come, easily, effortlessly. I felt myself tighten all the way to my core, hovering for a moment on the brink, before dissolving into the liquid bliss of release.

"I want to feel you," he murmured, withdrawing his fingers. Almost immediately, his hardness touched my slick lips, pushing into me, this fuller penetration causing me to spasm again, so that it was now his turn to groan.

His hands slid under my buttocks so that he had complete control of me, angling me so that each thrust he made pushed into my G-spot, making hot bursts of pleasure ripple through me. He fucked me slowly, sensually, his gaze locked on mine. His pupils were dilated, making his eyes look darker than usual, and it was easy to lose myself in their mysterious depths.

The way he was looking at me; the expression on his face, was tightening a cord inside me. I could see that Patrick was holding nothing back. He was making himself vulnerable to me, and at that moment I was certain that the "love" he'd included in his email to me was more than just a word. He was showing me, now, how he felt. This connection between us was far more complex than physical attraction alone.

It was not only the erotic delight of feeling him inside me that was making me breathless. It was the magnetism in his gaze, which forbade me to look away. I realized this was far more than sex…this was lovemaking. The emotional intensity of the experience was adding a richer layer to the physical. It was a sensory avalanche that blotted out everything except the immediacy of this act. All there was, in this moment, was us.

I feasted my eyes on the sight of the man above me, his chiseled face, cheekbones and jaw prominent, that generous mouth slightly parted. The lean, defined muscles of his shoulders and arms. I ran my hands down his spine to his buttocks—the only place on his body where there was a trace of fat, and there only enough to lightly cover those taut, rounded globes. They flexed and clenched as he drove himself into me. Touching them felt incredibly erotic. I dug my fingers in, loving the feel of the steely muscles under the sensual layer of softness.

The pressure of my fingers made him gasp. His strong hands adjusted my position, opening me fully to him. He thrust into me deeper, going faster, so that the explosions of sensation turned into one escalating rush.

I cried out as I felt my climax consume me, a melting sensation that began in my core and rippled outward, bringing such intense delight that it felt as if every cell of my body was being unmade. Sweat pooled on my skin. Wild with the need to express my desire, I ground my hips against his, clawing his buttocks with my fingers, showing him the intensity of the physical sensations that were suddenly too much for me to bear.

With a groan, Patrick gave himself up to his own orgasm, thrusting furiously into me, his breath sobbing in his chest as his arms crushed me. Our bodies were welded together, skin and sweat warm against each other. The hot jets of his semen filled me as he gasped with his release.

I felt lightheaded, euphoric…my heart was racing, the pace of my breathing matched his. We rested for a while, entwined in each other's arms, in a moment of the purest intimacy that I wished would never end. And as I lay in Patrick's bed, our bodies still joined, I realized that what I had found with him was too precious to lose. It was something I would not—could not—give up. No matter what trouble came my way as a result, no matter how difficult my choice ended up being, I was going to turn my back on my past. I was going to say no to Dave and College Sport.

CHAPTER 25

"I guess we should get up," Patrick said eventually. He stroked my hair, caressed my face with his fingers, tenderness evident both in his gesture and in his eyes.

"We should talk," he explained. "There are things I need to tell you."

"Okay." I felt apprehensive at the prospect, but was willing to trust him.

"I'm going to make us some coffee. If you want to put on some clothes, I can offer you…" he checked in his cupboards and turned to me with a rueful grin. "This robe. Not the height of glamor, but more comfortable than getting back into your ball gown."

The robe, patterned in vivid red and black, was too large for me, but the fabric was silky-soft against my skin. It felt strange wearing Patrick's clothes, but good at the same time.

By the time Patrick returned with two steaming mugs, I was out of bed and sitting on the leather sofa with my feet curled under me.

"Here," he said, handing me my mug carefully before sitting down beside me. Placing his own cup on the coffee table, he put his arm round me.

"I'm sorry about what happened last night. It ruined—well, no, it didn't do that. It marred an evening I wanted to be really special for you. Really happy. I'm angry that your husband was in that club—hell, I'm furious about what he's done to you."

"I'm confused," I admitted. "I don't know how long this has been going on. My husband and my best friend… it's unthinkable." I blinked hard. How naïve had I been not to realize it? Now that I looked back, there were clues I'd missed. The scarf, for instance. There was no way I could have accidentally packed it into my gym bag when we had separate lockers. She must have forgotten it at our house after visiting Dave, and had quickly invented a story in case I discovered it. And then there had been her shocked expression when I'd opened the door to her the previous evening. She'd come to see Dave, not expecting me to be there at all.

"I can't tell you when it first started, but they were definitely an item a year or so ago," Patrick said, and I stared at him, astonished.

"You mean...?"

"The photos I told you about? They were of your husband and Monika."

Seeing that my coffee was about to spill, he hastily took the mug from me.

"Why didn't you tell me?" I asked him, and I could hear the sharpness in my voice.

"Because you asked me not to," he countered, in a reasonable tone. "In fact, you begged me not to. You said you didn't want to know. Don't be angry with me for doing as you asked, Claire. I didn't know Monika was your best friend."

"Was," I repeated bitterly. There were so many questions whirling in my mind. When had Monika gotten together with Dave? Had it been before or after our marriage cooled off... had it been the cause?

I started to shake violently. Patrick's arms were all that lay between me and another flood of tears. I'd been betrayed in the worst possible way, by somebody who I'd considered to be a trusted friend.

Patrick handed me my coffee again. The rich, strong drink was soothing, and so were his words, but the knowledge that a friend had done this still burned inside me. I thought I'd never be able to forgive Monika, although perhaps, in time, I could understand.

"We need breakfast," Patrick decided, when I'd finished my coffee. "And you need clothes. Gorgeous as you look in that gown, I imagine you'd prefer to go home wearing something else."

I nodded. Unbelievably, I found myself smiling. Unburdening myself had helped me feel a whole lot better. It had been cathartic to share what was in my heart.

"I'll go out, then. Get you something to wear, and us something to eat."

"Do you cook?" I asked him curiously. It was an art I'd never mastered.

"I haven't had time to learn how to do it well," Patrick told me. "But the little I do, I enjoy. And I'm capable of not burning bacon and eggs, most times."

He leaned over and kissed me, his lips lingering on mine.

"I'll be about an hour," he said.

I checked the time on my phone when he left the apartment, seeing that it was just past nine a.m. and also noticing that my phone's battery was very low.

What could I do to pass the time in this luxurious but unlived-in space?

I could have a long bath in that magnificent sunken tub.

I walked into the bathroom and got the water running. It cascaded into the deep bath, filling it quickly. By the side of the bath I saw some oils and foams—a gift pack, with just one product opened. I wondered if they had been a gift from Patrick to his ex, or vice-versa. At any rate, I was going to try them. I poured a generous dollop of jasmine-scented bubble bath into the water and its fragrance quickly filled the room.

A sound from outside the bathroom—what was it?

I walked out to check, and hurried over to the bed when I realized it was the ringing of my phone.

An unfamiliar number, one I didn't recognize at all.

Wary, I let it ring, and waited for it to go to voicemail. Then I listened to the message. A woman's voice—she sounded elderly.

"Hello, Claire. My name's Maude and I live next door to your parents. I'm so sorry to worry you on a Sunday morning, but there's been an accident. Please call me back."

Oh, God, something had happened to my folks…my worst nightmare realized. I felt icy cold inside. Quickly, I pressed the "Call Back" button. Would I hear her well enough over the noise of the water? Hurrying into the bathroom, I snapped off the tap, stopping the deluge.

"Hello, Maude?" I almost shouted as soon as she answered. "It's Claire. What's happened to my parents? Are they okay?"

"Hi Claire." Her voice was quavering. "Your father's out of town for the morning. He got a part-time job driving a delivery truck. He asked me to come in and help with your mother. I'm so sorry, but I couldn't hold her when I was transferring her to the chair. She fell on the floor. She's knocked herself out, and it looks like she may have broken her arm. I've called the ambulance, but I just wanted to…"

And then it happened.

With a musical tingle that signaled the battery was empty, my phone died on me.

I stared down at the useless instrument in horror.

"Shit, shit," I shouted. "Shit!"

Did Patrick keep a spare charger anywhere? Oh, God, let him keep one somewhere.

Frantically, I ran through the apartment. The kitchen, the study, the lounge—nothing. Finally thinking straight, I sprinted back to the master bedroom and checked his side of the bed.

Thank goodness, there was one, plugged into the wall. But my relief was premature when I discovered it was not compatible with my phone.

I was sobbing from sheer frustration. There was a perfectly good landline right here in the bedroom, but I had no idea what my mother's cell number was—she'd given up her contract when they moved and went onto a new pay-as-you-go phone. The number was stored on my phone, but not in my memory. There was no landline at their new house. And with my phone having died, I couldn't get Maude's number.

Only one option left…and I had to take it.

Grabbing Patrick's cordless phone, I dialed my father's cell number from memory.

CHAPTER 26

To my utter relief, my dad answered the call within four rings. He didn't know who was speaking at first, with me phoning from a strange number and sounding hysterical with frustration and worry. It took him a minute to work out who I was.

"It's me. Claire. Dad, I need Mom's number." My voice sounded high and squeaky from stress.

"Sure, hon. Why? What's up?"

Dad always sounded calm; I'd never known anything to rattle him. Just as well, since he was driving while we were speaking. Panicking wouldn't have done him any good. Probably, it wasn't doing me any good either. With a huge effort, I fought for control, and managed to win the battle for long enough to tell him what the problem was.

"Oh, dear God," he said in a totally different tone, and I could pick up on his frantic anxiety as well as something else… was he angry with himself?

For a moment, I put myself in my father's shoes and realized what it must have taken to make the decision to leave my mom with someone else while he went off to try and earn some money, striving to claw his way back into the job market, one part-time job at a time.

"Don't worry, Dad," I said. Now I'd taken on the role of comforter. "It was an accident. They happen. I'll sort everything out and I'll be in touch with you soon as I can. Drive carefully, okay?"

I keyed the number he'd given me straight into the cordless phone, then pressed the dial button with frantic haste, praying that my mother's cellphone was somewhere that Maude could hear.

I thought it was going to go through to voicemail, but at the last moment Maude answered, sounding stressed.

"Claire? I've been trying to call you."

"My phone died. I'm so sorry."

"The ambulance is on its way."

"Where are they taking my mom?"

"I don't know. I'll call you as soon as I know. She's conscious… well, she's been asking for you. I'm scared to move her, though."

"If she's conscious and breathing, it may be safest just to leave her, if the ambulance is coming," I said. My heart was breaking for my mother, sprawled on the cold floor, trapped by her immobile body, and I felt terrible on behalf of poor Maude, who had been doing a neighborly favor by trying to help.

"I'm going to get over there as soon as I can. I'll call you when I'm on my way."

I asked Maude for her cell number, realizing I had nowhere to write it down. I hadn't put a pen in my clutch bag. I opened Patrick's bedside drawer, feeling like I was invading his privacy. There was a pen there. No paper, only a few business cards for PR agencies, printers, electricians. I scribbled Maude's number on the back of my right hand.

Then I closed the drawer again. I had to go, right now; this was an emergency and every second would count. I didn't know Patrick's cellphone number, so I couldn't call him to tell him what had happened. I felt awful knowing that he'd come back to find me gone. I thought of leaving a note, but had no idea what to write, and jotting something on the back of a business card seemed rude. As soon as I had the chance to charge my phone, I would call his landline and explain.

I picked up my red ball gown, which was draped over the back of the leather sofa. I slipped Patrick's dressing gown off, and it fell onto the carpet in a whisper of silk. I put on the ball gown, stepped into my heels, unlatched the apartment's front door and let myself out, closing it behind me so that the latch locked again.

It took me nearly an hour to get home, and when I arrived, I felt my hackles rise to see Dave's Audi at its usual careless angle in the driveway, but they rose even further when I saw Monika's car parked on the other side of the road. They must have spent the night at her place, believing I was here. Perhaps when Dave had arrived home and seen no sign of me, he'd called Monika to say the coast was clear.

I had a vision of them writhing in passion on our king-sized bed, and quickly suppressed it. Hopefully I'd be able to sneak in and out before they realized I was here. I didn't want to get involved in a confrontation now – not when I had more serious issues to worry about.

I opened the front door as quietly as possible and tiptoed inside. I stood in the hallway, listening.

And then my fists clenched so tightly my nails dug into my palms.

I could hear Monika's voice coming from the living room.

My earlier shock was replaced with fury, which surged inside me as I thought about how she had lied, pretending to be my best friend while having an affair with my husband. Now, here she was, conversing with him in my home, as if she owned it.

I stood and listened, heart thumping, undecided whether to storm in and confront them, or sneak past and grab my keys from the spare bedroom. But the conversation seemed one-sided. I realized that she must be on a phone call. Well, hopefully she wouldn't hear me as I tiptoed past.

But as I headed down the passage, a face flickered into my mind. Somebody I knew; a man I hated and feared. I recognized his lean, bearded face, and that oily-looking dark hair. It was Carlos… but in this image, his camera was nowhere in sight. Instead, he was speaking rapidly on his cellphone. Speaking to…

The vision gelled into memory and gooseflesh prickled up my arms as I realized who was on the other end of the line. These episodes hadn't made me feel dizzy for years, but now I had to put a hand on the wall to steady myself from the impact of the cruel, clear reality that had etched itself into my mind.

"You need to do it," Monika said pleadingly. Using the wall for support, I crept back to the half-open door, still not able to believe the truth of the picture I had seen, and the words I was now hearing. "No, she will have spent the night in his apartment. There's nowhere else she could be now."

Monika paused, listening. "Well, find it!" she snapped. "I thought you said you have good connections. You know his name… it's the same guy she was with when you took the pictures in Ireland. Patrick Maguire. It can't be that difficult to get his address, but you need to be quick, so you can be there when she leaves. I need those photos, Carlos. I have to have them today."

I felt cold all over and my stomach clenched as I took in the full extent of Monika's betrayal.

Even while my heart was screaming, "No, not possible," my brain was racing to analyze the evidence. Monika had been at all the events where I was photographed. She'd handed me the alcoholic drink and practically forced me to take a sip, so that Carlos could shoot the compromising image. She'd tipped him off about the private party, and had probably helped him get into the building. It had been her, all her. Monika had singlehandedly set out to destroy my career.

The shock of this discovery prompted me into furious action. Before I knew it, I was storming through the doorway to confront her.

CHAPTER 27

"What the hell are you doing?" I spat the words at Monika.

She was dressed in jeans and a sleeveless top, standing on the other side of the room with her back to the window. She spun round when she saw me, snatching the phone away from her ear, and the expression of horror on her face was as much of a confession as I needed.

She fumbled with her phone, stabbing at the disconnect button. Blood flooded into her face, turning her usually sallow skin to crimson.

"I... I... er, hello, Claire. Dave was worried about where you were. He said you didn't come back home last night, so he called me and I came here to help him search..."

"Don't bother lying," I told her icily. "I saw you dancing with Dave last night. And I've overheard enough of your conversation to know exactly who you were speaking to, and why."

Her mouth worked, but no words came out. Usually so quick with her repartee or her blade, my accusations had disarmed her completely.

"I was just speaking to a friend..." she whispered eventually.

"To a paparazzi photographer friend. You were briefing Carlos to take another photograph of me." My voice was filled with outrage. "Why, Monika? I thought we were best friends, for God's sake. You've been having an affair with my husband. And now you're trying to destroy my reputation."

She physically flinched away from the words.

"I'm sorry..."

"Sorry?" I repeated incredulously. "You think you can just apologize and everything will be all right?"

"You don't understand." Monika was blinking tears out of

her pale blue eyes. I noted this without any trace of sympathy.

"Oh, I understand all too well." I spoke through clenched teeth.

"No, you do not." Now there was a thread of defiance in her tone and she lifted her narrow chin. "You have no idea what it is like to live in your shadow, Claire."

"What do you mean?"

"You've always been the golden girl. The beauty who gets the sponsorships and the publicity, the fame and the money, who's so nice and friendly and squeaky clean. It's all fallen into your lap. Even this strange mind-reading gift of yours… you're not nearly the fastest fencer, not even the most skilled. All the coaches say so. But every so often you just seem to foresee where your opponent is going to move, and that makes the difference; it scores you points. It's unfair. All the coaches have noticed it; have said you would never have been on the teams if it wasn't for this weird ability that kicks in from time to time and wins you certain matches."

I stared at Monika, unable to believe her words as she continued, "If you knew how hard I have worked, and how many tears I've shed, and what a struggle it's been for me, you might see it differently. I mean, your parents get financial support from other sources, right? Dave told me so. Meanwhile, my parents also need help; I have to try and help them with my pittance of an income, and my earnings will always depend only on how well I do. I don't have telepathy or whatever it is to help me out, or a sponsorship to fall back on. You don't have a clue what pressure that creates."

"But I…" Now I was the one gaping in disbelief. I couldn't believe that Dave had fed Monika such a huge untruth about my parents, and that she had swallowed it. They had no other sources of income…they never had.

"You think I'm just a cheerful training partner who loves to party, but you have no idea about my life." Monika's words felt like blades. "You don't understand how much I worry about every parry I flub, about every muscle twinge that could mean an injury, or a missed competition. Yes, I admit, even though we're friends, I've been jealous of you for years."

Her words made me recoil. I blinked hard as she continued.

"I didn't start the affair with Dave. He started it. And that's all it was… an occasional affair. He said you were frigid. So from time to time, we'd go out and dance and have some fun, and sleep together. You know, at first I thought it would lead somewhere. That he would leave you and start a life with me, especially when you went off and started fooling around with Hassan. But even there, I didn't get what you had. Dave never even contemplated divorcing you. I was just a sideline for him; some entertainment. From time to time he'd help me out financially if I had a bad month, give me cash or buy me things. But I always had to ask nicely. To beg him, more like." She scrubbed tears from her face.

I could find nothing to say that would stem the tirade of bitterness that Monika had kept locked inside.

"Carlos is an old school friend of mine," she explained. "He needed money, and so did I. We set you up and shared the profits from selling those shots. Dave never knew about it. I was angry and I wanted to hurt you, so that you could see what it felt like to be pulled down. And I thought maybe, if the affair with Hassan became public knowledge, Dave might change his mind and leave you. I… I started hating you, Claire. And that's why… I'm sorry." Her thin shoulders sagged as she stared down at the floor.

"We were supposed to be best friends," I said. My voice sounded hoarse. "I trusted you. You can't believe how wrong you are about so many things, because you never bothered to find out the real story. Because you were so quick to believe lies, and jump to conclusions without asking me for the truth. You wanted to destroy my life? Well, you succeeded beyond your wildest dreams. Not only in destroying my life, but my parents', who are in desperate financial straits. You came very close to destroying Hassan's future, too, in a way you don't even understand and which I'm not going to explain. Well done. Are you happy now?"

She was crying now; bent over with her hands covering her

face as her shoulders shook with huge, racking sobs.

I turned to go, but stopped at the door. "I hope you and Dave get together eventually. One thing I can truthfully say is that you deserve each other."

Then I closed the door and headed for the spare room.

Luck was not on my side. As I passed the master bedroom, I almost collided with Dave, who was coming out. He must have been showering; he was wearing a different shirt and I could smell his freshly applied deodorant.

"Claire! Where the hell have you been?" I could see his mind working at full speed as he tried to come up with an explanation for Monika's presence. Obviously deciding attack was the best form of defense, he continued, "You're still in your evening gown and you never came home. Do you know how worried I've been? I called Monika to see if you'd spent the night there, and you hadn't. Where were you?"

A little voice inside me said, "Ignore him, just ignore him, let the lawyers deal with this."

I decided to ignore the little voice.

"Last night, I was in the Bohemian Ballroom," I spat out, and had the satisfaction of watching his mouth drop open.

"I..." he began.

"Dave, it's over. Everything. Our marriage, the sponsorship deal. I can't renew a contract based on nepotism, or spend my time doing P.R. for a firm whose management treats me like shit. Maybe you can suggest that Monika replaces me, because I'm done with this. You'll be hearing from my lawyers." As soon as I'd worked out how I was going to afford them.

"You'll be hearing from *my* lawyers!" he shouted. "Claire, you must be crazy. Look what you're throwing away!"

"I don't care what I'm throwing away. I care about a future where I'm happy. Where my husband doesn't screw around behind my back. Where I can trust my friends, and where those friends don't hire paparazzi photographers to try and incriminate me."

Dave's mouth dropped open. I could see from his stupefied expression that he hadn't known.

"Maybe you should ask your lover about her school friend Carlos, and find out why she asked him to take those pictures of me," I said. "And now, I'm out of here. My mother's had a fall and I have to go and help her. Send my apologies to Toby and Daniel for the meeting tomorrow. Tell them the answer is no, I'm not renewing the contract. And wish them a nice life."

I marched, as best I could in my high heels, to the spare room. Opening the wardrobe, I quickly chose a pair of jeans and a pretty, cream jersey that my mother had given me a few years ago.

I pulled on socks, Skechers, dragged a brush through my tangled hair and tied it back. I made sure I had my phone charger, together with my wallet and I.D. I was desperate to call Patrick. I'd charge my phone as soon as I reached my parents' house; there was nowhere in my car to plug it in. I was panicking twice – mostly for my mother, but also at the thought of him coming back to his apartment and finding me vanished, Cinderella-like.

The journey seemed to take forever. I tried my best to keep calm, to drive sensibly, even though I was still seething inside as I relived the awful confrontations I'd just had, and struggled to come to terms with the shock of what I'd discovered.

The weather was dull and overcast; the sky grey, the grass and trees taking on the sepia tones of late fall. A time of change. Winter was coming. Now that I had made this radical decision, what would this new season bring? How would I manage to earn some money? Perhaps I should ask my dad if there were any other truck driving opportunities.

I turned off the main road, taking the avenue which led to my parents' neighborhood. This section of the journey started off as a pleasant drive, through well-treed suburbia, pretty houses with neat gardens flanking the road. Then it headed past a small town center, after which it ran through the depressed, and depressing, suburb where my parents now lived.

I parked hurriedly, near the crumbling wall that surrounded their apartment building.

"Claire?"

The speaker was a black woman with graying hair and a concerned expression who was standing at the building's front door.

"Maude." Yanking the key from the ignition and slamming the door, I ran over to greet her. "How's my mom?"

"The ambulance left ten minutes ago," she said, and told me which hospital they'd gone to. "She seemed okay. They didn't say there were any complications… dear God, I really hope there aren't." I could see she was battling to hold back tears. "I was only trying to help."

"It's all right," I soothed her, following her to the front door of my parent's apartment, noticing her worn blouse and the faded print of her skirt.

"She slipped out of the harness and I couldn't hold her in."

Now the tears were flowing. I felt terrible for her. I knew how she must feel, wretched with guilt, waiting apprehensively for my anger.

"You tried your best," I told her. "You mustn't worry. That hoist is very tricky."

My father knew how difficult it could be. I was sure that my mother must have encouraged – insisted – that he take the work and leave her in a stranger's hands. My mother could be incredibly forceful when she'd made up her mind. She hadn't been thinking of herself; but rather of him and of me.

"I'm not angry," I reassured Maude still further. Then, feeling bad to have to say the words at all, but feeling I should, I added, "And we wouldn't dream of suing you. My parents and I aren't that kind of people."

I could see from the relief in her eyes that this was an outcome she'd been dreading.

I called my dad to update him on the news. His cellphone was engaged, but I left a message telling him what had happened and giving the details of the hospital. Then I hurried through the small house, packing my mother's essential items into a small carry-on bag. While I straightened the house out and made the bed, Maude mopped the floor near the hoist where some blood and urine had spilled.

Then, pocketing my mother's phone, I picked up the carry-on bag and headed to the back door, where I said goodbye to Maude and thanked her again.

I walked quickly around the corner and headed for the street, and it took me a moment to realize what I wasn't seeing.

My car had gone. While I was inside the house, it had been stolen, together with my purse and my cellphone, which I'd forgotten to take out when I rushed to meet Maude.

CHAPTER 28

I stared in horror at the crumbs of smashed glass on the sidewalk; the only evidence that remained. I'd been inside for only fifteen minutes. This was terrible luck, in every sense of the word. I needed to get to the hospital fast, and I now had no phone, no cash and no car.

This was a disaster in every way... my life had been turned upside down.

"Think on your feet, Claire," I admonished myself. I was supposed to be so good at that. Fast footwork, both physical and mental, had been my forte, but I was all out of good ideas.

"Did you see anything?" I called to the only pedestrian I could see; a young woman carrying grocery bags, walking away from me on the opposite side of the road. Perhaps she'd noticed something... "Excuse me!" I called to her again, and jogged along the curb, the suitcase bumping my calves, waving my free hand to try and attract her attention. I realized she must have headphones on and be listening to music, because she did not respond.

I wanted to sit down on the suitcase and burst into tears. I felt so frustrated, so helpless. And worst of all, I couldn't contact Patrick. What must he be thinking by now? Worry tore at my heart.

There was only one solution I could think of. I knocked on the door of Maude's apartment and asked her if I could borrow twenty dollars for a cab.

She had to go into her house to find the money, and from the collection of crumpled notes and change that she handed to me ten minutes later, I suspected she'd had to scrape together all her available cash.

Promising I'd give her the money back as soon as possible –

hopefully I could borrow some from my father at the hospital – I used my mother's phone to summon a cab, and five minutes later, I was on my way.

My dad called me when I was almost there, anxiously watching the taxi meter which was already standing at eighteen dollars. When it got to twenty, I'd have to climb out and walk… but to my relief, the hospital gates were ahead.

"I'm on my way," my dad told me.

"Have you finished the job?" I asked, confused.

"All done. I've been moving equipment for a rock band to a new venue after their show. I started out at two a.m. and now I'm back. I'll be there in a half-hour."

"Okay," I said. I hadn't realized the job involved such crazy hours. No wonder he'd had to get in extra help to look after my mother.

So much stress, so much exhaustion, such a struggle, and all for what? To do a few hours' work… but it was more than that; more than the money, necessary as that was. It was the need for independence. My parents had been trying to encourage me to follow my heart by proving to me that they could manage without my help.

But in fact, all this had shown me was that they couldn't.

My mother's ward was empty when I reached it. The matron told me that she'd been X-rayed, and then taken into surgery. The news was as good as I'd dared to hope for – the concussion was not serious, and the only other injuries were a broken right collarbone and two fractured fingers, which were now being surgically pinned.

I sat in the waiting room and used the last of my mother's minutes to report the theft of my car and stop my credit cards. Soon afterwards, my father arrived.

"Sorry to have caused you so much worry," he said, enfolding me in a huge bear hug. "How's Roseanne doing?"

I updated him on my mom's condition, and then on the more serious problem of my own stolen car and missing belongings.

"Damn it all," my father said. "I'm so sorry, Claire. This has been a dreadful run of luck. Here. Take my bankcard and run down to the ATM. You can draw some money and do what you need to do. Take as much as you'll need for the next few days. Here's the PIN code."

He gave me the code, and I repeated the four digits in my mind, over and over, as I hurried down to the ATM in the hospital lobby.

I decided to start by buying more phone time, and ordering two of the biggest coffees they had for sale. Then I could finish making all the calls I needed to. And I'd have to draw some extra cash to get home…

Five hundred dollars should do it. I hoped my father's bank balance would stretch to that. I couldn't help feeling a sense of relief when the machine whirred and the fifty-dollar bills riffled out of the slot.

How much had I left him with? I was worried I'd drawn excessively. I knew I shouldn't peek at somebody else's finances, but after all, I was seriously concerned about their predicament. This was an exceptional case; I needed to know, just to set my mind at rest.

I asked for the balance printout, and waited while the stub of paper fed itself into my hand.

I checked the figures.

Then I blinked, staring down at the paper incredulously. I reread it twice. I hadn't made a mistake… but somebody must have made a bad one, because this was impossible.

The balance was far higher – crazily higher – than it should have been. My eyes widened as I took in all the zeroes. There could be no reasonable explanation for this. This must be fraud, a scam, and I only hoped my father wouldn't get into trouble because of it.

I abandoned my plans. No coffee, no minutes. Clutching the slip in a hand that felt suddenly damp, I raced back upstairs to the waiting room, running the three flights of stairs in record time, rather than waiting for the elevator.

As I charged into the small room, my father looked up, surprised.

"Dad, I think your account's been hacked. Something bad is

going on, and you're going to need to sort it out, fast."

"Hold on, hold on," my father said, raising a palm, his calm tones only serving to inflame my anxiety further. "It's okay, Claire. I meant to tell you about it, but you rushed off. This would probably be the man I spoke to earlier today. He told me he knew you. He basically explained to me that he needed to pay me some money urgently."

"Dad!" I howled. "My pictures have been in all the papers. Anyone can say they know me. How were you taken in so easily? These are Nigerian scamsters! You've had two million dollars transferred to you. Two million! It can't be real. It's fraudulent. And the next thing you know, they'll tell you to pay the money back, and end up cleaning out your account."

My father's mouth dropped open.

"Obviously, you don't mean two actual million dollars, Claire."

"Yes, I do. I mean exactly that, Dad."

I held the stub of paper out. It was slightly creased, but the figures were unmistakable. Two million, four hundred and sixty-two dollars exactly.

I saw my own shock reflected in my father's face.

"He sounded so nice… he said he was going to help me," he mumbled.

"I'd better call the bank now," I said, pulling my mother's phone out of my pocket before remembering that my quest to buy more time had been derailed by my scare at the ATM.

"Can I borrow your phone, Dad?"

He handed it over, but as he did, it started ringing.

We both tensed, staring down at the phone as if it was a poisonous snake.

My father peered down at the screen.

"It's the same number," he said. "The same person who called earlier. Should I answer it?"

"Let me," I said.

Gathering my courage, I took the call, drawing in a deep breath and pressing the phone to my ear.

"Listen here," I said. "If you think you can scam an innocent person, I'm telling you now, you've picked the wrong one. We're going to get the police onto you faster than – faster than you can wriggle out of this. I suggest you go to the bank right now and get that fraudulent transaction reversed, because my next call is going to be to the FBI, and they're going to trace your number and lock you up in jail!"

I was about to disconnect and do exactly what I'd promised when, to my surprise, the caller spoke.

"Hello, Claire," he said.

I sat down hard, feeling as if a rug had been yanked from under me.

It was Patrick.

CHAPTER 29

"Patrick!" My voice was squeaky. My face felt hot, as if it was turning a furious red. "What the hell is this? What are you doing?"

In contrast, he sounded calm. "Right this minute, I'm walking out of the bank."

The bank where he'd just deposited a ludicrous sum of money into my father's account?

"How's your mother?" he continued, taking the wind out of my sails as I was about to shout down the phone that what he'd done was unacceptable, that I was going to get this money paid right back to him, pronto.

"She's – she's in surgery for her broken arm. The concussion wasn't serious. She should be back in the ward within the next two hours."

"Which hospital?"

I told him its name, frustrated that all these questions were distracting me from my main goal of shouting at him. I was about to get back to that when he said, "I'll be there in a half-hour. Can you meet me outside, Claire?"

"Yes, I can."

"Good. See you then."

He disconnected.

"So what did he say?" my dad asked, sounding anxious.

"Not much. He's on his way here now. I'm going to meet him downstairs."

"Well, make sure you ask him for his banking details, to pay this money back," my dad told me.

"Maybe you shouldn't have given him yours, in the first place!" Unfair as it was, I was taking my annoyance out on my father now.

"Seriously, you'd have done the same," he told me. "He sounded so concerned. He said you'd been staying at his place. He told me he'd gone out to get breakfast, and you'd obviously had a crisis and had to leave. He saw you'd made a call to my number on his landline, and he was trying to find out what had happened. I told him who I was, and why it had been so urgent for you to reach me. When I explained what the problem was, he said he'd like to help out in case there were any medical costs above our insurance."

Which, I realized, there would definitely be.

"He said it's what you would want him to do, and he was going to insist on helping. So, before I knew it, I was giving him all my details. I expected him to deposit a few hundred at the most. If I'd known it was going to be anywhere close to this, I would also have told him no, Claire, of course."

I let out my breath in a long sigh.

"Sorry for snapping, Dad. You didn't know. I would have done the same."

"We're both under stress right now. Doesn't mean we don't love each other." Standing up, my dad enfolded me in another big hug. "Now, you'd better go downstairs and wait for your boyfriend, so we can get this sorted out. Take your mother's phone; I'll call you as soon as she's out of surgery."

He gave one last, disbelieving glance at the ATM slip before wadding it up into a tiny ball and tossing it into the dustbin.

In fact, Patrick got there sooner than I'd expected. I'd only been waiting ten minutes before I saw a white Mercedes Benz pull up, and recognized him through the lightly tinted window. He leaned across to open the door for me, and I breathed in the smell of leather as I climbed into the air-conditioned space.

I closed the door, turned to him, smoldering all over again with anger – or at least, I thought it must be anger. I felt short of breath; my heart was pounding faster than it should have been.

"So, tell me…" I began, but he pulled me towards him and stopped my words with a kiss.

The feel of his mouth on mine was electric. The softness of

his lips; the sensuous rasp of his stubble – in the chaos of the morning, he'd obviously been in too much of a rush to shave.

I met his kiss with a need I hadn't realized I had been feeling, my mouth crushing his own in my need. My anger and confusion melted away in the strong embrace of his arms as he pulled me close, my own hands reaching over his broad back to hold him tightly.

We could have stayed that way for a long time; would have, except a horn from behind told us that his car was blocking traffic.

Hurriedly, we broke apart, Patrick raising a hand in apology as he put the car into Drive and pulled away while I did up my seatbelt.

I stole another glance at him; the unrepentant expression on his handsome face, the fall of his bangs pushed into disarray by our kiss.

"So what's the plan now?" I asked.

"You need to be back at the hospital soon, so we don't have much time. I thought we could go to a park nearby and take a short walk while we talk.

"Okay," I agreed.

The park proved to be a large, well cared for space with a lake, groomed expanses of grass, and paved walkways lined with trees. We climbed out and headed up the hill, towards a forested area. There was a strong wind blowing, turning the morning to somewhere between cold and refreshing. Leaves in autumn colors blew from the trees and scudded over the grass. It whipped my hair back from my face and I was glad when Patrick put his arm around me. I wrapped my own around his waist, and together, we walked into the park.

Despite the chilliness of the morning, there were several other people enjoying this outdoors space. A few joggers, braving the wind in nothing more than short-sleeved shirts, and a small group of elderly women wrapped up in coats, enjoying a walk that seemed to be more gossip than exercise. I saw a couple pushing a pram while their young daughter, clothed in a symphony of pink, toddled behind them.

"I'm going to pay that money back to you," I told Patrick. "You should never have done that."

"Why not?"

A question I hadn't expected. I had first, angrily, wanted to tell him that it was interfering. But it wasn't; he'd obtained my father's permission.

"Because – because it's too much," I said.

Patrick shook his head. "Not at all. It's what they need to enjoy the rest of their lives in comfort and without worry. If you'd told me about it, I'd have done it sooner."

"Well, I couldn't. My mother wanted it kept private," I tried to explain.

"You see, Claire, to me your situation was like a puzzle," he continued. "The decisions you made were confusing me. Your hesitation to turn your back on that sponsorship contract didn't make sense… it was as if there was a missing piece that I didn't know about, that would help the whole picture to become clear."

I nodded. I understood where Patrick was going with this.

"You never said a word to anyone about your mother's injury. I was appalled when I realized what she'd gone through, and what your family had been living with. What a struggle it was, and how you'd been trying to help." Seeing my eyes widen, he added, "Your father didn't tell me everything, but I was able to read between the lines. Unemployed, out on a part-time job, a recent move with a new neighbor helping—and not in a great neighborhood, either. I know that part of Camden."

"Okay," I said.

"Everything made sense, then. You'd been supporting them, with some difficulty, I guess, given your estranged husband's love for spending money."

"That's right," I admitted, ashamed.

"I wanted to help them and to help you. They are two brave people who deserve it. And you were too proud to ask me." His fingers smoothed my hair back from my face before his arm clasped my waist again. "You're so afraid of being vulnerable. I understand that. I know why you find it difficult to trust. I thought my words haven't been enough to persuade you… you've still held back. So there's only one way I'm going to be able to make you trust me, and that is through my actions."

"Okay," I said softly.

"That money will give them the security they need. And it'll allow you to make the best choices about your future, without having to worry. I had to pay it directly to them, because I knew if I offered it to you, you'd say no. And I didn't want you to feel you were entering into another contract." He gave a rueful grin. "This seemed like the best way. The money's all theirs, by the way. The tax has already been set aside. I'll ask my accountant to call your father and give him the necessary information."

I was blindsided by surprise all over again. He'd thought of everything. This incredible gesture was one of pure generosity, done in a way to cause my parents no extra stress. Suddenly curious, remembering what he'd said about the castle, I asked him, "Was it your head that made the decision? Or your heart?"

Patrick smiled. "Head and heart together, in perfect agreement. This was more than wanting to help, Claire. It was a way of showing you how I feel—that I am in love with you."

Well, at that, my legs refused to take me a step further. I turned to face him, wrapping my arms around him tightly as he continued.

"I want to be with you for the rest of my life. I want to make love to you every single night, and again in the morning. I want to be your partner, through the good and the bad. I've been crazy about you ever since that moment we met on the plane. If I'd had any sense at all, I'd have proposed to you right then. I let you go and it took me ten years to find you again…and I'm not going to give you up a second time. I can't."

Tears were streaming from my eyes at these words…tears of pure happiness.

"Claire. I want you to come and live with me," he continued. "And when your mother's better, and your parents have moved somewhere safer with a full-time nurse to help them, and when your divorce is finalized, I'm going to invite you away, to the most romantic location I can possibly think of, and I'm going to ask you to marry me."

My head was whirling. Looking into Patrick's hazel-green eyes, touched with fire, I finally summoned up the courage to speak what was in my heart.

"I'm in love with you too, Patrick," I told him. I sniffed hard, spoiling the romantic moment, but he didn't seem to notice and his eyes softened at my words. "I'm totally crazy about you; I always have been. If I'd had any sense, I would have gotten in touch with you after that plane ride. I wouldn't have let all this time slip by and made other decisions that turned out to be wrong. Thank you for helping my parents, and thank you for giving me the freedom to choose what I want to do. And what I want, right now, is to be with you."

"Thank you, Claire," he whispered. "Thank you for opening your heart to me and letting me in. I love you."

Sometimes, not often, I can glimpse what's going to happen. It's a strange ability. It happens randomly, but it's never been wrong. It comes in pictures. And as we were walking back through the park, not caring that a light, spattering rain had begun to fall, I saw a picture in my mind.

Patrick and me, lying in each other's arms in a room I'd never seen before, the morning sun shining through the large window, causing the diamond on my ring finger to reflect a pattern of light onto the white wall opposite. He looked older—by how much, I didn't know, but at least ten years or maybe more, although time had been kind to him, etching the handsomeness deeper into his lean face.

This was my future I was seeing; our future.

We were together. And we were happy.

Also by Jassy Mackenzie

Drowning

"The sexual chemistry bursts from every page..."
—Publishers Weekly

Sensuous but stifled New York City photographer Erin Mitchell thinks going to South Africa on assignment will be the perfect getaway. But when a flash flood washes away Erin's vehicle and she is stranded at a luxury safari lodge, Erin's romantic working vacation takes an interesting turn. She awakens from her near-drowning and meets her rescuer, Nicholas—hot and brilliant, successful and caring—not at all like her abusive husband. At Leopard Rock in the steamy South African heat, Erin faces the toughest choices of her life.

Nicholas is ripped, he's smart, and he's "no strings attached." To give in, or not to give in drowns Erin's senses as she struggles with two impossible goals: ignore the exquisite physical charms of her host, and conceal every last detail whenever her controlling husband calls. On the other side, Nicholas faces impossible choices of his own, as the bon-vivant playboy may just possibly collide with feelings more powerful than lust.

Erotic. Exotic. Wild. Drowning sizzles in the African heat as one woman is stretched to the breaking point by the strength of her vows and the intensity of her seething primal desires.